WITHDRAWN

RUN, SARA, RUN

Sara Tindall seems among the most fortunate of people; she's beautiful, in love, has a baby she adores and her name will soon be in lights above one of London's West End theatres. But in fact, her life is darkened by a terrible shadow, the hatred of someone whose identity remains a mystery; someone who has pursued her, year after year, with lies, rumours and threats, whose inexplicable, corrosive loathing cannot be appeased even by murder. Deep in Sara's subconscious mind lies the key to unlock the mystery.

Books by Anne Worboys in the Ulverscroft Large Print Series:

EVERY MAN A KING
THE BARRANCOURT DESTINY
THE LION OF DELOS
RUN, SARA, RUN

ANNE WORBOYS

RUN, SARA, RUN

Complete and Unabridged

ULVERSCROFT
Leicester

First published in U.K. 1982

First Large Print Edition
published April 1984
by arrangement with
Severn House Publishers Ltd.,
London
and
Charles Scribner's Sons,
New York

British Library CIP Data

Worboys, Anne
Run, Sara, Run.—Large print ed.
(Ulverscroft large print series: romance)
I. Title
823'.914[F] PR6073.A/

ISBN 0-7089-1122-6

To Dulcie Gray
for her kindness

Published by
F. A. Thorpe (Publishing) Ltd.
Anstey, Leicestershire
Printed and Bound in Great Britain by
T.J. Press (Padstow) Ltd., Padstow, Cornwall

1

August

NOW that he had made up his mind, excitement feathered in him, replacing the black anger he had felt when he read that notice in the newspaper.

GALAXY THEATRE
Opening Wed. 26th

RAINE MATHIESON
in
TWO'S A RISK
WITH SARA TINDALL

The Galaxy! She had made it to the top in spite of everything he had done to prevent it. And now he had heard the rumor that she was likely to marry Max Ritchie. Again, Sara with everything. Sara with her outward submissiveness, her unacceptable brains, beauty, and popularity. Sara winning, in spite of all he had done. In spite of him.

Time to strike again.

Sara, glancing over her script, lifted her head. If she had been a beast in the wilds, one would have said she scented danger. Ten-month-old Primrose put a hand on her mother's foot and looked up into her face, crowing. Sara swept Primmy up into her arms. She held her tightly against her breast. There was a blackness creeping into her consciousness like a forewarning of disaster.

Raine said, "What's the matter, Sara? Someone walking over your grave?"

The Preceding May

He thought Sara Tindall was the loveliest girl in the world. Perfect bone structure. A blue flash of a smile. Beautiful curly golden hair. Skin like porcelain. And she was popular. Women who should be envious liked her, even loved her. There was something novel in being able to feel sorry for someone who, by the ordinary laws of nature, ought to totally eclipse everyone else.

Patrick Delvaney, the play's director, a small man with a clever face and a shock of black curly hair flecked with gray, faced Sara across the table. His manager, Ted Lonigan, badly wanted Sara for the part of Claudia in Two's a Risk. She was a natural, he said.

Brilliant, virtually unknown, she could be a future Bernhardt. And he'd also said another thing. Since her first day at the Royal Academy of Dramatic Art, all through Repertory and provincial tryouts that had never made London's West End, she had earned a reputation for working hard and well.

"D'you know about her past? Her private life?" Delvaney had said.

"Listen, Patrick, Sara has never, through all the misfortunes of her young life, let anyone down but herself. Give her a fair trial. That's all I ask."

Delvaney had seen this situation before. When Sara reached the top, Lonigan wanted to be able to say that he had given her her first part. But Delvaney knew that the manager would withdraw his request that Sara play the part of Lady Claudia if Delvaney felt strongly enough against her or wanted another actress. As it turned out, no one who came to the audition could compare with Sara.

"Why don't you marry Max?" Patrick asked Sara bluntly. She looked away. Delvaney felt the room throb with her silence. "Well?"

She said in a soft but very definite voice,

"I'm still in love with Guy. And I don't see what this has to do with the play."

Delvaney searched his mind for words that would shock her into exposing herself. "Everything has to do with the play. You can't be in love with a corpse," he said slowly, deliberately.

The astonishing blue gaze faltered and he saw her flinch. "You can be brutal, can't you?"

"What did Guy have that Max hasn't?" He thrust his small, bearded chin forward. It was terribly important that he be sure of her emotional stability before he gave her the part. "Can't remember, can you? And we've got to have a straight talk about the child before I make up my mind." His fingers tapped on the chair arm. "I don't mind telling you I'm worried about giving Claudia to you."

"There's no reason why you should worry," she replied. Though she had perfect vision, Sara bore the curiously vulnerable, in-need-of-protection look of the nearsighted. "I can always get a baby-sitter. That's what's bugging you, isn't it? Getting married isn't going to automatically provide a baby-sitter, you know. And Max is scarcely the type."

Delvaney shifted uneasily in the chair. The

o know of her success. Guy who
found in Sara's flat shot through the
ng a gun in his hand. There we
erprints on the weapon except his ow
been happy. He had only that
nounced his engagement to the gi
ored. The postmortem said he had be
ood health. He had to be medically fit, h
n airline pilot. He was handsome, st
ergetic, and well able to defend hi
ably short on ene

would allow my per-
sonal circumstances to upset things now?"

"You realize that no matter how ill the child becomes you will be expected onstage."

"I understand."

"Gasping its last breath."

She said sharply, "Don't be silly."

"I want you to take this warning seriously, Sara. It is a warning, you know."

"I understand," she repeated soberly. "Of course I do."

"All right. You shall have the part of Claudia." But he crossed his fingers superstitiously under the desk.

August Again

All day Sara had been sliding obsessively back into the past. Wanting Guy, wherever he

ymous letter he had
rackled in his pocke
ngertips, uncertain ev
d confront her with it
houghtfully, "A girl who
in adversity is one thing.
bloody-minded and lookin
other. Which one are you?"
wanted to have Guy's child,
heatre has meant everything to
ten. Do you think I would

Besides, he was noticea

His family and friends declared it must have been murder. But there was no evidence. Guy Fortune left this world an apparently insolvable mystery and a pregnant fiancée.

Sara was playing in Repertory at the time. The baby was small, and because Sara's health was good she was able to keep acting until three months before Primmy's birth. Then she took backstage jobs. Primmy arrived a week after she stopped working. Her birth brought love and sweetness into Sara's life, but not peace—the black shadow of Guy's death lingered over them both. Guy's brother was the only one who actually accused her of the murder. James Fortune told the police he had evidence that in spite of the just-announced engagement, Guy had wanted to break up the relationship. When the police pressed for details, James produced a message put together from letters cut out of a newspaper, a sample of the anonymous letter that had dogged Sara for years. But nothing could be proven on such flimsy evidence.

If Guy had no enemies, Sara did. At every important stage of her life these damning anonymous letters had come. Her entry into R.A.D.A. had been shadowed by one of them. This girl is of very bad character. And more than that. Considerably more. She had come before the principal, who had been kind and had given her an opportunity to clear herself. The people who wrote anonymous letters were the ones to be condemned, he had said kindly. But he had grilled her all the same. Her ability and total dedication had brought her to R.A.D.A.; now they were to be her saving grace. She knew she would be closely watched, knew she must never do anything wrong. She worked harder than she might have had there been no problems, and inevitably she became a star pupil.

Sometimes, when she was on tour with a repertory company, her landlady would receive a slanderous, unsigned message. Someone who knew a great deal about her movements wanted to destroy Sara Tindall. The hospital where she gave birth to Primmy received one that was more frightening than the others. More vicious. Sara Tindall is a prostitute. That one had been considerably harder to ride.

Raine, her flatmate, a tall, slender girl with sooty black hair and direct, dark eyes, flung herself through the doorway of their sitting room in the flamboyant way she had perfected for the part of Jassy, the cheeky maid and leading role in the play. "Tea? Tea? Who's for tea, m'lady?" Unlike Sara, who saved her energy for the stage, Raine played her parts offstage as well as on. If she slipped back into her own personality, she declared, she would be lost. But since she was seldom out of work, scarcely anyone was familiar with her own personality. She was a delight to live with.

"Thanks. I'd love some tea." Sara was on the sofa holding Primmy in her arms. A mother and daughter idyll, Raine thought uneasily, looking down at the golden head bent toward the blond one, at the big, long-lashed eyes soft with love yet haunted because Guy was always there in the rounded point of the child's chin, in the breadth of her delicate brow. Guy Fortune, who refused to die because his child lived. It was scary the way Sara clung to that child with a primitive sort of obsession, as though she felt something menaced Primmy. Raine gave herself a mental shake, remembering the ordeal of her own first night in a West End play. Sheer blind panic. And it was true: If you weren't strung as tight as a violin string, the chances were you wouldn't be very good. "Believe me," Raine had told Patrick Delvaney, "You'll be glad you gave Sara the part." But today something had changed, and Raine's conviction was wavering. Sara seemed out of reach. Frighteningly so. And for the first time Raine began to think of her own security. For the duration of the play's run, she and Sara would be crucial to each other.

Raine said in a quick, nervous voice, "We must leave for the theatre at six. What time is the baby-sitter coming?"

"Anyone would think this was your first West End appearance instead of mine," Sara said smilingly. "Ruth will be here on time."

The sitting room was large and pretty. A town room with a country look. Faded loose covers on chairs bought at an auction. An ancient Turkish carpet acquired cheaply from a friend when her dog, suffering a false pregnancy and building a nest, chewed a corner beyond repair. There was some junk furniture Sara and Guy had bought in a hurry when they moved into the flat in Notting Hill. Two large gilt-framed mirrors, the kind that go for a song because of their size. One very good desk Sara had taken from her old home along with her bedroom furniture before her brother Elliott sold it. Mr. and Mrs. Tindall had died together in a fire. Their country cottage had gone up like a tinderbox while they slept. Now Elliott and his wife, Lil, were the only family Sara and Primmy had left.

"By the way," Raine said, "Max rang. He said he might drop in." She looked delighted.

Sara glanced away quickly. It was disconcerting the way everyone was trying to push her into marriage with Max. Raine swung around from the window in a practiced movement that flung her big skirt up to swirl around her buttocks. It was a Jassy trick, calculated to shock the Lady Claudia onstage. "I thought that car looked familiar. He's pulling into the curb now. Great! I'll let him in and make the tea."

Max came through the open door. He was tall, strong-looking, flamboyantly masculine, an extravert with dark hair that crinkled at the hairline, then straightened to lie thickly across his head. He had good teeth, toothpaste advertisement teeth if they had been straight, but they weren't, and his grayish eyes were steady. A cut lip from a charity boxing bout—he had gone five rounds in the ring with the famous Sam Sieger, hopelessly outclassed, emerging a mini-hero—had left him with a small scar on his underlip. "Well?"

They smiled at each other over the child's head. Sara felt guilty because Guy had dominated her thoughts all day.

"'Ere's the tea," announced Raine in her Cockney, Jassy voice, dumping the tray on the coffee table. "I'm orf. I'll be back by six."

2

MAX and Sara had met at a Chelsea party when Primmy was less than a month old. As he entered the room, he had seen her sitting quietly on a low window seat between two magnificent tropical plants. He thought immediately, with wry amusement, that this girl with the long, elegant legs, the straight back, the proudly lifted chin, had placed herself deliberately and with conceit in that very paintable, very photographable position so that any young Snowdon or Messell might in the moment of his arrival have her image unforgettably printed on his mind. Later, when he knew her, he realized that Sara was drawn to beauty. She wasn't innocent of her own good looks. How could she be? But she didn't flaunt them. She didn't have to. He sensed that, mysteriously, she was almost afraid of her beauty. He had seen her react oddly to a stranger's compliments as though looking behind the words for some obscure threat. It was one of the things about her he didn't understand.

"I had a baby a few weeks ago," she had said that evening in answer to his smiling, teasing flattery, "and I've been rehearsing all day for a TV play. I need to sit down." She told him that the child was in the guest room, in her carrycot.

"All the beauties are taken," he said regretfully. "Which is your husband?"

"I'm not married. And the child's father is dead."

"Oh."

It seemed to Max that he never saw another woman after those first few startled moments. He was overtaken by a wild, crazy desire to ask her to marry him then and there. And when the euphoria went away it was replaced by a deep inner consciousness that he and Sara belonged together.

He had run into her the next day in the city, the most unlikely of places. "I absolutely never come down here!" she said. She had looked up at Max in a haze of astonishment. "Just today, to see a friend for lunch. He had only one free hour, so it was better for him—better for both of us—if I came to his office."

Max wasn't listening to what she said or he might have been daunted by the knowledge that she had crossed London to meet a man.

He was looking at the soft powder-blueness of her in her pretty suit with the sharp wind catching her hair in feathery fans and tossing it high. "You've nothing to go back for, have you?" he asked, guiltily pushing aside the picture of a mountain of work lying on his desk.

"No."

He took her arm, dashing her away from the traffic toward the river. It was a bright, sunny October day. The turgid Thames glittered falsely silver as it ran fast on a receding tide and the chestnuts scattered their first autumnal leaves on the Embankment. "Where's the baby?"

"If Raine hasn't got a matinee she'll often take over."

"Raine?"

"Raine Mathieson. We share a flat. She's in Ten Times Truly at the Haymarket. If you haven't seen it, you should go. It's frightfully funny."

"Would you come with me?"

"With pleasure."

"And you? When you're not looking after little babies, where are you likely to be working?"

"I've never been on in the West End. Not

yet. But I will." She was good-natured about it. "You can't have all of the things all of the time. That's in the rules."

On a freezing November day, he took her to Brighton on the Veteran Car run, both of them wrapped snugly in rugs. Glowing from beneath a wide hat tied by veiling under her chin, she sat beside him in his father's de Dion Bouton as they motored serenely through Sussex.

Later, they danced the night away, Sara beautiful in a long, flowing dress. "By simply draping rags over yourself, you make them look like that?" His arms came tightly around her, his cheek touched hers. She had this odd ability to puzzle and surprise him—to block his throat sometimes with an emotion beyond his control. She had an intense vulnerability he had never seen in anyone before.

That she was not going to make the ideal wife was spectacularly clear. People pointed the facts out to him, and so did Sara.

"I shall be going on tour when a play calls for it."

"Of course. I shall be lonely. Especially lonely if you take Primmy with you."

"Do you realize what it's like to be married

to a woman who works in the evenings, when you work during the day?''

''Not yet, but I shall.''

''Every evening,'' she persisted gently. ''I am only happy when I'm acting.'' But her eyes were on his, closely, and there was uncertainty in them. ''You don't seem to be getting a very good deal.''

''It's the deal I want. I love you, Sara.''

A brief moment of hesitation. Then, quietly, gravely, even a little nervously, ''I love you, too.''

Friends told him about Sara's unexplained and apparently inexplicable past. Being none of his business, he thought, it couldn't touch him.

''Well?'' In the Osbon Square sitting room, on the day that Two's a Risk was to open, Max spoke softly.

''Well?'' The blue eyes shimmered up at him, then slid away. He kissed her, and felt her lips tremble beneath his.

''Why don't we use the party tonight to announce our engagement?''

''Oh, Max.''

''Oh, Sara,'' he mimicked. Sitting beside her on the sofa he gently prized one of her hands from where it lay across the back of the child to hold it between his own. "You're never going to marry me if I don't bully you into it and give you a deadline. What about midnight tonight? Deadline midnight!" She was like a madonna, with the sleeping child in her arms. Max wanted her now more than he had ever wanted anything in his life. He had never been bothered by Guy's ghost. Given a sanction, he felt he could exorcise that. He thought he could have swept Sara off her feet, but something told him not to weaken his position by using force.

Max was thirty. Born to privilege, with a father who was head of an industrial firm, he had sown his wild oats early. Expelled from a top public school as an "example" for smoking some pot offered to him in a pub, he went with perceptions heightened by anger through grammar school to Oxford and a first-class degree. This was followed by an American M.B.A. and a lengthy bus and camping tour of the United States. Then a period of uncertainty for his family while he tramped around India with a pack on his back, and finally, a journey east via the trans-Siberian railway. On his return home he had joined the advertising company where he was now a partner.

Max liked ambitious women. His ideal wife would have interests of her own. And he was prepared for marriage on a totally sharing basis. From the hard beginnings of a small fire outside a tent in India, Turkey, Ohio, and Tennessee, he had come to be a good plain cook. He was intrigued, even pleased, with the thought of turning his proficiency into an art during the evenings when Sara was onstage.

"You shall have a Cordon Bleu meal every night after the theatre."

"But if I get fat with all this attention I won't get parts." Always the theatre was in the forefront of her mind.

The afternoon sun was slanting through the chintz curtains. Primmy was quiet. It was already five-thirty.

Max leaned toward her. "Well? What about midnight tonight for the announcement?"

Sara felt herself slipping, giving way. She reached out in panic for the tension she had lived with for so long that it seemed a part of her safety. "You haven't met my family yet."

"I wasn't intending to marry your family." Max looked down at the child, touched the soft, rounded baby cheek. "She likes me. But I don't have to pass muster with your brother, do I? What's his name, Elliott?" Raine had told him a bit about Elliott. Raine avoided him, perhaps only because he had once pursued her. Not wanting to get involved with your friend's brother was a situation in itself, he guessed.

"No, of course not. You'll meet Elliott and Lil tonight."

"We're sitting together?"

"No. It wasn't possible to get everyone together."

"Well," said Max, drawing in a deep breath and starting again, "by say, ten-thirty or so, I'll have met the family." He wondered why she hadn't taken a block of seats together for her family and friends. Because she hadn't really faced up to the fact that they were to meet? And if so, why? He turned her to face him and looked into her eyes. "Sara, will you marry me?"

Both of them were sharply, poignantly aware that the child lay between them. Aware of a symbolism in her presence that neither wanted to identify. The past flooded around Sara in a scattering of memories. She had to beat it. Max's timing was perfect. Her West

End debut was a new beginning. She must rip away the past. The anonymous letter she had expected the manager or the director to receive had apparently not arrived. Perhaps this really was the new beginning. "I love you, Max." She felt a new sense of exultation before panic gripped her again.

"That's all I need to know, because I love you, Sara," Max said. "Let's make tomorrow the first day of a new life. You and I—with Primmy." The pause was deliberate. He planned to move the child kindly, and with intelligence, into her proper niche.

"Oh, Max!" A picture of Guy lying dead in a pool of his own blood overwhelmed her with fear. She gripped Max's hand, her knuckles whitening. "Max—"

"Yes, darling. It's going to be all right."

Dr. Charles Halbert was a tall, leggy, brown-haired, rather untidy man with an air of light-hearted good nature that hid a clever, complex personality. Those who knew nothing of his private life respected him greatly. Those who knew the effects but not the causes (especially his patients) regarded him uncertainly, hoping that what the gossips said was not so. A thinking man, Charles did not console himself with excuses. He found his burdens a challenge. He was a man's man who loved women. A man who had never lacked friends of either sex. A man who thought positively, reacted sensitively, and, surrounded as he was by friendship, love, and approval, inexplicably managed to make a mess of his private life.

Rounding the corner as he left Kettle Lane after visiting his elderly patient Mrs. Cavelley, he set off across Osbon Square. He was smiling to himself, thinking of the evening ahead. An opening night with a party afterward was something new for him. Regrettably, he would not be able to stay up with the cast to see the newspaper notices because morning surgery was at ten o'clock. The night birds could sleep all day if they so wished.

Fifty yards along the road the doctor hesitated, then turned back and took the route that would bring him past the building where the two women lived. They would be leaving for the theatre within half an hour or so. He decided to drop in to wish them luck. He had already sent them a bouquet of flowers apiece, Raine's more shyly significant with red roses and forget-me-nots. He quickened his step, thinking of Raine. How he wished, in his more sober, less stimulated moments, that he was not fated to lust after unsuitable women. One blatant matrimonial error had already smudged his career. Even today, with the change in feeling toward divorce—why even Royalty were separating, and marrying divorcées—a broken marriage was hazardous for a doctor. He'd lost patients when he and Caroline split up. Lost the faith of others. As the dear old lady in the lane had said, "A man who can't keep his own life in order . . ." One or two of the older and more fastidious women patients had left his list and nearly a half dozen middle-aged adventurers had swamped him, embarrassingly, with their attentions.

Over on the curb of the little road that ran off the square, he could see a Mercedes parked outside the Off-License liquor store and a man, unsuitably dressed for a hot day in tweeds and a cap set low on his forehead, staggering toward the open trunk with a large and clearly very heavy box in his arms. The man looked around guiltily, almost furtively, as he dropped the lid. What was he up to? Charles watched him with curiosity, then shrugged. Probably he was only nervously anticipating the arrival of a traffic warden.

Parking was hazardous in this area. The meter wardens were implacable, and the

Council refused to remove the double yellow line from outside McGarry's Off-License in spite of continuous applications by his clients and himself. Charles always had to walk to his patient, old Mrs. Cavelley, in the lane. There was nowhere to park there, either. The man in the tweed suit slipped into the driving seat and the Mercedes purred away.

As Charles approached number seven he saw that the double-fronted doors of the garage were slightly open. He moved several paces into the driveway where he could see if Raine's car was still there. It was. Turning, his eyes on a level with the sitting room window, he saw two figures locked in an embrace. He went more slowly toward the shallow steps leading to the front door, raised a hand to ring the bell, then paused. His hand dropped to his side and he turned away, hoping that whatever was going on there meant marriage. If ever a girl needed to be married, it was Sara.

Recently, as Sara's doctor, Charles had been aware that something considerably stronger than a normal attachment had developed between this mother and her child. Sara had become overprotective, overindulgent, over-absorbed with the small creature that she had deliberately brought into her already crowded world. It was almost as though Sara was afraid of losing her. Sara, in Charles's view, was a bit neurotic, perhaps slightly immature. But wasn't Max just the sort of fellow to set a girl back on her feet? Max was strong, normal, with a bubbling sense of humor. And he seemed to love Sara for the right reasons. Besides, and Charles smiled to himself suddenly as he bounded off across the square toward his own flat, her breaking away would leave Raine alone. Everyone said he should have married one of those highly suitable nurses his fellow medical students tied themselves to prior to qualifying, instead of the luscious, disastrous Caroline. Someone who, answering his telephone and his doorbell, would give the suffering world he inhabited a picture of unblemished and unblemishable respectability. Ah, well . . . Raine was a challenge and a delight. He ran up the steps, taking two at a time, and put his key in the lock.

Across at number seven Sara was saying breathlessly, "Yes, I will. I will marry you." Of course it was bound to come to this in the end—Max wasn't the type to give up once he had made up his mind. "I just hope you're not sorry. You don't know me very well. Not really very well." She was thinking about the past. She had no wish to involve him in the dark part of her life, the part she kept telling herself was over and which she knew perfectly well was not. There was too much that she could never share with him. The nightmare world that harassed her between two and four o'clock in the morning when her defenses were low. The secrets. The fears.

"Let's get married quickly and quietly." Make it a fait accompli, she meant.

There was a tightening of the muscles around her mouth, a flash of what could only be terror on her face. Max said swiftly, heartily, "Settled. I'll clear out the spare bedroom for Primmy."

"Oh, Max!" She was crying and laughing at the same time.

"Why don't you teach Primmy to crawl so that she can exercise a little tact and turn her back when I want to kiss you? You'll have to meet my parents," he added.

"They'll think I'm unsuitable."

"I expect so," he replied, deliberately laconic. "It is usual, even obligatory, where an only son is concerned."

"You know that's not what I mean."

"I do know. You heard me say I'm not

marrying your brother. By the same token, you're not marrying my parents. But they will love you dearly, anyway. And I'm sure I'll like your brother."

She wished she could talk to him about her parents. About the aloneness that was more than mere loneliness since their death. About Elliott's marriage and consequent withdrawal. "I'm very fond of Elliott."

"I'm glad."

"We used to be close before he married. I wanted so much for him to marry Raine."

Surprised by the emotion in her voice, he said consolingly, "Perhaps Lil was a better choice. And it's right that your closeness to Elliott should have been shaken when he married. It wouldn't be much of a marriage, would it, if he put you first? And if you're worried about my parents, they're the kind who would make a point of loving my wife, even if she had two heads."

They laughed together and the tension split into fragments.

3

HE went down the steps to the cellar. The gun was in the first niche on the right. He picked it up, unwrapped it, and slid it into the inside pocket of his jacket. Then he put the silencer into another pocket, switched off the light, and closed the heavy door. The garage was securely locked, the car standing beside the big buttonhole rose tree that grew at the edge of the drive and shed its pale petals all over the ground. He liked roses. He stopped to pick a bud, set it in his lapel, climbed into the car and drove off. There was a telephone box three hundred yards down the road. He braked. A woman using the phone glanced up. He accelerated, averting his face as he passed. He cruised down the road looking for another box. Not finding one, he drove back slowly. The woman was gone. He jumped quickly out of the car and went inside. He put the piece of gauze over the mouthpiece and dialed. A quick, bright voice said, "Hello." He spoke with his mouth nearly closed, the way he had practiced. "I'm ringing for Sara

Tindall. She decided to take the baby to friends for the night, so she won't need you after all."

Silence. Then the girl said resentfully, "She might have given me some notice. I turned down an invitation . . ."

He broke in quickly. "She asked me to say she'll pay you. It was unexpected. She'll explain."

"Okay." The girl sounded faintly mollified, but disappointed all the same. "Okay. Thanks."

He looked around carefully. The road was deserted. He climbed back into the car and drove fast toward Kensington.

The feeling of elation had gone. Sara hung the dress she had been wearing in her wardrobe. Only a moment ago she had been sitting on top of the world, right on top for the first time since Guy's death. Now she was down like a damp squib. Turmoil within, and a growing premonition of disaster. First night nerves? No. No. No. She glanced at the small gilt clock on her bedside table. Fifteen minutes to baby-sitter time. Tell Max. Tell him now.

She went with fast-beating heart down the passage, then stopped dead. Voices. Raine was back. Sara swung around and returned to her room. Max's bouquet was propped up in a broad, shallow dish on her dressing table. Charles's on the chest. How kind everyone was. Cling to that. Their generosity. Their trust in her. Their faith. Control the black fears. Keep busy. Get things ready. But there was nothing to get ready. Everything she wanted this evening was already at the theatre, safely in the hands of her dresser. The stage makeup was there, and the new pleated chiffon dress she had ordered especially for the party. Think about the party. About breakfast in Covent Garden. The first editions of the morning papers on the streets.

Think about Patrick Delvaney, strung up with excitement, prancing in Covent Garden market, waving the papers containing the rave notices he so confidently expected. Think about that, the success of the play. Don't call the engagement off. There's happiness here. Forget the past. It won't happen again. Her heart was listening, but not her brain. She closed her eyes, willing herself to be calm, fixed an actress's assured expression on her face, and went back to the sitting room. The baby was propped against a cushion in an armchair. She looked up at Sara, waved both arms, and gave a triumphant yell. "Aaah!"

Cold fear clutched at Sara's heart.

"Ruth hasn't arrived," said Raine, looking anxiously at her wristwatch.

"She's never been late. She isn't due for another five minutes." Then, with a quick intake of breath, Sara turned to Max. Everything she had tried to push away surged forward again. "Max, I've been having second thoughts. Let's not—"

He grasped her hands. "Let's," he said, his mouth smiling, his eyes grave.

His strength flowed into her, pressing down on the sharp edges of terror that cut through her assumed calm. Her smile held the tremulous quality of a vulnerable child.

Momentarily, Max was conscience-stricken about saddling her on this night of nights with perhaps too great a weight. But the guilt passed because he felt sure that their marriage was right. Patrick Delvaney was certain this play was a winner. A winner for Sara's first night in the West End! Max wanted badly to make it the biggest and best night of her life. He was more cognizant of her problems than she guessed. Patrick Delvaney and Raine had filled him in. They sensed the depth of his love.

So the baby-sitter had never been late, Max thought. Could this be the one night that she missed the bus, was held up by a telephone call, had an accident en route? "There's no point in hanging around if you're ready," he said calmly. "I'll stay until the girl comes. You two go off." He rested a hand on Sara's shoulder and gave her an affectionate little push. "Take her away, Raine. Just give me the baby-sitter's name and telephone number."

Sara's smile shimmered and that cold finger on her heart eased a little. Being with Max was like having the "iron" as they called the safety curtain, between her and the fire. "Ruth Willis is her name. Her number is on that pad on the desk."

"I'll ring her if she's more than a quarter of an hour late. And you know I would never leave Primmy alone, don't you? You'd trust me with her?"

Their eyes met. Of course Sara trusted him. With her life. She looked down at the small creature in the chair. The child gurgled, crowed, kicked her legs in a joyous, uncontrolled movement, and flung her arms invitingly wide. But not with her baby's life. She didn't trust anyone with that. She gathered the child up warmly, kissing the top of the round, golden head. She handed the bundle to Max. "Good luck, both of you," he said, waving them away. "I'll come backstage as soon as I get there."

"Please."

He kissed Sara tenderly. Then, so that Raine wouldn't guess—because they had yet to tell her of the engagement—he kissed her, too. "Good luck," he said again. He stood at the window watching Raine back her little Triumph Spitfire out of the garage. He lifted the sash with one hand. "Don't bother with the doors. I'll shut them when I go." Raine shook her head, mouthed "Ruth" from the street, and waved one arm in a swishing movement, indicating that the baby-sitter would use the garage for her own car. From the passenger seat Sara smiled and waved. The little car shot off across the square.

Max closed the window and looked down at the child in his arms. Primmy stared gravely back at him. He said aloud, "We're going to be family now." She was a bulky little bundle with her dress spread wide over whatever it was babies wore underneath. Tiny feet in yellow shoes, a soft woolly jacket. Rather like a doll, he thought, and wondered if it was their doll-like qualities that made unmarried mothers want to keep their babies. He held up a finger and she grasped it and held it tightly, though still looking at him with that uncertain expression. He smiled. She began slowly to smile in return. He felt flattered. Odd to be a father, almost, before he was actually a husband.

He had not introduced Sara to his family because he knew they would be no more pleased about the baby than about the mystery surrounding the death of Primmy's natural father. Not that he intended to discuss it. But he had never been naive about human nature. His marriage must be a fait accompli before the busybodies at his mother's bridge club dug out the scandal. He knew his parents well. They would not distress him with criticism and disapproval once Sara was their daughter-in-law.

He glanced at his watch. That girl Ruth was indeed late now. He crossed to the desk and stood looking down at the list of names, dates, and numbers that composed the baby-sitter roster. Ruth Willis's number was at the top. Then he heard a car swish up the driveway and through the window the tail end of it disappear into the garage. Ah, good. He went back to the baby, lifting her onto his knee. The back door was open. Sara had said the girl would walk in.

Max looked up as the door moved. It opened slowly, very slowly, as though a cat smoothed itself along the length of it. There had been no banging of a car door, no footsteps. Max's brows furrowed into a faint frown and his mind opened to surprise as he watched the door edge moving toward him through the silence. He asked uncertainly, "Miss Will—?" and then it was flung wide. Distorted features in a pinkish face enclosed in a nylon stocking, a cap low over the forehead, a gun pointing directly at him. He tried, clumsily, to leap to his feet, tried to fling the child behind him, shielding her. "What the hell!" The gun went off with a dull thump. He fell across the child. She was too astonished to yell. He managed to hurl himself upright, staggering. His left arm dropped limply to his side. He let fly with his right fist, wildly. The man side-stepped. Max saw the butt of the gun rising above his head. God in heaven! This was it! There was nothing he could do to avoid it. Then he felt the blow on the back of his neck, lurched in a desperate, futile effort to save himself, and fell forward with a thud on the carpet.

4

"BUT he did say he would come backstage," Sara reminded Raine. They were made-up and ready to go on. Sara wore a magnificent gown, dark green with gold flecks. No cost had been spared in this production. With her golden hair swept smoothly into a flat coil at the back of her head, she looked every inch the wife of a high-ranking diplomat. She wore crocodile accessories, exquisitely made, the gift of Bond Street shoemakers who, looking for publicity for their new shop, had encountered Patrick in one of his most persuasive and ebullient moments. And diamonds. Cartier had offered to loan the real thing, but the management was unwilling to tackle the security problems. Besides, good paste looked real.

"No," Raine replied, "I didn't hear Max say that." It was not the moment for Sara to lose control. Raine added, "But if he did, he'd remember afterward that visitors are allowed in the dressing room only up to the half."

That meant thirty-five minutes prior to curtain time. "If he didn't," she added for good measure, "as you know very well, he'd be stopped at the stage door." In an effort to redirect Sara's attention she spun around in a circle, her parlor maid's skirt lifted audaciously to expose the very last inch of her thighs. "I've got that to a fine art, now." Her eyes gleamed mischievously. "One millimeter higher and the coachloads from Bradford would walk out in disgust."

Sara smiled, obsessed with the fact that Max had not turned up. Nor telephoned. Something had gone wrong . . . Her fingers beat a small tattoo on the dressing table, and the untidy pile of congratulatory telegrams fluttered to the floor. Bouquets lay everywhere: on the couch, on chairs, propped against the wall. The air was heavy with their scent.

"I'll move the bouquets. You should be resting on that couch." Raine spoke like a mother talking to a child. She supposed the truth of it was that the baby-sitter had let Sara down. But Max would cope. He'd rustle up somebody, or take the child somewhere, before the end of the first act. Max had many friends. She smiled at Sara and Sara smiled back. It was not the first time they had acted together. They knew how to bolster each other up.

"Half an hour, please, ladies and gentlemen." The voice burst in upon them from the speaker, and Sara jumped.

"Well, that's it." Raine turned away to hide her relief. There was a potent excuse, now, for Max's nonappearance.

With a quick tap at the door the dresser entered, carrying some hangers. Sara asked her to run up to the stage door and see if Max was there. Hannah was back swiftly. "Nobody."

The stage director put his head in at the door. "Everything okay?" He frowned faintly at Raine and she slipped away. The cast were supposed to be in their own rooms at this time.

"Okay," Sara assured him. He moved on to check the other dressing rooms.

Hannah smoothed a loose strand of hair, then gave Sara's skirt a small tug. "You look marvelous, dear."

"That's sweet of you, Hannah," she said, but her mind was on Max. On Primmy, too. Where was Max?

"Shall I stay with you, dear?" she asked.

"Thanks." Sara sat down on the divan and stared blankly at herself in the big mirror opposite, seeing only Max with the child in his arms. Hannah began to tidy up the bottles and jars. By average standards this was a palatial dressing room. The Galaxy was the manager's own theatre. He had made a small fortune from a farce that ran for eight years at the Prince. He had spent some of the money renovating the Galaxy. "There's nowhere to go but down after this," Raine had declared exultantly when she saw her own dressing room. With star billing, she had the best.

Where was Max?

The stage director's voice sounded, low but clear, from the speaker in the corner. "Act one. Beginners please. Act one. Beginners please. Miss Mathieson. Miss Tindall."

Sara swallowed. Hannah brushed aside the floral curtain and smiled in her calm, motherly way. "Good luck, love." Sara tried to speak, failed, and nodded an acknowledgement. Raine joined her outside the door. They went together in silence up the stairs to the double doors, then quietly through to the wings. Raine moved ahead. When the curtain went up she was supposed to be dusting furniture. She went onstage and got into position. A pause, then the big velvet drapes slid silently apart. There was a burst of clapping, Sara moved into place for her entrance. Then suddenly everything to do with her private life faded away and she was Claudia, strung tight, it was true, but not afraid anymore. She strolled casually into the audience's view, smiling. "Good morning, Jassy," she said in that clipped, upper-class accent that belonged to the Lady Claudia. "Has his Lordship gone?"

Nobody clapped, because Sara was not an established star. Raine was, and the public knew and liked her. Two's a Risk, with Raine Mathieson in lights outside the theatre. Raine Mathieson above the title on the billing with and Sara Tindall below.

As the curtains closed after the first act Patrick Delvaney bounded across the stage. "Great! Great!" he exclaimed. "Not only beautiful, but clever. You were transported, Sara, my darling. Out of this world! You're marvelous!" If he hadn't been three inches shorter than she, he would have swung her off her feet.

"And me?" said Raine, standing elegantly, one knee bent in front of the other, pretending to sulk.

"Magnificent, darling!" He pushed them

upstage a little to avoid the iron as it came down. "You were all splendid."

Sara turned to Raine, her voice taut, her beautiful face drawn. "Max was not in his seat. He should have been in the center of the third row of the stalls next to Barry Trent. Barry was there. Max's seat was vacant."

Delvaney heard and reacted quickly. "Perhaps he changed it. The third row is a bit far forward."

"He wouldn't change his seat." Sara's voice was a little out of control. One of the other members of the cast, passing in the hallway, looked at her in surprise. "He knows I can see Row C from the stage," she said.

Silence. Those who had moved ahead hesitated. One or two turned back, gathered around Sara protectively. They were gentle, concerned. Delvaney said cheerfully, "I should think the baby-sitter has let you down."

"She doesn't let me down. Ever."

"Okay, there's always a first time. I'll go out and see if I can find him, just to put your mind at rest. He'll be there. I can't see Max missing the first night. Can you?" He didn't wait for an answer, but when he had walked a few steps he turned. "If I don't get back, don't worry. The theatre's packed. It won't be easy. Wait in your dressing room." He spoke with authority, director to cast. Sara knew it was an order. She knew also that Max was not in the theatre.

Raine said, wheedling gently, "Come on, ducky." The rest of the cast stood silently. They knew controlled panic when they saw it.

Sara scarcely heard Raine's words. She was watching Patrick Delvaney's receding figure. Behind her Raine asked wryly, "Don't you trust anyone, Sara?" She didn't answer. They went back through the wings, down the wooden stairs, and along the corridor to Sara's dressing room.

The dresser was standing by the wardrobe holding the outfit Sara was to wear in the second act. Ignoring her, Sara slipped out of the door and into Raine's dressing room. The star had a telephone. It was buried beneath an avalanche of bouquets. She lifted the receiver. "Bert, give me an outside line, please." She dialed. The ringing went on and on, interminably. Sara allowed it to continue long after she knew there was no one in the flat.

"What's going on, Sara?"

"There's no reply." Sara's eyes were wide with fear. "Ruth isn't there."

Hannah came into the dressing room. She said gently, "Let me help you change, dear. Time's passing."

"Perhaps she's in the loo," Raine suggested, trying to sound off-hand. "Or perhaps she has taken the child for a walk." She took Sara's arm, turned her around to face the dresser. "Go on back to your own room. As Hannah said, there isn't a lot of time."

Sara side-stepped, avoiding Raine's hand. Her face, under the stage coloring, was ashen. "Raine, someone must go to the flat."

"Yes, of course. But what on earth could have gone wrong?" Raine asked. She was calm. Reasonable. There was no hurry for her. She didn't have to change. Her wardrobe mistress was watching in silence. "If Ruth didn't turn up, Max would take Primmy to a friend's place. That's logical. He wouldn't want to miss the show if there were a way out. Come on." They led her back to her own room.

"Sara, dear, let me have your jacket." That was Hannah, beseeching.

Expertly, Sara ripped the buttons undone, shrugged the garment off her shoulders, and took the new one. In a blind flailing of arms, her dress half over her head, she swung back toward the door. "I'll ring Ruth. I'll ring her at home."

Raine grasped her arm, turned her forcibly back to the dresser. Hannah was tight-lipped, faintly distrait. "Not now, Sara, not now. There isn't time. You've got to change."

The stage director's voice whispered over the speaker, "Act two. Beginners, ladies and gentlemen. Mr. George. Mr. Dupont. Miss Tindall."

"Hannah, I'll write down Ruth's number," said Raine. "You ring." She picked up a pencil from beside the telephone.

The pent-up tension broke and Sara lost control. "My child has gone," she screamed. "My child has gone! I knew—" She broke off as Raine hit her sharply, but not hard, across the face. Raine began to write down Ruth Willis's telephone number. She wasn't even sure if it was right. She didn't care. Hannah would cover up. The voice on the loudspeaker whispered anxiously, "Miss Tindall."

The dresser said in a sharp whisper, "Your hair," and began to smooth the coil at the back of Sara's head. "Miss Tindall!" The stage director's voice was sharp, demanding. Raine was holding the door open. Sara flashed through it, along the corridor, up the stairs two at a time, and into the wings. She smiled tightly at the stage manager and he wiped his brow in return, flicking imaginary drops of sweat from his fingers to the floor. Sara straightened. At every crisis in her life she had been able, miraculously, to turn to the stage for comfort. She emptied out the agony, purged herself of everything except Claudia, and walked calmly on. "Malcolm, I want a word with you before the Ambassador arrives."

Delvaney, waiting in the wings, hidden behind one of the flats, moved silently to Raine's side, his face closed, his fingers gripped so tightly that the nails bit into his palms. Wasn't this what he had been afraid of? Hadn't he mistrusted the bloody girl? Even knowing she was magnificent, wanting her desperately for the part of Claudia, he had not, in his heart, felt safe with her. Illogically, his sympathy had been heightened by the anonymous letter. He had thought that whoever wrote it needed putting down, thought that any girl with a bastard like that on her back deserved a break. But there was no room for sentiment when so much was at stake. He'd been a fool. He had gambled with chance and lost.

Raine whispered, outwardly cool. "Is Max here?"

"No."

"If the baby-sitter didn't turn up, then she didn't turn up at six. Three hours ago. Max has had plenty of time to either get someone else or take the child to a friend. He would do that. Max would use his brains." She said tensely, "Things have gone wrong, Patrick, and Sara knows. Can you get someone around to the flat?"

"Sure. But who?"

"Her brother Elliott's here somewhere. I glimpsed his wife in the crowd earlier, but I don't know where they're sitting. The trouble is, all our friends are in the audience tonight, and that includes Charles, her G.P. who lives across the square from the flat. Charles is in Row D. Seat number nine."

"There's no one in D9," returned Patrick with conviction. "It's directly behind Max's empty seat, that's how I noticed. It's vacant, too." Raine looked at him stonily.

"I'll ring The Jolly Fox and ask them to send someone around to your flat."

Afterward, Sara didn't remember anything about the second act, but everybody else recalled that she played it magnificently. With her panic trapped behind a closed door of sheer professionalism, she transported herself into another being. If she looked at the vacant seat in the third row of the stalls she did not allow herself to recognize it for what it was. When she came off for ten minutes at one point, Delvaney met her with a bland smile. All was well, he lied. The baby-sitter had been taken violently ill after eating oysters. She had telephoned and Max persuaded Sara's doctor, Charles what's his name, to run over to her. It was a pity Charles and Max were having to miss the first night, the director added. He was doing a brilliant acting job himself as the falsehoods fell one after the other from his lips, but everyone was saying the play would run for years.

He had reckoned without Sara's sixth sense, which was more than a sixth sense where the child was involved. She knew that he lied out of concern for the show. No matter what is happening in your private life, you will appear onstage and will be expected to give your best. She crept into the dressing room like a torn wraith. Hadn't she known, ever since accepting Max's proposal, that something was going to happen? Wanting Max was not in the rules, just as wanting Guy had not been.

She looked up sharply as the stage manager opened the door. What was he doing away from the prompt corner? "Are you all right, Miss Tindall?" He had never spoken to her like that before, with compassion. To him the cast were cogs that made the machine of the play run. She rose, closed the door tremblingly on her private life, and walked along the passage, up the stairs, through the double doors, and into the wings. Claudia. Stately, calm Claudia, ready to do battle with her recalcitrant maid.

Raine appeared, apparently from nowhere, transported into her own part. Sara knew they had kept Raine away from her because Raine had been told what it was that had gone terribly wrong at the flat. Knew, possibly, what had happened to the child. "Gasping its last breath," Patrick had said when he agreed that she should have the part of Claudia.

Even with Primmy and Max gasping their last breath, the show had to go on.

5

IT was a converted Elizabethan farmhouse only ten miles from London. There were fields in back of the houses, an old ruined church, a pony, a donkey, barns, chickens, a little group of shops, a village green gone to ruin because there was no village now. Suburban London was encroaching, with ribboning lanes and highways. The big house on the knoll was an old people's home now, the little school had given way to a vast outer London comprehensive school. It had stopped being the kind of place where people cared about each other.

The gravel drive cut through a high hedge and ran around to the rear of Wild Hatch. He parked, jumped out, and unlocked the back door of the house which led to an Elizabethan kitchen recently modernized for renting to highly paid oil men such as Retenmeyer. A modern eye-level grill, a glass-doored oven. A big inglenook fireplace. An oak table. Half a dozen copper pots hanging high on the walls.

The door to the cellar was made of heavy

planks reinforced by hand-hewn crossbars and fitted with enormous, hand-wrought iron hinges. An original Elizabethan door, possibly made from ships' timbers. On the inside there was no catch. No catch! He gulped, wiped great beads of sweat from his face. How easily he could have locked himself in when hiding the gun! He returned to the kitchen, abruptly conscious of unseen traps, of the need to be painstaking and sharply alert, of not letting his emotions muddle his brain. He put the gun down on the kitchen table, went back to the door.

He stood trembling with excitement, taking in the size and thickness of the door, then raised the wooden bar and pulled it effortlessly back. He let the door go and watched with demonic wonder as it swung silently closed. The end of the wooden latch bounced against the door jamb, then settled.

The light switch was on the stone stairs. The cellar was made in the shape of a cross, more like a crypt than a cellar. The light, flooding out from a naked bulb, did not reach the tunnel. The beginnings of real excitement rose up in him and grew. This cellar was truly impregnable. Built in the Dark Ages of eleventh-century stone, Hermann had told him, and he had had the information from the estate agent. Underground for God alone knew what vile purpose. A place for the condemned. To bring them closer to God. He went to the bottom of the stairs, then slowly, his eyes dilating with the evil and the hope in him, walked across to the tunnel. A shaft of light, opaque and cobwebby, came down from an outside grille. A small stack of coal gleamed damply where the rain had seeped through. His eyes darted in all directions, narrowed, gleamed; his breath came through his teeth in a sucking, whistling sound. The sweat oozed warmly in his groin.

It was a manhole cover, that round iron plate with geometrical cutouts. Used as a coal hole. A big man could push it away with his hands, yell loud enough for the neighbors to hear. He'd find a heavy weight to put on top. Not one of the lions, of course. They would attract attention if anyone came into the garden. Besides, they were to have their own function. He allowed himself the joyous, ghoulish pleasure of picturing Max drowning. Drowning with the weight of the stone lions. He felt suddenly cocky. He might even decide to keep his prisoner longer than twenty-four hours. Play with him. It would depend upon how the rest of the plan went. He could drop food through the manhole. Talk. Watch the prisoner sweat.

Passing through the kitchen, he paused to take the largest copper pot down from the wall. One or two of the biggest stones from the rockery would fill this, and he would camouflage it with greenery. He put the pot down by the back door and went to check on Max. Peering in at the car window, he saw that the dark head had risen. He ducked out of sight. A quick, furtive glance around the garden. He reached into his pocket for the nylon stocking and pulled it over his head.

Max was sitting erect now, the gag still in place, looking groggy, as though still in the process of regaining consciousness. Leaning in, he grasped his prisoner beneath the armpits and hauled him out. Max, his feet tied, fell heavily on the gravel. Blood on the leather upholstery! Blood! He sucked the breath in sharply between his teeth. He'd have to get a damp cloth. And now, was that blood on the gravel? Anger rose out of apprehension. The plan had seemed so simple. So straightforward. But it was forged with tripwires and growing into a maze of complexities. He hauled the prisoner roughly to his feet, dragged him to the back door of the house, jolted him over the step. Max moaned.

Blood on the linoleum! That feverish sensation of panic shivered up through him. He dragged the body across the kitchen, down the short passageway, paused at the top of the steps leading to the cellar. Sweat poured down his face. Edge the body over the top step. Push it. Max half rolled, half fell down the stone steps to the cellar floor. A faint, agonized moan drifted back. He went down the steps, hauled Max into a sitting position, leaned him against the rough stone wall. Max was writhing now, trying to loosen the bonds. The bandage still held. The gag seemed safe.

He stood on the bottom step watching while the hazards melted and the slow warmth of fulfillment welled up inside of him. It hadn't been like this with Guy. He had fired, placed the gun carefully, then run. Unlike anonymous letters, too. He never saw Sara reading them, never saw the pain in her eyes, the fear.

This was immediate. This was satisfaction beyond belief. For the first time in his life he felt himself richly winning by his own efforts, and the excitement of it blazed through him in a panegyric of sheer joy.

Searing, agonizing pain. Where am I? What's the matter with my arms, I can't move them. Can't move my wrists. Sweet Jesus, my wrists are stuck together. My arm! Where am I now?

Max struggled. Cliffs of pain rose giddily before him. He tried to speak. The numbness around his mouth became, unacceptably, outrageously, a bandage. A gag. He tried to shout. Nothing. He raised his good shoulder, bent his head, rubbed the bandage against his shoulder. Rub hard. Push the band down, down over the chin. You can get it off. Ignore the pain. Ignore it. You can get the gag off. Jesus, who has done this to me? Why? Keep rubbing. The bandage is moving. Try harder. You can get it off. The pain! Oh God! The pain. Get the gag off. Get the gag off. Rub. Something moved. Someone. Max looked up and the bandage slid onto his chin.

A man was standing over him, looking down at him, his features pinkly contorted by a nylon mask. It was that same unreal man who had burst into Sara's flat. Behind the mask there were strange slit eyes, a tight mouth, a nose pressed sideways by the tug of the material. An evil face.

"Who the hell are you?" His throat was dry. Dry as dust. He swallowed hard. The creature looked grotesquely back at him. "What did you do with the baby? Where's Primmy? Is she here, too? Answer me, you bastard. If you've hurt that child . . ."

Nothing. No sound, no change of expression in that weird, half-demented, flattened face. "You devil!" Max shook his head and the gag slipped a little further, he tucked in his chin, and it fell to his chest—like a noose. "For God's sake, say something. What did you do with the child?" They stared at each other. He was a big man. He wore a heavy tweed suit and a tweed cap that hid his hair.

Max's forehead and chin hurt where they had been grazed when he was pushed down the steps. And he could taste blood. "This has to do with Sara, hasn't it?" he asked. The strange pink face with the narrow distorted eyes was still. Horrible.

Keep cool. "Couldn't you undo my hands?" he asked. "I'm in considerable pain." No reaction. No movement. Max's arm throbbed until his mind went dizzy and he lost control, said what he had not meant to say. "You crazy madman. You'll get life for this." No reply. No reaction. Keep calm. Don't make him angry. He could kill so easily. Then why hasn't he? "What have you to do with Sara?"

Anonymous letters. The death of Guy Fortune. "What's Sara to you? Did you kill Fortune? Jesus, will you answer me? I can't get free. At least tell me why you shot me and brought me here . . ."

The man turned slowly and went back up the steps. Silhouetted against the open doorway, he switched off the light. Max released a violent shout of protest. "Do you have to do that?" His jailer was coming back, blocking the light behind him. He moved close to where Max crouched against the wall, almost too close, as though deliberately taunting him. He reached up toward the ceiling and, in the pale light that again came in from the door, Max saw with horror what he was about to do. He hurled himself forward, flung the weight of his whole body at the man's legs, and fell heavily on the damp, greasy bricks.

The man swore, gave an angry grunt, kicked out, miraculously missed Max's face in the darkness, but caught his shoulder. Max rolled over, gasping with pain. "Leave the light. For pity's sake, leave the light." There was no reply, only the soft, mouselike sound of the bulb being removed. Max swung his trussed legs round and up, swung them hard. They bumped softly, ineffectually, against the man's legs. "You bastard!" said Max violently. "You bloody psychopath." The man in the mask went up the stone steps. Silhouetted against the light from the open door, he placed the bulb in one of the niches halfway up the stairway. Then he closed the door and darkness came.

Darkness like suffocation. Like a black, damp weight. Like mustiness and despair. Dropping his head so that it rested on his knees, Max gave a long anguished sigh and closed his eyes on the present.

Sara! None of this had anything to do with him. It couldn't. He'd made no enemies. Attached no mysteries to himself. Sara! Why hadn't he listened when they told him that Sara received insulting anonymous letters, that people concerned with Sara received communications spitting with lies about her? Why hadn't he questioned her? Well, he knew. He thought anyone with Sara's looks was bound to have rejected suitors. He didn't believe he had a right to question her about her past. He thought she'd had bad luck. Been attracted by the wrong sort of man. If it happened again he was fully prepared to go straight to the police. No one was going to send anonymous letters to his wife and get away with it.

Guy? Guy got himself murdered. Full stop. If you loved a woman you did not, or could not, see her as a murderer. You didn't fall in love with anyone capable of murder. Murder was not in your books. You listened, shrugged distastefully, and put stories like that out of your mind. You did until a maniac with a gun attacked you, tied you up, and imprisoned you in a cellar.

Time to start thinking.

Curiously, after that first accidental meeting it was Sara who did the running. Max had told her he owned a cabin cruiser called Little Mint berthed temporarily above Chelsea while some work was being done on the engines. She had turned up the following Saturday morning in Raine's little car. "Come aboard," he had shouted. Happiness had exploded into the day.

"I've got Primmy."

"Bring her. Wait a sec, I'll give you a hand." Pulling on a T-shirt, he sprinted up the ramp, and showed her where to park. The tiny baby was asleep in her carrycot. Sara lifted her out of the car. Max had forgotten how tall Sara was. How elegant. He'd thought her merely beautiful. But when they stood side by side to cross the road back to the river he discovered he was towering over her. She was not, after all, so tall. It was the way she stood. She wore a cheap, salmon-colored polo shirt that quixotically went with her hair. Tight jeans. Life was throbbing through her. The sun was on her face and behind it. Vitality seemed to overflow. They put the carrycot in the cabin. "I'll make you some coffee. Cocoa? Tea? Beer?"

She smiled. "Yes, cocoa would be nice. Max, I've got some wonderful news. I've been offered a new part."

"Congratulations. Did you come down especially to tell me?"

She nodded, bright-eyed.

"I'm greatly flattered." He found himself speaking with idiotic gravity, overwhelmed by the potency of her attention, by his too great luck. "Is this a West End part?"

Those very blue eyes danced. "West End! Cor!" she said, twisting up the beautiful face like a Cockney comic. "Well, it's the next best. We open at Brighton on the twenty-eighth. There will be West End managements down to see it."

"You mean people go down to Brighton to look the play over? Sum up its potential?"

Max knew nothing about the way the theatre worked.

"That's right. Brighton's a shop window. But anyway, if it did go to the West End I wouldn't necessarily go with it. I could audition for my part because it's a secondary one." She was bubbling with happiness, the words falling over each other. "Providing, that is, it all happened after the Rep season ends. Putting a play on in the West End is more involved than you'd think. There has to be a theatre available at the right date. There are all sorts of considerations. You're talking about hitting the jackpot." But she looked ready to receive the jackpot, sitting there with the cocoa in her hands and stars in her eyes. He seemed to be walking on air himself. There was an element in her that had the power to lift him, too, carry him forward on a bright thread of optimism.

"What's the name of the play?"

"Topaz. Topaz."

"Funny name."

"It's a funny play."

"D'you know, you've got the most alive face I've ever seen. Has anyone else said that?" She went quiet and he thought with gravity, though not with any sort of despair, yes. That other chap. Guy. Don't push your luck. Even later, when he knew Sara loved him, he never fooled himself into believing that she had forgotten the child's father. He knew only too well whom she was thinking of when she looked at the baby, her beautiful eyes like dark sapphires, the light gone from them.

That morning on Little Mint Sara talked knowledgeably about boats. "You're an experienced sailor?" he asked in surprise.

"No. But my brother, Elliott, has a cruiser. I used to go out on it."

"Don't you go out on your brother's boat anymore?"

"He's married now."

"Oh." Max waited, but she didn't volunteer any more.

After that, while rehearsing for Topaz, Topaz, she came often to Little Mint when he was working on her, bringing Primmy with her smart little carrycot lined in Laura Ashley patchwork and her fluffy toys. Max watched the child grow from doll size, watched her fill out. Max never minded her coming. She was part of the relationship. He was in love with them both, he discovered, rather to his surprise. Sometimes, when Raine looked after the child, he had a feeling of incompleteness. And Sara would be a little on edge.

Just before Sara left for Brighton they spent a whole day on Little Mint. Sara cooked a meal in the galley, a marvelous feast of chicken with yogurt, tomato puree, selected herbs. Max produced champagne to drink a toast to the play's success. As they cruised upriver past Hampton Court, Sara said, "There's my brother's boat. The Sally Blow." Max turned from the wheel, saw a smart cruiser, white-hulled with a blue waterline.

He said, "It's a beauty. Is Elliott rich?"

"He is, rather."

"A tycoon?"

"Nothing like that. My father had a manufacturing business. You've probably heard of it. Silofoam Industrial."

"Everyone's heard of Silofoam Industrial. Does your brother run it?"

"No. Our father hoped he would. He was involved with it when he first left school but not very enthusiastically, and when my parents died he sold it." She volunteered nothing of what he was to hear later from others. The fire at Carmarthen. Sara's exclusion from her parents' will.

The cast of Topaz, Topaz assembled and

went to Sussex. Desolation. A light gone from Max's life. He dashed to Brighton for the opening night, then twice during that week, and again for the two weekends. It was not, after all, such a funny play, and the leading man let down an otherwise good cast. It never got to the West End. But Ted Lonigan saw it. Saw Sara, met Max, put on his thinking cap. Made inquiries. There was little enough Max could have told him at the time, and what he did know he kept to himself. But Patrick, when he came to consider Sara for the part of Claudia, inevitably learned of Sara's background. Inevitably took fright. Max knew how the manager of Two's a Risk had had to argue to get Sara in the cast.

6

CHARLES HALBERT, carrying his little black bag, went wearily up the steps to his flat. He was no longer thinking of the first night showing of Two's a Risk, or even of the party afterward that he could still attend if he wished. Earlier in the evening, when he was about to begin dressing, the old lady's son had telephoned to say she had taken a turn for the worse. That, unbelievably, was nearly three hours ago. Time had telescoped in the drama of keeping the patient alive. He felt washed out now, depressed. He checked his watch and remembered his engagement. The second act would be barely over. Oh hell! He let himself into his flat, stood indecisively in the middle of the room. Should he have a quick drink and rush off to see what he could of the show? Or should he have something to eat and relax, then turn up in time for the party? Or, he thought longingly, merely go to bed. His patients were right. He needed a wife. A proper one. A picture of the beautiful Raine

Mathieson flashed across his mind, her hair a thick, tossing dark mane, her mouth laughing, her slender feet dancing. Raine, vital, flamboyant, bold. She was not, probably never would be, a suitable wife for a doctor any more than Caroline had been. I had better repeat that to myself twelve times daily, he thought, knowing he wouldn't.

The flat looked depressingly empty. He made a snap decision. He'd go to the theatre and cheer himself up. He went to the kitchen and filled the kettle. In the refrigerator, looking for milk, he found a foil-wrapped little bundle labeled: "Heat for 25 mins at 425." He peeped through the foil and found one of Mrs. Macready's lovely pies, switched on the oven, replaced the foil, put the parcel on a baking sheet, and went off with a small spring in his step to take a shower. People were great! They were worth all the trouble it took to keep them alive. Losing sleep. Missing first nights. Macready, his daily woman, had known his ex-wife Caroline. She was always urging him to marry again. "To the right one this time, Doctor," she would say coyly. She would recognize Raine at first glance as the wrong one again. Oh well . . .

He was toweling himself dry when he heard

the wail of a police siren and glanced out of the open window. The long blue car dashed in from the Knightsbridge end of the square, swung around the corner, and disappeared beyond the trees. The wailing stopped abruptly, too abruptly, just by the corner. Charles stood still with the towel in his hand. An uneasiness crept over him and took over. He dressed quickly, went into the kitchen, and took the lukewarm pie out of the oven. Lukewarm. A pity. Never mind. It tasted good. He ate it swiftly, standing at the kitchen sink. Brushing the flakes of pastry from his fingers, he picked up his wallet and car keys, then let himself out of the flat.

He saw the police car immediately, and with a sick sense of shock realized that it was parked outside number seven. He swung left, pulling in at the entrance to the garage where Raine kept her car. When the engine was switched off, he could hear the child's hysterical screaming. He leaped out of the car, slammed the door, and hurried around to the front. A uniformed policeman, an immensely tall man, met him at the partly open door. The policeman had a benign baby face and large round eyes.

"I'm Dr. Halbert," Charles said, "Miss

Tindall's doctor. I happened to be passing and saw your car. Is there anything wrong? Is there something I can do?"

The officer said, "Come in, Doctor." He led the way into the familiar chintzy sitting room. A hefty policewoman held the screaming child in her arms, rocking her back and forth, concentrating as though trying to remember how she had been tutored for just such an occasion. There was blood on the carpet and the sofa, blood over the child. Charles stared, appalled. He was introduced to Superintendent Oliver, a tough-looking man with sandy hair and a steely look. "Perhaps you can help," the officer acceded. "The mother's an actress?"

"That's right. She's onstage at this moment." Without preamble Charles went to the policewoman and took the child. "Is she hurt?" The little dress was stiff where the blood had dried, the small round face was white and blotched with crying.

"I don't think she's hurt," said the woman, "but heaven knows how long she's been here, alone."

"I'll have a look at her." The child strained away from him, screaming. Deftly, he removed the bloodstained outer garments. He was already fairly certain she was unhurt. He quickly looked over the small form. "She's all right. Thank God for that." He held her against his shoulder, and after a while she calmed. He looked down at the blood on the carpet, shuddered, and turned away. It had sprayed across the cushions and the end of the sofa.

"Who was the baby-sitter?" the Superintendent asked. "What was her name?"

Charles shook his head. "There are several. Miss Tindall keeps a roster when she's working." He saw a sheet of paper lying askew on the desk and went over to look at it. "Yes. Here are the names. Today's date—a Miss Willis."

The Superintendent came and stood beside him. He looked down at the list. "There's no address. Do you know where she lives?"

"I'm afraid not. You'll have to ring that number."

The policewoman picked up the receiver and dialed. Charles walked to the end of the room and back. The child gave a hiccuping sob. Poor little mite, she looked half dead.

He went into Sara's bedroom, took a blanket off the cot, and wrapped it around the child. Everything looked normal enough. The frilled net cover on the small antique four-poster was straight, the pretty Georgian dressing table was covered with the normal scatter of little boxes and brushes—all, he thought, in reasonable order. The window was closed. He went back down the hallway. The policewoman was still on the telephone. He heard her say, "A man's voice? Didn't you recognize it? Didn't he give a name . . .?"

He came to stand beside her as she put the receiver down. She said, "Someone rang the baby-sitter about five-thirty telling her she wouldn't be needed after all."

Charles was aware of the Superintendent watching him curiously. "*Miss* Tindall, you said?"

"Yes. The child's father is dead." Compulsively, Charles's eyes came back to the bloodstains. Guy Fortune had died in the flat Sara had lived in before coming here. As her doctor, Charles had been told about the anonymous letters. He wondered how much, if anything, he ought to tell the police, and decided to hold his tongue because they would soon question Sara and nothing he could tell them would save her from that. The baby's head had fallen onto his shoulder. She lay quietly now, mouth dropping. Gently, he extricated his left hand so that he could look at his watch. "Miss Tindall's play will finish about ten-twenty. I'd like to be there when she comes offstage," he said. "Who telephoned you, by the way?"

"Someone from the pub down the road. The stage doorkeeper at the Galaxy Theatre got in touch with them," the Superintendent said. "The mother had rung the flat and got no reply. They said there was a baby here and someone was supposed to be looking after it. Blake," he indicated the youthful-looking policeman, "came around to investigate."

"So she knows there's something wrong." He had better get moving. He turned to the policewoman. "Is it possible for you to come with me to the theatre? I want Miss Tindall to see the baby when she comes offstage. Before she hears the news." Seeing was believing. The officer began to object. Charles said with authority, "As Miss Tindall's doctor, I must insist on this."

Max's arm was throbbing. Sheer, black agony. Twist this way. That way. He had to get the cords undone. Don't lose consciousness. What was that, seeping warmly down over the back of his hand? Don't think about it. But he did.

He knew that if the bullet wound was bad enough, he might bleed to death. Twist. Pull. And it was the twisting and pulling that brought the blood. He would have to stop. Keep conscious. Think.

Sara! Where was Sara! He leaned back against the wall, dazed with pain. What had Sara done? Why hadn't he asked himself that question before? Asked her? He had been taken in by her exceptional air of innocence. Blinded by his love into forgetting about cause and effect. Nothing happened to anyone without cause. Sara's troubles were an effect. What was the cause?

Oh God! The pain. But he had to stay conscious. Pull at the cords. No. He could not stand any more of that. He'd have to rest. Take his mind off the pain by working things out.

Sara had not wanted to accept his proposal tonight. Tonight? How much time had passed? He had pushed her into promising to marry him. Was his presence here in the cellar the effect of that cause?

Guy had wanted to marry her. Guy had died. Did she destroy those who loved her, those who might stand between her and her obsession for the theatre? Was he delirious?

Oh God, the pain! Push, pull. Push, pull. Sweat ran into his eyes. He gritted his teeth. Try again. Keep your mind off the pain.

Where the tunnel ran out of the cellar there ought to be, though Max hadn't noticed it when the light was on, a right-angled corner. If the edges of the stone were sharp enough, they might cut through the rope. Awkwardly, he inched along over the gritty, uneven bricks, using little jerking movements that sent spasms of pain up and down his wounded arm. But there was relief in trying something new. It was slow, clumsy, and his buttocks chafed painfully through the thin material of his trousers. Was he going the right way? His good sense of direction was no use to him in the inky darkness. That warm, sticky substance was once again dripping down to his hands. The more he bumped, the more he was going to bleed. He tried to hurry, fell over, and then there was the agony of jolting himself upright again without hands.

His knees hit the wall first. He swung his feet forward. A gasp, half pain, half relief, as his left ankle cracked against the corner. Planting his feet firmly on the bricks, he edged his body back. Edge a little further, just a little further. Now he could feel the sharp stone-work against his shoulder. Lean back. He raised his elbows, brought his wrists into contact with the right-angled stone.

He moved his hands methodically up and down. The binding cords caught on tiny rough spurs and snagged. He jerked away in a spasm of pain. Pain like fire. Pain like knives. Up, down. Up, down. Agony was driving out his spirit, letting in faintness, a dreadful nausea. And the blood kept coming, filling his mind, telling him if he did not stop soon all the blood in his body would pump itself down his arm. But don't give up. Don't lose consciousness. Somehow, hang on and keep going. Keep going! Think of Sara.

Oh hell, this agonizing pain! Think of Sara. Why had she been excluded from her parents' will? Why? Well, only because they hadn't approved of her way of life. Because they hadn't liked the idea of a "love child". Because the son always inherited a business. What about the house? Maybe it was mortgaged to the business. What about the cottage in Wales? Sara could have had that. Maybe it wasn't insured. Why hadn't he asked these questions when he'd had the opportunity?

Am I now actually suspecting . . .? Oh God, the pain!

Sara, bewitching in tight jeans with her hair caught up in a ponytail cooking dinner at his flat. Hurrying off to change Primmy while the potatoes burned. "It's her fault. It's my daughter's fault. I'll thrash her later when I find the time. Anyway, potatoes are fattening. Oh Max, this is such fun."

There's a lot you don't know about Sara. That's what you're supposed to be thinking of.

Sara, rehearsing the part of Claudia. Blowing him a kiss, then totally absorbed, forgetting his existence in the stalls. "Jassy, did that young man actually sleep on the sofa last night? Actually sleep there?"

"Yes, your Ladyship. Why not? He had to sleep somewhere."

The bewildering darkness. The pain. Was he conscious or unconscious? Were these thoughts or dreams? Was he clinging to Sara, instead of analyzing her?

You cannot analyze the person you love.

7

CHARLES was standing in Sara's dressing room with Primmy in his arms. She came offstage radiant from the final curtain call. Sara saw him, saw the calm sleeping face of the child, the policewoman standing behind. She gave a small, tortured cry, put a hand up to her face as the past telescoped through to the present and she saw Guy's contorted body, his face twisted with pain.

"Sara, dear—"

She leaped forward, tore the child from Charles's arms, clasped it convulsively to her. She looked up at him, blue eyes swimming in a stark white face, her mouth trembling. "It's Guy, isn't it?" The baby jerked awake, opened her mouth to yell, and saw Sara. With an exhausted whimper she fell forward against her mother's shoulder.

Raine glanced uneasily at the policewoman, then back to Sara. "Something seems to have happened to Max, dear. He wasn't at the flat. We think he's had some sort of accident.

Primmy was alone, and there were signs that something—er—that someone might have been hurt."

"Guy," repeated Sara, her mind fuzzing over, confusing the two men because in a way they were the same man now. She tried to remember what had happened to Guy. Still holding the child close against her shoulder, she sat down on the couch. "Max is dead!" She said it in a flat, empty voice.

"No, dear. But he may have had an accident."

"He's dead." She had done this terrible thing to them both.

With her left hand Sara began to smooth the baby's curls. "I should not have said I would marry him. I shouldn't have done it."

"Don't distress yourself, Sara. Max isn't at the flat, that's all. There are signs of a fight."

"No! Oh no!"

"The baby's safe, darling. Look, you can see. She's perfectly all right. Not a mark. And Max can look after himself."

Sara said in a thin, bleak voice. "There was no anonymous letter this time," as though its existence would have saved Max, then covered her mouth with her hand.

Raine turned just enough to hide her face

from the policewoman. She whispered, "There *was* one of those letters. Patrick told me about it. He didn't take any notice. He didn't want you to know." Sara's free hand dropped from her mouth. She blinked. "Patrick can't bear anything like that," Raine said. "Victimization. Cruelty. Crucifying. Whatever it is."

"He should have grilled me, as they did at R.A.D.A. when they got the letter." Or thrown her out as had that awful landlady in Birmingham. Superstitiously, she thought if she had taken her usual punishment it might not have come to this.

Sara looked down at the sleeping child. She didn't want to go home to the flat. Didn't want to be questioned. She wanted to go away with Primmy to hide. She would rather die herself than relive everything that had happened when Guy died. When her parents died.

"The police will get to the bottom of it," Raine said with confidence.

Sara looked up at Charles, gravely professional, standing beside Raine. "Is Max dead?" She asked the question quite straightforwardly, without emotion.

"We don't know where Max is," he replied. Then, hesitantly, very gently, "I don't suppose you know his blood group?" A kind, compassionate man, he didn't want her to walk into the flat, to see what he had seen, without warning.

"Yes," she said dully, "there's blood. They would want to know if it's his, if he isn't there." Her mouth twisted. "The blood will be his. Never mind the group." She stared at the plethora of bouquets. Roses. Delphiniums. Sweet peas. Irises. And lilies. Funeral flowers, she thought blankly.

"Come on, Sara." Charles helped her to her feet. "What about these bouquets?"

"They'll find him," said Raine. "Don't worry. They will find him." She said it in a thin, angry voice, lacking in confidence. When "they" found Guy it had been too late.

Sara glanced across at the other bed, her eyes warm and loving as they rested on the sleeping child. She felt the agony of guilt. Max! I knew. I knew it was going to be like this.

But he left my baby. My baby is safe. Angelic little face with its frame of damp curls, long golden lashes lying on a flushed cheek. She wanted to lift the child, hold her to her heart. But she must not waken her because of what she had been through last night.

Max! How can I live with myself now! Max, I loved you. Is there a life after death? Are you aware? Do you know that I truly loved you? God has kept my baby safe.

She wanted to rush into the sitting room and turn the radio on for news, but she was afraid. Afraid to hear for certain that Max was dead. She looked across at the mess spilling out of her suitcase. Baby clothes. Towels. Shoes. She scarcely knew what she had brought with her. The Superintendent had said they could go back to the flat in a day or two, after forensic tests had been completed. Meantime, Charles had offered to put them up. Raine was in his room and he was sleeping on a sofa in the living room.

In spite of the sedative, Sara had lain awake, the Superintendent's questions shivering through her mind, pounding at her head. "What have you done, Miss Tindall, that someone should want to persecute you? What about Mr. Fortune's family? Do they bear you any ill-will?" She had had to tell them the truth, that James and Deirdre Fortune bore her a great deal of ill-will. If she hedged, the police were bound to interview them and find out the truth.

Max's parents had been informed. They

were coming down from Yorkshire. She spoke to them on the telephone. They were confused, upset. Their son had never mentioned Sara to them. She was going to have to see them. Talk to them. Face their accusing eyes.

That hard-faced policeman. "Did you and the—er—late Mr. Fortune intend to marry?"

"Of course." There had been the faintest suggestion of a sneer on the officer's face. Illegitimate child. There were people who called Primmy that, her own brother's wife included. The Superintendent would no doubt have approved of a quick, secret abortion. Lil and Elliott—or Elliott, through Lil—had suggested it too.

"Why didn't you have the child adopted?" Such impertinent questions.

"Would you give away a precious gift, Officer? Or hand over such a responsibility?" He dropped the mask of official politeness and she saw through to the man beneath. One who made judgments. But she had long ceased to care what people thought. Only God had a right to judge, and He had given her the child.

She found her robe among the mess of clothes sprawling around the suitcase. She scarcely needed it in this heat. The flat was airless. The window was wide open, but the curtains were still. She put the robe on, sank down on her knees before the sleeping child. Oh, my darling. You're safe. You're safe.

Sara crossed the hall. The sitting room was long and narrow with two windows that looked out on the trees of the square. A gate-legged dining table stood in the bay. The chairs were from a medium-priced, well-known line, reasonably comfortable. The carpet was Chinese, and secondhand. There were good pictures on the walls, some military bric-a-brac, an untidy pile of medical books in a small bookcase. A male room, its bareness highlighted by the two bouquets Charles had sent the women the day before which were balanced fanwise in bowls on the mantelpiece above an electric fire. Nobody said why Max's flowers had been left at their own flat.

Raine was staring gloomily out of the window. She was dressed in a flowing gown of sprigged lavender cotton, bare-shouldered, caught beneath her small breasts, and molded to excite the senses. Raine only wore undergarments when she was cold. Already the thermometer had risen to eighty degrees. She heard the soft whisper of bare feet, sensed her friend's presence, and swung around, suddenly bright and smiling. "Hello, old thing. How do you feel?"

Sara said, "Alive, more or less."

"Good," said Raine cheerfully, as though Sara had told her she felt on top of the world.

"Is there any news?"

"No. I've made coffee. Just look what I chose in the heat of the moment last night!" She kicked out the skirt of the gown with one knee. "It's rather more suited to practically anything than cooking the lunch. Still, it's cool and if it brings a smile to the lips of the po-faced visitors we're likely to have today it will have done its bit."

Sara smiled as Raine had intended she should, and the wretchedness faded a little. Raine swung off toward the kitchen. "Has Charles gone?" Sara called after her.

"He had an emergency. That old lady he visits in Kettle Lane is very ill. We're to make ourselves at home. I've rung the flat. They've got it sealed off, but the Superintendent agreed to let me go over and get some stuff from the kitchen. Come and have a cuppa coffee, love."

"I want to ring Elliott first." Raine's mouth tightened. Sara crossed to the telephone and picked up the receiver. The dial whirred. "Is

Mr. Tindall in . . .? Thank you," said Sara faintly. She replaced the receiver and went in silence to the kitchen, her face closed, drawn into herself. She picked up the percolator. "They're both asleep," she said to Raine, looking crushed. "They went to a nightclub."

Raine said angrily, "Why didn't you ask that woman to wake him?"

"She said he left a note saying not to."

"For God's sake, Sara!"

Sara put the percolator down, put a hand to her head, and burst out hysterically. "Why couldn't you have married him?"

"Sara, dear, it's too late for that." She turned her back and began to walk away.

"How I hate you for not marrying Elliott," Sara burst out passionately. "You could have married him. You should have married him." She flung herself on the sofa and fell to pieces in a torrent of sobbing.

Raine looked down at her, tight-lipped. Then she moved quietly into the kitchen and picked up the coffeepot. The room was small and strictly functional. There was nowhere to sit down. She put their cups on the table in the sitting room window bay. The sun came through the glass like a furnace. Sara was still crying, but the sobs were quieter. Raine said in a controlled voice, "Pull yourself together, Sara. Come and drink this coffee. You'll feel better then." The sobbing stopped, but Sara didn't move. Raine added, more gently, "It's futile to blame Lil." There was a lot more she wanted to say, but she didn't dare. She had never seen Sara lose control like that. She wondered with fear if her friend were losing her reason.

Sara sat up. Her face was blotched, her hair awry. "I can't drink that. I'm sorry, Raine." She rose unsteadily and stumbled out of the room. Raine ran to the telephone and dialed. "I want to speak to Mr. Tindall."

"I'm sorry, Mr. Tindall isn't up yet."

"Then get him up," Raine snapped.

"He left a note saying—"

"I don't care what he said, wake him up, please. Tell him it's Raine Mathieson and I'm ringing about his sister who is in trouble." Her eyes flew to the open hall door. She decided to risk shutting it, hoping Sara wouldn't notice. It was a long time before Elliott came on. There was a muted click, then he said sleepily, "Tindall here."

"Elliott, it's Raine. Can you get dressed in a

hurry and come over? Elliott, are you there? Elliott!"

He cleared his throat. "What's that?" he asked croakily.

"Elliott!" she implored. "Wake up. Sara wants to see you."

"What for?"

"What for?" Raine echoed in disbelief. "You must know her friend Max has disappeared. Have you seen the papers?"

Elliott sounded bored, irritated. "No, I haven't seen the papers and I can't involve myself in Sara's affairs."

"Elliott," said Raine desperately, "Sara needs you."

"She didn't seem to need me last night."

"What do you mean?"

"We waited in the foyer," he said peevishly. "Nobody came to collect us, did they? In the end we were turfed out, so we went around to the stage door, but the doorman wouldn't let us in. He said everyone had gone."

Raine was speechless, remembering how they had been bundled into police cars and rushed away. The cast had been told the party was off and had been asked to leave as quickly as possible. The stage doorkeeper had been told not to talk to anyone. Everyone had forgotten about Elliott and Lil! Sara, clinging to the child, distraught because of the police questioning, leaning heavily on Charles, had forgotten her brother and his wife who were waiting, puzzled, because no one turned up for the party! She groaned. "Elliott, please come around to the flat. No," she corrected herself feverishly, "not to the flat. We're both at Charles's place. You know, Sara's doctor. Charles Halbert. Number twenty-two, on the opposite side of the square, almost directly opposite The Fox. Please come right away. Please. I am most dreadfully sorry about last night. I'll explain when you get here. Something ghastly happened. There was no party. It's in the papers. Front page. Please, Elliott, come and see your sister." She heard the bedroom door open and replaced the receiver in time to be standing at the window when Sara appeared.

8

THEY heard it on the eight o'clock news.

"A man has disappeared from a flat in Osbon Square, Kensington. He is Mr. Maxwell Ritchie, a business executive of Melson Place, Pimlico. It is understood he was babysitting for the actress Sara Tindall, who appears in the stage play Two's a Risk, which opened in the West End last night. Bloodstains were found on the carpet and furniture, but the baby was unhurt. Police would like to interview anyone who saw Mr. Ritchie after six P.M. or anyone who knows of his whereabouts.

"The situation in the Leyland strike—" Deirdre Fortune leaned across the breakfast table and turned the switch. "Jamie!"

As the moment of shock ebbed he said viciously. "I hope they get her behind bars this time."

Deirdre cried, hand to mouth, trying to control rising hysteria, "It won't bring Guy back. Nothing will bring Guy back."

"She eats them. What's that insect . . .?"

"Jamie, please."

"Praying mantis, isn't it? Eats its mate? Sara Tindall is a human being who eats men."

"Jamie, don't. Don't talk like that. I can't bear it."

He looked into her face, his eyes burning. "Deirdre, don't you realize that's our tiny niece who is involved? Guy's baby is our niece." He looked slightly mad. "Guy's child is having to grow up with this crazy woman."

"Crazy woman? You loved her for years."

His eyes narrowed as he looked at her. Flinching, she knew what she had never before allowed herself to believe, that James, loving her, still dreamed of the beautiful Sara Tindall whom his brother had captured.

"When one man dies in a girl's flat it could be anything," James said. "But when it happens twice you've got to stop and think. Deirdre, would you be willing to take the child?"

"Take it?" she echoed.

"Yes. It will have to be removed."

She looked shaken. "Of course. But she's less than a year old. One can't take a baby that age from its mother."

"One can, if she's crazy. If she eats her

lovers. If she gets convicted and goes to jail."

Deirdre wanted to shout, You're mad! You're mad! because he *was* mad. It was written in the glitter of his eyes. She began to feel numb. Numb and scared.

James had known Sara and loved her before she went to R.A.D.A. She had not wanted to be serious then and had asked him to wait. He had taken it badly, knowing her beauty would attract many men. But he had not given up hope. He kept her away, very deliberately, from his twin brother, Guy, until unfortunately the three of them had met by chance in the street and he had no recourse but to introduce them.

A twin was more a part of you, perhaps, for wanting what you had. Taking it. They had always been adversaries as well as friends. James's marriage would not have separated the twins, but Guy's friendship with Sara had. James had married on the rebound, trying to forget, and on the surface the marriage was a success. He and Deirdre had a small, pretty home on a top floor in the Kings Road area near Sloane Square, a one-bedroom town flat full of begonias in pottery bowls and elegant Swedish chairs. James was in insurance and doing well. He drove a Mercedes. They gave small trendy dinner parties in the kitchen/dining/living/drawing room. If Deirdre had hoped for something different, she wisely kept her own counsel—for the moment, anyway.

They had decided not to have children. James had decided, and because she liked her job she had gone along with him for the time being, shelving real decisions. Taking Guy's child would mean giving up her job.

"We'd have to buy a house. I wouldn't want to bring up a baby in this flat," she said wretchedly. They had the flat because there were to be no children. James had said life with Deirdre was complete in itself. She was a small girl with enormous hazel eyes and a short upper lip. James had said he loved her, only her, and she had believed him. Until there came an opportunity to love Guy's child! Sara's child. She felt suddenly hollow.

"We could use the money Guy left as a deposit on a house. That's what we kept it for. To benefit the child."

James was not a suburbs man. He liked town flats. Was this vengeance? Or a mad obsession to resurrect the past? To bring Guy back into their lives? Guy who was dead and should be left to rest in peace. "Yes—we could do that."

James rose abruptly, his eyes over-bright. "Come on. We're going to talk to the police."

She pushed her chair back with a scraping sound. "The police?"

"We — are — going — to — talk — to — the — police."

She had never seen James like this. Not even when Guy died. He had been numb then. When the anonymous letter arrived, he had come coldly alive. When that was thrown out for lack of proof, he had grown numb again. That dreadful suspicion came back. Had Jamie sent the anonymous letter to himself? She brushed it aside. He was already at the telephone looking up the number. *When a man dies in a girl's flat it could be anything. But when it happens twice you've got to stop and think.* She went to him, put a hand over his. "Jamie!" Irritably he pushed her hand away. With trembling fingers she picked up some dishes, put them on the kitchen bar. She stood at the tiny sink staring sightlessly through the delicate foliage of the flower pots to the haze of rooftops beyond. The plants were her children. Georgina Gloxinia, with pretty purple and white trumpets. Bertie Begonia and Citrus Sinensis, the sweet orange she called Sid. She talked to them, and told her self they grew better for the attention. She sighed and it came out like a sob. She had imagined all her troubles were over when she married James. But life was not like that. You never knew when it was going to take another swipe at you. Banned from having a baby of her own, she was now to be offered a Guy-substitute; a stranger's child, torn from a stranger's unwilling arms, to be obsessively loved by her husband and fought over bitterly when the mother came out of jail. A pain began in her temples and swelled, broke, settled into a steady throb.

Her husband's voice came sharply. "Scotland Yard?"

"Elliott's just rung," said Raine innocently.

Sara looked astonished, baffled. "I didn't hear the phone."

"I was standing right beside it. I was about to pick up the receiver when it rang. He's coming around. He didn't know." Sara looked blank. "Nobody told him. When you think about it," Raine pointed out, putting an arm around her friend's shoulders, "none of the people who were coming to the party know him—except Charles. And Charles was backstage. Elliott and Lil couldn't find anyone, so they went off in a huff.'' At Sara's horrified expression she added lamely, ''You can't blame them, Sara. They've just seen the papers.''

''And he's coming?'' Sara looked as though she were going to cry.

''Yes.''

''Thank God!'' She turned abruptly, went back into the bedroom, and sat down on the edge of the bed clenching and unclenching her hands. Elliott would give her the money to get away. But what about her clothes? Would the police allow her back into the flat to collect them? There were all Primmy's diapers. She couldn't travel light with a small child. Perhaps her brother would give her a check large enough to pay for a new wardrobe as well as their fare. She would be able to go because the police didn't suspect her. She had an alibi, as she hadn't when Guy died. Or when her parents died. Her passport was in order. Don't think about Max. Purge the agony of his loss in saving the child. She was not going to win any more rounds if she stayed here. She covered her face with her hands. Oh Max! Oh Max, my darling, I did this to you. Max, I told you I loved you and I spoke the truth. Forgive me, Max. Forgive me for loving you.

Primmy stirred. With relief Sara picked up the warm little bundle, holding it against her heart. Primmy whimpered, rubbed tiny fists in her eyes. She was soft as a puppy and smelled sweetly of talcum powder. Sara patted the child's back gently, lovingly, until she was fully awake. She changed her, then went into the kitchen.

"Hello, scamp. Awake at last!" Raine had the plastic cup full of milk ready on the bench. She added some boiling water. Primmy reached out to take it, drank thirstily, burped, gave the two women a lively, happy smile. Raine poured some milk and cereal into a bowl. "She's obviously none the worse for her adventure."

"Thanks. Thanks awfully, Raine." Sara looked miserably into her friend's face. "I'm terribly sorry I did that. I don't know what I've done to deserve you."

"Clearly something in a past life," Raine replied airily. "Perhaps you slew a dragon. Saved a king. Now come on, don't cry about it. Shall I feed little poppet while you go off and dress?"

9

THE telephone shrilled and Raine jumped. She crossed the room thinking of Ovaltine, Marmite, yogurt, vitamin B tablets. She couldn't afford these exposed nerves. "Hello, Raine Mathieson speaking."

It was Patrick Delvaney. "How's Sara?" He was too concerned for the "good morning's," the "how are you's".

"She's okay. Really, quite okay. She's bathing the child at the moment.

"Shall I come around? What do you think?"

"Better not for the moment. Her brother's coming."

"You know what I mean, Raine. Has she said anything about tonight?"

"I won't let her renege."

"I'm going to stick her name above the title. You don't mind, do you, Raine? She's made a huge success. Tell her that, will you? I'll bill her as a star."

Raine tried to think about Sara becoming a star in her first West End play. She'd had to work so hard herself to get there. Sara, in her first West End part, stealing the show from her best friend! "That's great!" she said.

"Shall I come around and tell her, or will you?"

"Leave it to me. There is one thing, though. She's not going to be willing to leave the child. Are you prepared to have Primmy in Sara's dressing room during the performance?"

"No!" he replied violently.

"Then think of something." She slammed the receiver down. Odd how things turned out, she thought with a rush of very real grief. Not only had she invested every ounce of energy into pushing Sara for this part in which Sara had now overtaken her, but her friend's disasters were threatening the run of the play. Threatening Raine's livelihood.

She went into the kitchen, took an enormous basket from a hook on the wall, then paused, looking at it with distaste. A left-over from Caroline's reign? She felt unreasonably disturbed that it should be there. She fingered the handle, thinking about Charles's wife. Somehow, it was easier to think about her than about Sara's unwillingness to talk. She didn't know Charles's wife. Didn't want to know her. He was half-way divorced, anyway. The beginnings of her love affair with Charles were sweet, indeed, but there were more important matters afoot. She shook herself back to the present and called out to Sara, "I'm going across to the flat. Is there anything you want?"

Sara appeared in the doorway, her face startled, eager. "Oh, yes. You could—" she broke off.

Raine waited. "Could what?"

"It doesn't matter." Sara turned and went back to the bathroom.

Shrugging, Raine let herself out of the flat, went down the stairs. Unless the lift was actually standing at the first floor, nobody bothered to use it. It was another day like yesterday, a hot breeze ruffling the limes and the sun glittering above a froth of cirrus clouds. The trees in the square momentarily hid number seven from view, but as she came around the corner Raine saw that there were two police cars parked outside the building. In the front of one of the cars a man sat in shirt-sleeves and peaked cap speaking into a two-way radio. Another policeman stood on guard outside the front door. Two women in flimsy summer dresses who were crossing the square turned to look back, and a man coming from the opposite direction stopped to speak to them. All three turned to stare at the police and at the house. Ghouls! Raine thought angrily. It's going to be like that tonight. The stage door will be surrounded. We'll have to ask for police aid. It will be hell.

The policeman went up the steps and opened the door for her. She had been asked to surrender her keys the night before. "Be as quick as you can, won't you, Miss?"

"Yes." She hurried down the hall. They were taking measurements as she passed the sitting room door. She was still shocked at the sight of the bloodspattered sofa, the blood-soaked carpet. In the old-fashioned kitchen she gathered some essentials. Butter from the refrigerator. Cheese. Biscuits. The remains of yesterday's cold chicken. Coffee. Some whole-meal bread from the bin. It was a little stale but it would do. There were some onions in a wire basket on the floor. She took them also. It was a friendly, roomy, untidy kitchen compared with the small, functional one in Charles's modern flat. The house had been built in the 1860s and, though it was now divided into three flats, it had never been properly modernized. Someone had been making tea. Cups had been left on the wooden bench. Some sugar had been spilled. They could have tidied up, Raine thought. She went down the hall, paused at the front door. The gawking people were still there. Back to her bedroom. Rummaging angrily in a drawer she found a large pair of sunglasses. The policeman came to the doorway and stood looking in at her. "What do you think I'm doing," she snapped, "removing evidence?"

"I've got a job to do, Miss."

"I'm sorry. I didn't mean to be rude. It's been a bad night."

"That's quite all right, Miss. Got everything you want?"

"Yes. There are people out in the square, staring."

"Do you want me to escort you over to the Doctor's?"

"No thanks. I'll be all right." There was a pale pink blossom on the floor. She stooped to retrieve it.

"What's that, Miss?"

"A dehydrated rosebud. I'll take it and put it in water. It probably came off one of the bouquets we took with us last night." She picked up the basket, averted her eyes as she passed the open sitting room door, and went out. With head held high and looking to neither right nor left, she crossed the square to number twenty-two.

A middle-aged man with a plump, untidy figure and ruffled fair hair lounged against the railings. She gave him a cursory glance as she went in. The basket was heavy and her arms were aching by the time she reached Charles's flat. She unlocked the door, pushed through, kicked it shut behind her. In the narrow kitchen she was putting the provisions away when she heard footsteps. "Charles?"

"Ossie Mount," said an unfamiliar voice.

She swung around. "You were outside. How did you get in?"

"It was easy," he replied with a self-conscious smile. "I came through the door."

Oh hell! She had been so certain she heard the latch click. "Are you in the habit of walking into private apartments just because the door happens to be ajar?" she asked acidly.

"Not often. I'm from the Morning Dispatch."

"Then dispatch yourself off," she snapped.

"You're Raine Mathieson, aren't you?"

"I'm Larry the Lamb and I'm none of your business. Now get out." She flung her head up, the dark hair swinging. "Get out."

"I haven't come to see you, anyway. I've got a proposition for Sara Tindall. My paper—"

"Get out!" She was angry with herself for being so careless with the door after what had happened last night. Angry, and a little unnerved at the realization that they were so vulnerable.

"I can't see that you've got the authority to turn down an offer I propose to make to Sara Tindall."

"Miss Tindall isn't interested in your offers."

"Are you really in a position to say that? She's in trouble. Is she going to have any means of support when she loses her part in this play?"

"Get out."

He backed into the living room, sat down on the arm of a chair. "Come on now. I bring good hard cash. There's a real story here, and my paper's willing to pay a top price for it."

"She's not at home."

A child's squeal of delight emerged from the bedroom. The man grinned. "She's a lady with a past, isn't she? Parents died violently and she was involved."

"She was not involved."

"Miss Mathieson, I do know my facts. There were fishy circumstances. Then her fiancé gets knocked off in her flat and where's her alibi? Now—" he broke off as Raine swung around. Charles's late father had been a major in the Grenadier Guards. His sword hung on the wall. In a flash she had unhooked it.

"Oh come, Miss Mathieson. Isn't this a little over-dramatic?"

She walked toward him slowly, sword raised. Mount jumped out of his chair, took a step backward, then another. "Miss—"

"Get out!" He went in a scatter of slippery goatskin rugs. Raine slammed the door behind him. She marched back to the living room and sat down with a thump in a deep chair, the sword supported across the arms, her heart beating furiously, nerves tingling. Someone must have come upon Max like that, she thought with fear.

Sara came through the door carrying Primmy. She was wearing a flame-colored tube of a dress. Even with her hair dragged back into a rubber band, Sara could still make a garment look good. "What on earth are you doing with that?"

"I went over to the flat and when I came

back I stupidly left the outer door open. I've been chasing away an impertinent reporter who wanted to make you an offer for your memoirs.''

Sara's lids drooped, her face became still. ''Thanks. Thanks very much,'' she said in a small voice.

Raine jumped up, put the sword back on the wall, and went through the flat to the kitchen. The rosebud was lying on the sink. She picked it up. ''My good deed for the day,'' she announced flamboyantly, waving it in the air. ''I've saved the life of a rose. It must have fallen out of your bouquet last night.'' Sara looked up. Momentarily she was rigid, then she raised a hand to her eyes, covering them, as though shutting out too bright a light.

''Now, is this yours or mine? Poor little flower,'' Raine said, touching it to her lips. She crossed the room to stand in front of the bouquets on the mantelpiece. ''It's about time I sorted them out. But I don't imagine Charles has much in the way of vases and I daren't ask to go back again to our flat.'' She glanced down at her own bouquet, frowning. Red roses and forget-me-nots. The pink bud clearly did not belong here. She turned to Sara's flowers. Apricot shades. ''Well,'' she said in surprise, "I can't think where that came from." The flowers Max had sent were still in Sara's own bedroom, across the square. She didn't want to mention them. She tucked the bud between two stalks and left it. "Maybe somebody dropped a buttonhole," she said lightly.

10

SARA's face was white and still as a mask, as if all life in her had crystallized into endurance. Raine went swiftly to her. "Do you feel all right, love?" Sara nodded faintly. "It's catching up with you now. That's inevitable. What can I do?" She raised the window sashes. They were already down at the top. What breeze there had been had dropped.

Sara said, "If—if—things go wrong, I shall need money. Primmy will need it. You shouldn't have sent that man away."

"You wouldn't!"

Sara still wore that dazed expression, slightly blank. Then she burst out in a rush, "Does it matter? Does anything matter? It will be a nine-day wonder, then some Middle Eastern potentate will be shot in the center of Piccadilly and everyone will forget. I may as well take the money."

Raine stared at her in disbelief. "Sara, dear . . ."

She clasped the child to her, eyes filling

with tears. "I may as well give up, Raine. If I don't . . ." Her face went blank again.

"If you don't, what dear?"

"If I don't, I'll lose Primmy."

"Lose Primmy? Why do you say that? If that was going to happen, it would have happened last night."

Sara said, still wearing that numb expression, "I'll take the money and run away."

"You can't run. Where would you run to?"

"Away. Really away."

"Sara, you can't do that."

"I must. They want to take everything from me. Everything."

Raine knew it too. Someone out there, some nebulous stranger, for he had to be a stranger, was bent on destroying her friend.

"I'm to be stripped. I'm not to be allowed anything. You've got to see, Raine," Sara said, urgent now, tearful again, obsessive. The white skin was pulled tightly over her cheekbones, the soft mouth was rigid. "Think back to everything that has happened."

"You mustn't upset yourself." Sara's tears spilled over and ran down her cheeks. "Stop it, Sara! Pull yourself together. You've got to." Raine's anger splintered through the room, hitting out against the perpetrator of this atrocity, against Elliott for not being here, smashing into Sara for giving up, twirling into sharp, spiky circles, pursuing the man from the Morning Dispatch who wanted to make hay out of human misery and who was possibly going to succeed because such people always succeeded. Because, however grotesquely, they paid. And money always did, always could, help. There was a long silence. Both women were aware that the thin screen between calm and terror, between balance and madness, had been pierced too often during the terrible hours since they had left for the theatre the night before. Survival depended upon both of them working to keep the calm intact.

"Raine, last night I told Max I would marry him." Sara said it without looking up.

"That's good," said Raine at last in a hollow voice. "I'm glad." Inside of her icicles formed, cold spikes of shock and dread. There was no connection . . . of course there was no connection with the fact that Guy had died on the day he and Sara announced their engagement. She had to believe it. "No one knew about you and Max, did they?"

Sara's fingers drummed sharply against the

table. "There was no one here to tell. Only you."

"A macabre coincidence. Forget it. Listen, Sara, Patrick rang. He's putting your name up in lights."

"You mean, starring me?" The child collapsed onto Sara's lap, looked at Raine wide-eyed with Sara's eyes. They were both still.

"Yes. He's having fireworks set off in your honour." Presenting the news extravagantly like this helped with the warring emotions inside her. "Your name is going in above the title." Raine's face softened with affection. "Isn't it super? Congratulations. You deserve it, you know."

"Raine," said Sara gravely, "you know the reason for this. Patrick's afraid I'll drop out. He's a fighter, and he'll use any ploy, dirty or otherwise, to win."

"No, Sara. The show was you last night. You lifted it into a new dimension. People are going to turn up to see you, not the play."

Sara said nervously, "Let's not talk about it."

Raine's mouth went dry. She pulled a chair over and sat beside Sara. "You're not thinking of opting out, are you? You can't do that, you know."

"I've got a perfectly good understudy. Marion can take over. She will have to."

Raine sat in appalled silence. A horn blared in the street, there was a screech of brakes, then the powdery burr—rr of dry tires on a dry road. She said at last in a hollow voice, "What about the rest of the cast? What about Leslie George? And Alan Dupont? You have a duty not only to Patrick but to everyone concerned."

Sara's face twisted. Then her self-control cracked. "I know all about my duty," she cried. "Don't make it any harder for me, Raine. I know what I'm doing and I know it's a terrible, unforgivable thing." Then, in a rush, "I can't leave Primmy, Raine. I'm going to ask Elliott for some money, and I am going to take her away."

"Yes, yes. Do that. Take Primmy away," Raine urged her. "To some secret address and leave her with a trusty nurse until this is all over."

Sara shook her head. Her eyes were blinded with tears, her throat choked by fear. "It's not going to be over, Raine. Don't you see?"

Raine saw, only too clearly—until the killer

was found and dealt with, Sara and her child would have to disappear. Disappear? No. That, too, was unacceptable. She jumped up. "The police will find Max," she said with brittle, assumed confidence. "And they'll find the person who attacked him. You can't pull out of the play, Sara. Patrick won't let you, for after those notices it would sink without a trace. You were the success of the show last night, Sara dear. Can't you see what that means? It was you the audience wanted. They literally howled for you. I've never seen anything like it before. This play will run for years, if you stay in it. But only if you stay in it, at least for a while."

Sara's arms tightened around the baby. She steeled herself against Raine's argument, knowing that if she listened, allowed herself to take it in, she would be lost. She must not think of Patrick. She couldn't think of Raine, or Leslie, or Alan. Fear lifted her onto some distant level where the problems of her friends and colleagues could not follow. Where neither guilt nor compassion, not even her own ambitions, were able to reach her. "Nothing, and nobody, will part me from Primmy tonight. Nothing, Raine," Sara cried, running to the bedroom.

She stood, holding the child, looking blindly out of the window. Look at the shadows, the flickering shadows. A figure moved hurriedly across the landing and disappeared. Her arms tightened involuntarily around the child. Don't look. It was nothing but a shadow. Certainly nothing but a trick of light. Try to keep calm. Don't think of Max, he is dead. Don't raise hope in your heart. Just watch the moving shadows.

What is that? It's a man. What's he doing, running? Cling to the child. No, it isn't a man, it's a shadow. Oh God, I'm so frightened. Talk to Raine. You've got to talk to someone or you'll go mad.

Raine had returned to the kitchen. Sara could see her standing at the sink peeling vegetables. She didn't turn around. The morning paper was neatly folded and lying on a chair arm with the front page still hidden. Sara touched it, hesitated nervously, turned away, then with a feeling of inevitability opened it on the table and sat down. Primmy leaped dangerously forward, came up against the restriction of Sara's arm, and emitted a howl of protest. Sara put her down on the floor.

West End actress in offstage drama.

The love child of Sara Tindall, who appears

in Two's a Risk which opened last night at the Galaxy Theatre [see p. 14, Quentin Arlen's review] was found abandoned in her flat at approximately nine-thirty last evening. It is understood there were bloodstains on some of the furniture and on the floor. Mr. Max Ritchie, who had been left in charge of the baby, has not been seen since. A full police search is being mounted, and anyone who saw Mr. Ritchie leave the flat last night is asked to contact the police.

Mystery still surrounds the death of the child's natural father, Mr. Guy Fortune, who was found dead in Miss Tindall's flat in Westhoath Road, Notting Hill, eighteen months ago with a gun in his hand. The coroner said at the time he had no recourse but to issue an open verdict, but that he hoped the police would keep an open file on the case.

Sara looked up. Raine was standing in the doorway watching her.

"Read Quentin Arlen, Sara." Raine's face was soft, drawn with compassion and distress. Crunched up like that in the chair, Sara reminded her obscenely of a terrified rabbit waiting for the coming kill. Sara stood up suddenly, knocking the table with her knees so that her coffee, now cold, rocked and spilled. She stumbled against the table leg and went to the window. Raine was opening the paper at page fourteen. She could hear the rustling.

"Look, Sara. Read this."

She couldn't. If she read it she would have to go onstage that night. The sun was slanting prettily on the pale limes in the square. Women were hurrying to their shopping in Kensington High, and cars slipped by quietly heading for the Tulley Street exit, hidden behind the trees. She must not read the reviews because then she would know she couldn't let her friends down. She must run. This mad chain of events had to be stopped. Guy first. Then Max. Hadn't she known? Only she had thought it was going to be Primmy. They must get in touch with Patrick and Marion French, her understudy, who would play the part of Claudia tonight. She half turned. "Raine." The doorbell rang.

11

ELLIOTT was wearing a well-cut, summer-weight navy blue suit with a quiet tie. His blue shirt was immaculate, his shoes highly polished. "Aren't you being rather silly, Sara? Surely you owe something to this fellow Delvaney? I don't see how you can drop out after only one performance." As a baby, Elliott had a head of blond curls and the sort of digestion that produced a sunny nature, angelic smiles. He had been adored by his mother and aunts, spoiled, though in fact it had been said in the family that it was impossible to spoil such a lovely child. Now, he was prematurely bald. What hair remained was dark brown and straight, little more than a thick fringe encircling his head. There was a resemblance between brother and sister, but because Sara's astonishing blue eyes dominated her face and because of her exceptional beauty, few people noticed. Elliott's eyes were gray, round, and still.

Sara had forgotten, in her desperate need, that Elliott was not going to be any help.

Never had been. The past came flooding up in a panic-stricken wave. An image of Elliott, standing hands in pockets before the Adam fireplace in his big Georgian house in The Boltons, rocking backward and forward on his heels, saying, "How the dickens do you get yourself into these things, Sara?" Lil not speaking. Not saying a word. Lil, who knew and hated her. Guy, spread-eagle on the floor of the Notting Hill flat with the gun beside him. The policeman's eyes last night, coldly suspicious as he asked in that hard voice, "Were you going to marry Ritchie, Miss Tindall?" The crucifying look in his eyes. She shuddered. Elliott had to help. He was the only one not obliged to think of the play.

"Now, Sara, we've got to talk about this," Elliott said, not unkindly. He was looking around the living room with interest. His eyes rested on the sword, the big picture painted by Charles's father. He tested the carpet pile critically with a toe, fiddled with a box of matches. He looked faintly uncomfortable, but whether that was from the excessive heat or the situation was hard to tell.

Sara's arms tightened around the child. As though she felt her mother's need of sympathy, Primmy's small fingers closed over Sara's. "I want to go away, Elliott."

"But that's what I'm telling you you can't do."

She asked tightly, "You mean, you're unwilling to loan me the money?" She had nothing of her own. She had been cut out of her parents' will. That was why they suggested she had driven to Carmarthen from Bristol, where she was appearing in Repertory, had a row with her parents, failed to persuade them to reinstate her, pretended to them that she would stay the weekend, set the cottage on fire, and left.

"Sara, are you listening? You're miles away, aren't you?"

Sara dragged herself back from the nightmare.

"If I loaned you the money to run away, you'd be doing everyone a great disservice. You've taken on something and you're morally obliged to see it through," Elliott said. "Surely you see that, Sara."

"You don't want to loan me the money?" Sara's beautiful mouth trembled.

"It's not a question of money," Elliott replied impatiently. "Aren't you listening to me?"

Her face was lifted, her eyes pleading.

"Have you got two thousand pounds? I mean, that you could pick up in cash without having to sell anything? I'd pay you back. I'd find a way. I haven't got any money. I spent everything I had buying the flat."

Elliott's still eyes widened further in astonishment. "Two thousand pounds? Where are you going? Two thousand pounds would take you around the world and back here again."

"One thousand would do," she amended shakily. "In foreign countries a woman with a child needs something behind her. Elliott," Sara implored, "give me the money." He was staring at the carpet, his face expressionless. Almost expressionless. There was a faint flicker of irritation at the corners of his mouth. He leaned forward in his chair, shoulders hunched. He looked what he was, a man who had been dragged into an uncomfortable situation and who would like to slip away without becoming too involved.

Sara said in a small, haunted voice, "It's not as though one thousand pounds can mean too much to you, even if I never can pay it back—" She took a tissue from her pocket and wiped her eyes. Elliott, waiting for her to calm, straightened his tie, flicked a bit of something off his lapel. The irritation was under control. Sara said in a small, frightened voice, "Please help me, Elliott."

"It's stupid to run away," he said. He leaned toward her. "It looks guilty. Besides, I thought you were in love with this chap—what's his name? Max?"

"I wanted to marry him."

"Wanted?"

"Elliott," she said desperately. "Max is dead."

He started, looked at her sharply. "What do you mean, he's dead? How do you know?"

"He has been attacked by the same person who killed Guy."

Elliott was startled. Then he said reprovingly, "Now you're being ridiculous, Sara. How could he, eighteen months later?"

She was silent a moment, biting her lips. Then she went on. "I know that if I stay here I'll lose Primmy, too." She put her head down on the child's small shoulder, hiding her face, closing her eyes.

Elliott pushed both hands into his pockets, rattling some coins. "Give the child to me. Lil is perfectly willing to look after her." Sara didn't reply. He rose, walked out into the hall and back again, went over to the window, returned, and glanced in at the kitchen. Raine was pouring rice into a pan, preparing a risotto for lunch. She was still dressed in the indiscreet, beautiful gown, a semi-naked goddess filling the very ordinary little kitchen with magic, making a stage of it, bringing it to life with her swiftness and grace. She looked up brightly.

"Shall I make you a coffee, Elliott?"

"Thanks." He turned away, still rattling the coins, and sat down on one of the hard chairs at the table. He looked across at his sister. "I can't imagine why you sent for me, if you're not going to take my advice."

Sara raised her head. Her face was sheet-white now—with fear. She didn't remember sending for Elliott. Was she going mad? "I need help," she said shakily.

"I am trying to help. God knows, I've always tried to help. But I always come up against this blank wall with you, Sara. Didn't we offer to adopt the child in the first place?"

"You know I couldn't allow you to do that. She's mine, Elliott." Sara's passion came to life, her eyes burning like blue flames. "A million visits to someone else's child don't compensate. She's a part of me. Don't you understand that?"

He shrugged. He leaned back in his chair,

rattled the coins again. "It seems to me she would be better off in a normal home with two proper parents. This is a terrible background for a child."

It would be pointless now to say that Primmy was shortly to have had a normal home and two proper parents, because Max was dead. "Please," Sara's voice broke, "please loan me the money to run away. Please, Elliott, please."

"You're pretty irresponsible, you know," said Elliott, speaking gently, for him, affectionately even. "I don't want to be hard on you, Sara, but I'm bound to point out the fact that you've made a fair old hash of your life so far. What would happen to you in a foreign country?"

Her head spun with the awful knowledge that he wasn't going to help. With the terror of what would happen if she didn't get away, and the knowledge, too, that what she wanted to do was disloyal, against the rules. Her mind went blank. From somewhere in the distance there came a scream. It grew in volume until it filled the room. Someone slapped her and the noise stopped. "Sara, take a hold on yourself."

"Who was that screaming?"

"Don't you know? Don't you really know?"

12

PRIMMY's soft little hands clasped Sara's fingers, soothing her raw nerves. Elliott said with compassion of a sort, "If you were to run away, Sara, the police would be on to you in a flash." His voice dropped to a whisper. "They never stopped suspecting you for Guy's death, you know that. And don't forget—the other."

How could she ever forget? In Sara's dreams she still saw in the eerie light of dawn that ghastly ruin of a cottage, the wood still smoldering. Two charred bodies. Without reporting to the police, she had driven directly to London. The police saw guilt in her behavior, and Charles had problems convincing them that shock had set her running. He cited a dozen instances of equally bizarre reactions. At the time, Sara had only known she had to see Elliott.

He had been asleep when she reached London. Always asleep when she needed him, it seemed now. He came to the door in his robe, yawning, rubbing his eyes. His irritated half-awakeness held her at arm's length. She remembered leaning against the back of the closed door, looking across a yawning gulf of distance at him, and realizing how far apart they had grown since his marriage.

"I warned them, time and again, about those paraffin heaters," he said later, reducing the horror to a cold technicality.

Now she said miserably, "I had an alibi last night. I was with people all the time."

Men's voices sounded in the hall. Charles came through the door followed by Patrick Delvaney. Charles nodded to Elliott. They had met when Sara's brother came to talk to him about her pregnancy. He had followed his own conscience when Elliott tried to influence him with regard to the future of the child. Elliott had gone on at length about his sister's driving, unswerving ambition, had given his considered opinion that Sara's career would come first and that the child would necessarily suffer. Charles hadn't acquired the impression that Sara would be a bad mother. Her pregnancy looked to him more like professional suicide. Anyway, as he told her brother cryptically, it was not a doctor's function to tell an independent woman of twenty-four what to do with her life. Or, for that matter, what to do with her fatherless child.

Raine introduced Patrick. Sara's eyes fixed on the director's face. Charles said to Raine, "I've come to collect a few things. Mrs. Cavelley has offered me a room. Or rather, her daughter has."

"Oh no. We can't push you out."

Charles smiled. "The invitation was too effusive to resist. If your old mother was dying, wouldn't you be only too delighted if the doctor moved in?" He saw Elliott's cup and added, "I see the coffee lady's on duty." Raine strode obediently back to the kitchen and Charles followed her in. "Of course, if I could share my room with you . . ."

Raine looked up at him, eyes glittering. "That's all we need—for the Morning Dispatch snoopers to put their long-range cameras on your bed!"

"What's the matter, Raine?"

She kicked the door behind him with her heel, hissing, "Give Sara a sedative. That bloody brother of hers . . ."

He knew there had been something between Elliott and Raine. She was jumpy on the subject of Sara's brother.

He took a glass from the cupboard, filled it

with water, and went back to the living room. Patrick was saying persuasively, "But you've got to appear tonight, Sara. You've an obligation to the public, now that the reviews are out. They're rushing to buy tickets to see you. You, Sara, not the play."

"I can't." She shut her eyes, needing to recede from the world because everyone seemed to be coming at her from every direction and she couldn't fight them all.

Charles was unlatching his black bag, pulling out a little built-in drawer, extracting two white pills. Without opening her eyes, Sara said in a choked voice, "Patrick, I can't leave the child."

He was too buoyed up with the certainty that he would win to be angry. Or even to listen. He was a West End director of growing reputation. He had made exceptional commercial triumphs of two plays broadly considered to be uncommercial, and the theatrical world was sitting up to take notice of him. By making a success of this new play, he hoped to win acclaim from those who really counted, the critics and the boys who handed out the really big jobs. He saw himself in headlines: Patrick Delvaney appointed Artistic Director of Stratford. Or, Patrick Delvaney appointed

Artistic Director of Chichester. "Remember my words when I gave you the part? Remember what I said? If the child is at her last gasp! You didn't take me seriously, did you? Well, I was serious. I am serious."

Charles stepped between them, gave Patrick a warning look. "Here, Sara, take these."

Obediently, she opened her eyes, held out a hand, then put the glass to her lips. They all stared at her in silence. The child began to pull at Sara's collar. The small hand began to explore Sara's neck. She took a handful of hair, pulled, looked expectantly up into Sara's face for a reaction. "Patrick," said Sara, "Primmy's life is in danger."

Silence lay over the room. Then Patrick said heartily, "Well now, it's a matter that seems to me to be easily combatted." He turned to Elliott. "You're married?"

Elliott said in a voice untinged by either sentiment or rancor, "I've already offered to take my niece home. My wife and I wanted to adopt her in the first place and bring her up, but Sara wouldn't have it. We've always been ready to help. Sara knows that." He gave Charles an unfriendly, faintly aggressive look. "You know it, too."

Patrick said happily, "There you are!" As though the whole matter was settled.

Raine entered carrying a small tray. She put it down on the table, looked across at Sara, and noted that she was once more clinging obsessively to the child. She said gently, "Let me take her while you have your coffee." Sara didn't move. Like a holed-up animal, Raine thought again, surrounded now by a pack of dogs. Her own guilt in getting Sara the part of Claudia, in bringing Elliott here, burst through in a shocking wave. Suddenly, without warning and for no apparent reason, the child began to cry. Sara rose and left the room without a backward glance, closing the door behind her.

Patrick held out his hands in a gesture of despair. "You're her brother. You'd better do something."

Sara was sitting on the end of the bed with the child on her knee. She looked up as Elliott came through the doorway. "Sara," he said firmly, "I'm going to take the child home. You come, too, if you like, and see her settled. In fact, you're welcome to move in."

She looked up at him beseechingly. "Elliott, let's talk."

"Talk about what? We've talked. We've

done nothing but talk for the past hour, and where has it gotten us?"

She was silent. Then, "Elliott, you know Primmy's life is in danger."

"Why should you say that?"

"Because that's what it's working up to, isn't it? Guy, then Max. Primmy will be next."

He went on staring at her, his face, his eyes, still. At last he shook his head, saying, "There was a long interval between Guy's death and Max's disappearance. Why do you say—"

"Elliott, I know."

"For God's sake, Sara," said Elliott irritably, "put all these people out of their misery. I've got work to do. I can't hang around here all day." He bent down and took hold of the child. Sara's arms tightened convulsively. Primmy screamed. Sara screamed.

There were running footsteps and Charles burst in. "What the devil! Tindall, let that child go. Have you lost your wits?"

Sara collapsed on the bed, the shrieking child in her arms. "Do you mind?" asked Charles frostily, holding the door open.

Elliott glared at him. "Somebody had to do something."

"Not with a sledgehammer, you didn't,"

exploded Raine from the hall. "Why don't you go home, you insensitive clod."

He turned on her furiously. It was years ago, all over again, the hurt, the disappointment, the anger, the spite. "It was you who asked me to come."

"Okay. It's not the first stupid thing I've done and it won't be the last." The blaze subsided into despair. "Go home and forget about your sister if you can't do better than that."

Sara heard the outer door slam, and burst into tears.

Patrick went with Raine back into the living room. "Why does she insist Primmy's life is in danger?"

"She's in a state of shock."

"What are we going to do?"

"I wish I knew."

Patrick paced up and down. "Hell, Raine, I'm in a spot. I've shot my bolt now, putting Sara's name up."

In the bedroom Charles was saying gently, "Come now, Sara, you and I had better talk this out." He rested a hand on her shoulder. "You've got to put Primmy down. You can't hold onto her like this." The child stopped crying. He lifted her out of Sara's arms and put her on the floor, took a golliwog from the bed, and handed it to her. "Why won't you let your brother take Primmy home? She would be perfectly all right. I'm sure he and his wife would take the greatest care of her."

The sedative was beginning to work. Sara said wanly, "Perhaps I would have, but—"

"Yes, well, he did rather go about it like a bull at a gate. But he meant well. He's concerned for you." She nodded. "You've got to go on tonight. You accept that, don't you?"

She said pathetically, without hope, "I've an understudy."

"No, Sara. It won't do. You've seen the notices?"

"No."

"I feel sure you'll understand when you've read them." He put a hand beneath her elbow, helped her to rise. "Come and let Patrick show them to you." She turned convulsively toward the smiling baby, but he drew her back, adding in that same gentle voice, "Leave her, Sara. She's perfectly all right." Primmy was happily bashing the golliwog on the floor. He stood in the doorway waiting as she hesitated. "Sara!"

She turned, and he was shaken by the haunted expression in her eyes. Unhappy himself about what he had to do, he led her into the living room. Patrick pulled a sheaf of papers from his bag and put them on the table. Sara seated herself where she could look through the door and across into the bedroom. Across at the window, too, where she had seen the shadows earlier. Primmy was still engrossed with her toy. Obediently, Sara began to read.

Charles went to the window and looked down into the square. Elliott had come out of the building and was walking over to a dark blue Volvo. Even at this distance Charles could see the anger in his face. He felt a deep sensation of regret. Sara obviously loved her brother dearly. And clearly he meant well by her. Charles shrugged. Well, who did understand Sara? He went to the kitchen. Raine had returned to preparing lunch. She had partially covered her glamorous dress with a floor-length granny apron of frilled cotton. "I hope you're staying to eat with us. Do you have to be invited to lunch in your own flat?"

He smiled in return. "Is there enough? It smells fantastic."

"I did cater for you."

Patrick was waiting for Sara to finish reading the notices. He looked up, saw Raine and

Charles coming out of the kitchen, and signaled to them to keep quiet. Raine settled herself in an armchair. Charles returned to the window. Sara went on reading, looking up now and again, to check on Primmy. There was no sound in the flat except the rustle of paper and the distant baby sounds of Primmy talking to herself.

Patrick's mind fled back over what he knew of Sara's career. She had had her first part, a tiny one, when at school. Someone at Questers knew her parents. Indulgently, proud of their pretty daughter, they had allowed her to appear in an amateur production, and that enchanting experience had convinced her, Sara had told him, that her future lay on the stage.

She had been accepted at R.A.D.A., and Barry Heald, looking for a juvenile for a play he was directing, went backstage at their end-of-term show. It was Sara's last term. Barry offered her the opportunity to go on tour with a children's theatre company, and she had accepted. The company took the medieval play Everyman on a tour of schools all over the country, playing to adults in Chichester, York, and Norwich cathedrals. Patrick, who knew Barry well, had heard glowing reports of

Sara's integrity, her happiness in her work, her popularity with the cast. He also heard about the anonymous letters that were sent to Barry and two of their landladies. Letters that sought to blacken Sara's name. To nip a promising career in the bud.

"Didn't you try to trace them?" Patrick had asked at the time, interested in the sordid story rather than in the girl, for it was long before he had met Sara.

"I talked to her, of course," Patrick remembered Barry saying. "But what can you do? Take a list of her ex-boyfriends and put the police on to them? Not really. When she was at R.A.D.A., she was thick with Guy Fortune's twin brother, James. Most of the cast knew him. He seemed a decent young fellow. She refused to discuss any of her other boyfriends."

"So there's someone in her past, somewhere, that for reasons of her own she won't expose?"

Barry had shrugged. "One can only surmise."

In the next tour Sara had understudied the lead in The Immortal Lady by Clifford Bax. She took over quite soon and went with the play to the Bath Festival. After that there were

TV commercials and small parts in a series. She had told Patrick she didn't like TV, but they both knew it was the best shop window available. It had led her toward the West End. He had seen her, dressed in Victorian costume, singing "Only a Bird in a Gilded Cage" at the Players Theatre under the arches at Charing Cross. She had a pretty voice, true, but not strong.

Now, if they could get her back onstage, get through this terrible nightmare, she was going to be made. She'd be invited, he reckoned, to play a lead at the National or the Royal Shakespeare. Or to star in a film, if that was what she wanted. He had to get her onstage tonight for her sake as well as his own. If I die in the attempt, Patrick said to himself, I will bloody well get Sara back on that stage tonight. Beneath his nervous anger was a genuine fondness for this woman who was putting him through hell. She had been marvelous during rehearsals, offstage and on. She was obedient, cheerful, sensitive to the other actors, and utterly trustworthy. She never upstaged. True, she had taken over the play, but on her own worth, not by upstaging Raine. She never threw a tantrum. However idiotic, immature, or self-indulgent she might appear to her critics in her private life, in her work with the theatre she was a professional.

Eyeing her as she turned the final page, Patrick felt genuine pain deep in his gut. He hated to see her like this. Diminished.

"Patrick," she whispered, "I can't go onstage tonight. Please forgive me. Forgive me and let me go."

He jerked erect, all five feet seven of him flashing anger. The little beard rose aggressively and his eyes hardened along with his heart. "You can read those notices and say that? Bloody hell!" He snatched up one of the pages and read out loud, spitting the words:

"'Sara Tindall plays the Lady Claudia with an intimidating intelligence. Inexplicably, she has made of a secondary part an unforgettable experience. As has happened in the theatre before in a new play, someone has taken what appeared to be quite an ordinary part and brought it up to equal the lead. This is not to denigrate Raine Mathieson's masterly performance as Jassy—' Let's bypass that if you don't mind, Raine. 'Working with monumental control from within, Sara Tindall offers physical expressiveness that is by turns exquisitely funny and heartbreaking. She galvanizes into life a character both artificial and indestructible. Yet one feels—and this is borne out in the surprising twist at the end of the play—that beneath the suave exterior of the character there is a woman desperately afraid. Under Patrick Delvaney's excellent—' Never mind about that. Here's another bit . . . 'Sara Tindall's future and the future of this play is assured. People will flock to it not for the reasons that they flock to the smutty little farces and good-natured comedies that make a cheerful night out, but because Sara Tindall shows them what a woman is made of, and what she may become.' "

He put the paper on the table and gave Sara a long, frozen look. "You can read that and say you will let the cast and a theatre full of people down?"

Sara was again staring across the hall and into the bedroom.

"What about your career?" Patrick shouted.

"I'm a human being, and human beings are divided into men and women. And women, when they have children, are first and foremost mothers. That's how the world is. That's how it was meant to be, Patrick. In the end nature has the last say. Even animals won't desert their young."

There was silence, then Charles said quietly, gravely, "Especially animals."

"Animals! You're primitive, Sara."

"Perhaps I am," she replied. "Perhaps that's what makes me a good actress, being primitive. Perhaps that's what makes me a good mother."

Charles said gently, "There are more than eight hours until curtain-up. Can we shelve the decision until later? Sara has an understudy. I know she's not acceptable in the circumstances, but she's there."

13

IT was exciting, having the key. Knowing he could get into the flat any time he liked. At any time. He would choose an evening when Sara was onstage again. He climbed into the car, started the engine, and drove off, the ultimate picture flashing through his mind: Sara when she found the child gone; Sara screaming, the beautiful mouth drawn with agony, the wonderful blue eyes drowned in tears; Sara totally berserk, finally desiccated. Breaking Sara's spirit wasn't an easy job. It had to come slowly, a little more and a little more, with the final holocaust the loss of her child. Everything gone now. Sara the beautiful, the successful, the strong—stripped. His eyes gleamed evilly.

"What the hell d'you think you're doing?" He started, looking up into the irate face of a lorry driver who was belligerently waving him over to the left-hand side of the road. He swung aside. Shouldn't have looked. Remember the lesson from Wales. On the way home he had stupidly switched the interior car light on. And the next day he had run into Vernon Hills. "Thought I saw you on the M4 last night about midnight," Vernon had said. And while his Adam's apple bulged, his eyeballs glazed over, and the sweat soaked his armpits and dampened the palms of his hands, Vernon had added, laughing, "Some goon with the same car, similar registration, wearing dark glasses and a hat. Driving at midnight in dark glasses and a hat!"

A row of shops lined the top of the hill above Wild Hatch. He stopped in front of a small garage. A thin young man in overalls stood in the entrance, a spanner in his hand. Safer to go back to the big gas station on the main road. The thin man was looking at him curiously. He turned his face away, took his foot off the brake, and the car slid on.

CHINESE TAKEOUT MEALS. Hunger, raw and compelling. He pulled the car to the side of the road, switched off the engine, and went back. He'd have to take a chance. He must eat. Shop radio blaring. No one in sight. Bang on the counter with a fist. Hurry, before any other customers come. Mustn't be seen. A squat Chinese in a white shirt bustling, apologizing smilingly.

"Sweet and sour pork?"

"Will be twenty minutes. Can wait?"

"Have you got nothing ready?"

"No."

"I'll come back." He said it with his face averted. Must be careful. Some people had a good memory for faces. Back in the car. Christ! It was an oven. Turn on the cool air. Leather upholstery sticking to his shirt. Shirt stuck to his back. The car purred smoothly down the road. He dwelled with brutal relish on the fact that a piquant smell would drift down into the cellar through an open door. Max Ritchie would be crying out for food by now.

This was a splendidly narrow driveway opening—the garden protected from prying eyes, overlooked only by the ruined church. He parked the car under the drooping laburnum out of reach of the hideous sun and checked for bloodstains on the gravel. With the engine running, his foot hovering over the accelerator, his eyes swiveled around to take in the blank-faced windows. Warily, like a big cat, he looked and listened, his left hand on the gear lever, his right on the steering wheel. Then slowly, as the tension began to ease, he turned off the engine and climbed out of the car. A quick cheep came from the center of the buttonhole rosebush and he jumped. A triangular formation of geese flew over, honking and cackling. When they had gone there was only the midsummer afternoon silence, pulsating, burning, presaging death.

Stepping carefully only on the grass, he made his way around to the front of the house. The weighted copper pot was there over the coal hole, exactly as he had left it, foolish and forlorn with his camouflage leaves dried and wilting. He looked warily up at the front windows. Closed, glassy, and still they winked back at him in the bright sunlight. He retraced his footsteps around the house and across the gravel to the garage door, bent down, touched the handle. A clicking sound, a metallic cough. It swung up toward the roof.

He stood looking at the doorstops, breath held. They seemed to have assumed a personality of their own. Ther lions' eyes gleamed as though they knew and had their own plans. Hurriedly, he transferred one of them to the back doorstep, returning for the other.

Excitement rubbed at him, a scary black enjoyment that he remembered from the moment he killed Guy—actually killed a man, face-to-face, and broke through the normal pattern of human behavior with its inbred boundaries and taboos. He didn't count the fire in Carmarthen, not having seen the victims in their death throes. He took the key from beneath the rainwater tank and unlocked the back door, transferred the weights into the house, and locked the garage.

Head down, shoulders hunched, he examined the gravel where the car had stood the night before, pushed a pebble tentatively with his foot, picked it up, rubbed at it with his thumb. It was a reddish color but the red didn't come off. There were reddish patches everywhere! Blood? Feverish with fright, nerves tingling, he turned to the sky for help. The little dancing white clouds of the morning had gone and haze hung low and heavy. Rain! Rain! Rain would wash away the blood, if it was there.

A flower broke off as he brushed against the rose tree. It rolled across his shoulder to land quixotically in his breast pocket. He picked it out, was about to throw it away, then slid it through the buttonhole of his open-necked shirt. He loved roses.

The radio in the Chinese food takeout shop had been turned down when he returned. A small, dumpy woman with her hair dragged into a bun, a bright face, and black, slanted eyes came to serve him. She noticed the rose, indicated it with one finger. "Is very pretty. You grow?"

"No. It comes from the garden of a friend of mine."

She smiled. "I guess Mr. Retenmeyer, perhaps? Down road? He wear one very like."

He stared at her, not answering, his mouth dry with shock, mentally kicking himself for being a careless fool.

"That will be one twenty-five, thanks."

He climbed back into the car, tore the rose from his buttonhole, threw it across the pavement into the hedge. Incredible, the way his luck fluctuated. And then that inner excitement that came with hairbreadth escape was back again, almost sexual in its intensity.

Max must have slept, or lost consciousness again. Time had extended in a ghastly sort of delirium dominated by the pain and stiffness of his arm and the weighty darkness. Dominated by Sara, too. Sara onstage in that rather ordinary Topaz play, outwardly relaxed, inwardly keyed up. Sara, on the deck of Little Mint, soft as a cat, surprising him at every turn by her efficiency. Sara's warmth, her giving, that came from a generous heart. Sara's sudden withdrawal when she remembered—Guy?

There had been no sex in those early days. They had come to that later. Somehow, the child's presence precluded not so much the act as the morality of it. Sara thought she was still in love with Guy, and there was the evidence that she had been in the carrycot in the cabin. He had to take her very slowly along the new road, making certain she knew where she was going so that there would be no panicky rush back.

Max shook his head, shaking himself back to reality. Had the seesawing of his hands against the stone corner of the wall cut deeply, or even at all, into the fiber of the cords that held his wrists? There was agony in moving the stiffened, injured arm. His feet were numb, his ankles in clamps. He had fallen on his injured arm. Cold sweat, and the clammy blackness of the cellar all around, covered his body like mold. No knowledge of reality. Neither day nor night nor even hours passing. Just pain, and a confused inadequacy.

Then something began to creep through. He listened, turned his head. Was that a door opening? He saw the blessed shaft of light and in a moment the confusion went in the relief of contact with light, with humanity. "Who's there?" he shouted, and "Help!" Oh God, let it be someone other than that maniac!

A torch beamed down the stairs, wavered in surprise across the cellar, and caught him full in the face. There was a grunt of satisfaction or perhaps relief, and with it Max's flash of hope died in crumbling despair. His voice came up out of hell, with bitterness. "How long is this mad joke to go on?"

"Only until tonight." It was the first time Max had heard his captor's voice. He was positive he had never heard it before. Or was it disguised? "Are you hungry?" the man asked.

"What do you think? I've had nothing since tea yesterday. I presume it was yesterday."

"You've been sleeping?" The torch wavered downward and Max could see the dark form looming ominously in the doorway.

"Perhaps. I don't know. My arm is bad. I need a doctor."

"Doctor?" That seemed to amuse him greatly.

"Are you going to give me some food?"

"You're not doing any exercise. You shouldn't need food."

He had some food. The smell of it filled

Max's nostrils. Slow waves of hunger spread, sharpening, twisting his entrails. Like a dog, he salivated. "But you've brought food. I can smell it."

"Mine." He turned off the torch, sat down on the top step. Now Max could see the bulk of him, but no more. There was a rustling of paper or plastic bags, the sound of a fork or spoon rattling. The figure moved sideways to utilize the light. Max strained forward, but the man had only half turned. Momentarily, the light caught his features and Max had a glimpse of a largish nose, full lips that gave an impression of spare flesh surmounting a bony jawline.

Max edged clumsily, painfully along the floor toward the steps.

"Stay where you are."

"What are you up to?" Max asked angrily. "Why have you brought me here?"

"I am going to drown you."

The slow, deliberate, and very clear statement hung in the air, strangely unreal and without meaning. Max found himself asking light-headedly. "You're what?" Then, in the long silence that followed, the words began to sink in. Max made a convulsive, involuntary leap forward. Pain swept through his stiffened arm, pain that brought sickness and faintness. When he could speak again he said weakly, "I'd like to talk about Sara, because she's the reason for my being here, isn't she? You're persecuting Sara." He waited. No reply. "You've been at it for years," Max went on. "Writing anonymous letters aimed at ruining her career." When there was still no reply he added bitterly, "But they didn't work, so you had to turn to killing. Is it that you don't want her to marry? Why? Because she turned you down? She's not going to be allowed to have anyone else because she won't have you? You won't be free for long. No one gets away with this sort of thing a second time. They'll trace you, now they've got something to work on. Now the clues lead to a failed suitor." He could hear the man's slow, heavy breathing. "What on earth am I doing in this cellar if you're going to drown me?"

"There's someone else to come."

"No!" Max cried explosively.

He rose, crumpled the food bags in his fingers, and turned slowly away. The door was closing. "You bastard!" Max shouted. "You rotten murderous bastard! You'll not get away with this, I promise you. I'll see you in hell." The hunger had gone, the fear. "I'll see you in hell!'' he said with conviction, speaking quietly, almost to himself.

There was a sound like a soft laugh, or it may have been the rubbing of a latch against wood. Max's head came forward on his knees. "He can't. He can't drown Sara!" And then, in the silence something stabbed through to him and he lifted his head as though listening to a new voice. It's all over if Sara dies. All his fun, which has gone on for years. He can't be going to drown Sara!

Primmy? Oh God!

14

HE saw Primmy's little face, the round soft cheeks, the brilliant blue eyes so like Sara's, the trusting baby smile. No! Max pushed his heels hard against the brick floor, scraping backward on his buttocks until once again he leaned against the rough stone of the corner where the tunnel led off. He lifted his head, set his jaw. If he didn't let the pain in, there would be no pain. Up and down, up and down, he rubbed the cords against the stone. Up, down. Up, down. Fighting all the time to keep the pain out of his mind. Up, down. Up, down. God, I can't stand it! Waves of faintness and nausea. He held the smiling baby face in the darkness of his mind. Keep going. Don't feel anything. If you don't accept it, it isn't there. Cut the cord. Cut the cord. Cut the cord.

A long time later he was aware of a difference in tension. Slowly, tentatively, almost with disbelief, he moved his hands and they parted. His shoulder muscles fought back agonizingly as he tried to bring his right arm forward. He inched the fingers across his thigh and the arm came gradually until his hand lay on his knee. His left arm, with the bullet wound, was stiff. Bending down, using the fingers of his right hand, he worked on the knot at his ankles, pulling, teasing, twisting, jerking until in the darkness the cords were undone and he was free. Free in a black abyss with limbs that seemed scarcely to belong to him. Gradually, supporting himself with the aid of the wall behind, Max hauled himself to his feet. He leaned shakily against the stonework, eyes closed, before he staggered a little way and relieved himself.

It was some time before he could walk properly, even with the wall as guide and support. The light bulb. There was a sweet, wild justice in this, that he would utilize the very thing deliberately left here to taunt him. Keeping one hand on the wall he shuffled along, came painfully up against the corner, and turned left again. Half a dozen careful steps brought him to some sort of obstacle. He bent down, running his hand across a stone protuberance perhaps eight inches high. A step. One—two—three. Reaching upward, his fingers came into contact with the electricity panel on the wall—metal switch covers, glass faces, and bunched wires. The niche where the light bulb lay must be close by.

Turn the switch on first. Up another step and then another. He found it easily, flicked it on. Now, back down two steps. A smooth edge. One of those arched niches. His fingers explored it tentatively. With the utmost care, so very slowly and carefully, the fingers of his good hand crept inside. The bulb was there. His hand closed over the delicate glass. He came back down the steps, back along the wall. He transferred the bulb to the fingers of the injured arm. Moving carefully, very carefully, he explored the upper wall close to the ceiling with his right hand. He found the socket, put the bulb in.

The light blinded him. When he could see again he discovered his watch had stopped at seven o'clock. He came back up the steps and stood looking at the door. It was not a big door, but it was made of hand-hewn oak. He knew, even before setting his shoulder against it, that there was no way he could make it budge. He tried. The pain from his arm set him reeling and he collapsed against the wall. His sleeve was red with dried blood that clung to the wound.

What was this curious cryptlike place he was

in? Obviously it had religious significance, being in the shape of a cross with niches in the stone. He hazarded a guess that it belonged to one of those old farmhouses, possibly Kentish, but they could be found in other parts of the country too. No one knew their origin. It probably meant that the house was near a church. There could be a secret interconnecting tunnel.

He went back down the steps and crossed the main body of the cellar. There was the tunnel. It looked to be about twenty five feet long. If it had once run any distance underground, the exit had long been blocked up. There was a heap of black coal in the center and directly above it a round indentation from which cobwebs hung in long, thin veils. Slithering helplessly, he managed to find a footing. His fingers explored the rusted iron in the ceiling, the smooth segments behind. Smooth, and clean as the iron was not. Yes, his jailor would have put a weight on top.

He retraced his steps. There, beneath the large arch at the head of the cellar by the stairway, was a pile of firewood. He stepped in among the pieces, kicking them apart, looking for a stick. Nothing. He turned to look at the central heating plant that stood against the wall in the main part of the cellar. The front panel of the boiler came off easily. There were no rods that could be usefully unscrewed. He replaced the panel, looked around again. He went up the stone steps again and glanced over the electricity panel. Nothing there. But—a rubber tube with a metal stick attached dangled from a nail near the ceiling! A long metal stick!

It was a gas poker and it slid obediently through one of the holes in the circular iron trap over the center of the tunnel. Max pushed it so hard that he lost his footing and the coal crumbled and slid away beneath his feet, leaving him sprawled among the loose chippings and dust. His arm began to bleed again. He felt the warm stickiness running down toward his wrist. He climbed back onto the coal heap, pushed the poker upward, forced it sideways, sideways, and sideways again. He put his entire strength to the handle and pulled. Daylight! And with it a great surge of excitement. Of hope. The weight had risen no more than an inch off the ground, but "Help!" he shouted, his mouth as near to the iron grille as he could reach. "Help! Help!" With a resounding crack the metal broke and he slid painfully down the coal heap with the flaccid rubber tubing in his hand.

Enid and Willie Theobald had been living next to Wild Hatch for seven years. It was owned by an army family called Roberts, presently stationed in Germany, whose leaves, in spite of frequent change of tenants, freakishly avoided the periodic vacancies. In the beginning, the Theobalds heeded Colonel Roberts's suggestion that they extend a welcome to those who hired his house, but as time went on tenants came and went with a regularity that taxed their hospitality beyond the limits that they, as quiet, retired folk, were prepared to go.

It was a week now since they had first missed the regular-as-clockwork eight A.M. departure of the American in his big flashy Pontiac. More than a week since the little blond woman had sped past their front windows in her Fiat for the last time. And now, according to the owner of the laundromat down the road, there had recently been some local burglaries. Although she hadn't wanted to get involved, Enid's innate sense of responsibility was taking over.

"I've seen that big car come in three times," she said to her husband.

Willie was stretched out in the brocade chair with his feet on a pouf. He was seventy-five and thought he deserved to have an hour to read the paper in the morning. He looked over it now at his wife, spectacles sliding down his nose. "No burglar comes back three times, sweetheart. It's probably someone doing some work for the Robertses while the tenants are away."

"It's not that kind of car, Willie."

"What kind?" He liked to tease her. Enid was a dab hand at fairy cakes, and if she had never learned to change a fuse or a tire and never intended to learn he was quite happy to leave it that way.

"I do know an expensive car when I see one," she said with arch, prim pride, "and no workman ever owned that car. Not the one I've seen coming and going next door."

Willie twinkled. "What kind?"

She said with birdlike, charming defiance, "I think it's a Mercedes."

He dropped his paper in astonishment. "A what?"

"I think I do know a Mercedes, Willie. Ever since you told your cousin Jonnie I can't tell the Queen's coach from a Datsun—"

"I said that?"

"You know you said that. Ever since then, I've been looking at cars. I'm not stupid, you know. It's just that I wasn't interested before. But I saw a Mercedes in a showroom the other day. That car next door is a Mercedes," she said with confidence. "So don't you think now that we ought to investigate?"

"And what if we're caught?"

"I'll say Mary Roberts gave me permission to pick some of those little buttonhole roses—you know, the bush by the garage. They're in flower now. I'll say they're for the church," she added. "That will sound better. Come on."

He shook his head. "Not me."

"Willie!"

"Not me," he repeated, settling back and closing his eyes. "If you see a burglar, tell him to hang around while I phone the police."

"Willie Theobald! Have you no public spirit at all?"

"None," he replied passively.

Carrying the pruning shears, she walked boldly through the hole in the hedge. She crossed the lawn, looking up at the windows of the old house. They were shut, and intact. She went to the back door and tried the knob. It was securely locked. There were always wheel marks in the loose gravel, so those told her nothing. She cut a bunch of the tiny roses and went around the side of the house. Nothing here. Nothing at the front. She crossed the lawn above the rockery, passed the front door, and paused. Why on earth was that great mound of yew and lilac piled over the coal hole? She stared at it for a long moment, scarcely seeing it, marveling. There was no doubt—and she shook her head in puzzled disapproval—money was easy to earn these days. It would be a pea-sized brain, to be sure, that would think of piling hedge clippings over the coal hole. But maybe a young and inexperienced boy was helping with the garden. Some student whose father was away, perhaps, using his limousine? It could be an explanation. She returned to her own garden through the hole in the hedge.

Enid was entering her own back door when she thought she heard a cry. Thought also, though she was not certain, that it was a cry for help. It seemed to come, faintly, from the garden next door, but she knew that was not possible because she had just returned from there. Perhaps there had been an accident in the road? She hurriedly put the roses and pruning shears on a bench, ran out of the door and up the path. At the front fence she paused, looking up and down the road. An old man hobbled by leaning on a stick. Two boys sped along on bicycles, chattering happily. The traffic was thin at this time. Everything seemed normal. She walked up the road a little way in the direction of the shops. The woman who lived in the mock Tudor cottage was trimming her hedge. She looked up. "Good morning".

"Morning."

Enid said diffidently, "I thought I heard a cry for help."

"A cry for help?" the woman echoed, glancing briefly around at the encompassing orderly scene, then back in astonishment at the neighbour whom she had never spoken to before.

Enid flushed. "I thought I heard someone shouting."

The woman shrugged, raised the shears. Snip. Snip. "There have been children riding in the field behind here several times this week. One of them may have fallen off a horse. You're welcome to walk through and look over the back fence."

Enid muttered her thanks and wandered away. She could look over her own back fence, for that matter. It wasn't a child's voice she had heard. She was fairly certain in her own mind that it was the voice of a man. But there was no man there. She shrugged.

"It might have been a strange bird," the woman called after her.

"Very likely." It was cooler inside the house. She thought she would keep the doors shut until the sun went down. Willie was asleep. She put the roses into a vase.

15

SUPERINTENDENT Oliver closed the file and turned to Detective Chief Inspector Bill Pointon, who was seated at the table across the room.

"I'm sorry for Ritchie's parents, I really am. There doesn't seem to be anything we can say to them. I've advised them not to talk to Miss Tindall. Their meeting can do nothing but harm, the way things are. They've gone to the Hilton, and I've told them I'll keep them informed."

Pointon looked up. A dark-haired Cornishman, heavily built, he wore his squashed nose with the air of one who has gained it nobly, as indeed he had, in a successful fight with a bank robber, saving the insurance companies a hundred and twenty thousand pounds. Compared to his steely superior, on the surface he was a gentle, tolerant man. But in an emergency he could outstrip Oliver, and the Superintendent knew it. "Have you considered the possibility that Tindall writes the anonymous letters to herself?"

Oliver swung around in his swivel chair, put his feet up on the desk. God, but it was hot! The whole force was out in shirt sleeves. He lit a cigarette, threw the match into an already overcrowded ashtray. It was a large office but without roominess. Chairs stood about looking abandoned, deskless. Oliver had a habit of seizing one, thinking with a foot on the seat, an elbow on the back. When he moved, always abruptly, he left the chair where it stood. There were papers piled high on his desk; some files inexplicably on the floor by the filing cabinet, which was conveniently placed just inside the door. Maps spattered with red dots brightened the pale painted walls. His blotter was a jungle of irritable black doodling. "Some suggestion," he rapped out, but his hard face cracked into a grin.

"She's a right looker. Clever. Seems to have everything. Could it be a bad case of masochism? Life isn't putting up the hurdles, so she has to invent them?"

"Go on." Oliver leaned forward, picked up a pencil, battered the back of his hand with the rubber end.

"She had no alibi for Fortune's death. Why doesn't she find alibis? She didn't have one the night her parents died, either. Maybe she wants to be charged. Masochism again?''

''She doesn't need an alibi for Ritchie's disappearance. We know exactly where she was and who she was with from the time she left the flat.'' Through the silence came the dull drone of traffic, the screech of a horn.

''Why don't we go over her parents' death together, inch by inch? We might rustle up something in the way of an accomplice.'' Pointon glanced at his watch. ''We've ten minutes before the other victim's twin brother is due.''

''Shoot,'' replied the Superintendent crisply.

Pointon, hunched on a stool at a table a little to Oliver's right, glanced down at his notes. ''She was playing in Repertory at Bristol. Her parents were at their holiday cottage in Carmarthen. It's isolated in a valley, in a forest, and up a track a couple of hundred yards from the road. There's no telephone. Tindall, at her digs in Bristol, gets an anonymous letter with a smudged London postmark—'' He broke off and added shrewdly, ''We're not forgetting how useful the smudged postmark is. She could have recieved that envelope at any time, and held it for her own purpose. It was typewritten, no handwriting to trace. The letter says—we've got it on file—that her mother wants to see her. She tells her landlady and friends she's going to drive over to Carmarthen on Sunday morning, because her parents are there for the weekend. She's going for lunch. Instead, she sets out after the performance on Saturday night. She says later her mother rang from a phone box, sounding distressed.

"The landlady says Tindall didn't get a call. The girl says she happened to be on the stairs when the phone rang and answered it herself. The rule of the house is that guests don't answer the phone unless there's a note on it saying the landlady is out. And there was no note."

Oliver tapped the end of his cigarette against the side of the ashtray, missed, said, "Blast!" and blew the ashes onto the carpet.

"I've given a lot of thought to that phone call," said Pointon. "There's only one explanation, as I see it, and it doesn't make sense in view of what actually happened."

"Go on."

"There's got to be an accomplice, hasn't there? If so, did she use the same one in London? She didn't spirit Max Ritchie away herself. He's a big, heavy chap. About twelve and a half stone they say, and five feet eleven.

And she was at the theatre when he disappeared. Opposed to this is the fact that she left the baby with him. Does a mother leave her child with someone she knows is going to be done in?''

''That sort of mother, perhaps.''

''You're being too harsh. She's said to be devoted to the child. And she gave every sign of it last night.''

''Could be a better plan was bungled. Mightn't she have arranged to have the child removed before the crime was executed? There was all that hysterical drama last night. It might have been shock at finding she had put her own child in danger. Then again, she's an actress.'' From three floors down there came the blast of a car horn. ''Let's go back to Wales.''

''All right. Why does she have to invent the phone call to her digs in Bristol?''

''She botched things up by telling people she was going to Carmarthen on Sunday morning, so she had to invent an excuse for going Saturday evening. I'm not sure it's important, Chief. She may be just a messy thinker, inclined towards muddle.''

''You're forgetting, of course,'' Oliver put

in, "she was onstage in Bristol that night giving a perfectly good performance."

"She was also onstage last night," Pointon reminded the Superintendent, "giving a perfectly good performance. She's a dedicated actress. Maybe she can live in two compartments. Maybe when she's onstage she doesn't remember she's a villain. But why didn't she provide herself with alibis before? That's the weird part. Is she guilty? Or stupid, with luck on her side?"

Oliver ground out his cigarette, glanced once more at his watch, and put his feet on the floor. "So, after the performance in Bristol she hops in the car, drives into Wales, gives the parents drugged cocoa to ensure they don't wake up, sets fire to the cottage, then drives to London to tell her brother she's found the cottage burned to the ground."

Pointon rubbed a hand around his chin, gave his superior a humorous little grin. "Hell no. I don't believe it. Say she's not guilty. Say some other person did the drugging and arson, and wanted her to find the charred bodies?"

"Who? And why?"

"We don't know who. But it may have been someone who knows her well enough to expect her to react badly. Suspiciously, I mean.

Someone who knew she wouldn't do the normal thing of ringing the police from the nearest phone box or house."

A typist came in, dropped some papers on a side table, and went out again.

The Inspector gave Pointon his narrow-eyed, shrewd look. "What about James Fortune?"

"Why?"

"Vengeance. To reword a famous adage: Hell hath no fury like a lover scorned. Or, because he believes she's the cause of his twin's death."

Pointon, rustling through some of the pages on his desk, looked up. "He was the girl's lover or boyfriend or whatever years ago. She did dump him for his twin—the one who was murdered. But walking into Scotland Yard voluntarily to have a word with you doesn't sound like the act of a guilty man. What did you think of him when you met him before?"

"Emotionally very disturbed. It was to be expected at the time, though."

"What does he want to see you about today?"

"They couldn't get anything out of him on the phone. My guess is he wants the other business brought up. He's still after his pound of flesh. It will come up, all right. You've seen the anonymous letter Fortune received while the inquiry was on?"

Pointon looked down at the papers on his desk. He read aloud: Your twin was murdered by Sara Tindall. Pointon swung around in his chair. "These anonymous letters are all the same, I understand? Words cut out of newspapers and glued to a white sheet?"

The inspector nodded. "If she sends them to herself, she's got a death wish. She didn't behave like a girl with a death wish last night."

"No. But she's got a child to live for, now."

The telephone rang and the Inspector answered it. As he put the receiver down Pointon said thoughtfully, "The girl was said to be on good terms with her parents. Maybe she was until they told her they had changed their will. It was altered only that week, according to these notes. The mother may have given her the news in the phone call—if there was a phone call."

Oliver nodded, tapping a pencil on his arm. He was going along with Pointon because a new brain could sometimes come up with an idea, but the subject bored him. He had been over it too often. They needed a fresh lead.

"You believe Miss Tindall went to the cottage to protest, didn't get anywhere, and burned the place down with her parents in it? You believe that yourself?"

"It's the only theory that makes sense."

"Why wasn't her brother suspected, if he got the money?"

"It wasn't actually so much money, as property. A business. It's usual for the son to get a business. He was questioned carefully, don't worry."

"Did he mention anything about providing for his sister?"

"He said he intended to."

"And let's see, where was he the night of the fire?" Pointon looked down at his papers.

"He was in London. His sister corroborated his story. She drove straight to his house and got him out of bed. It was his evidence about the paraffin heaters that helped her. He said he'd warned their parents about them."

Pointon sucked the end of his pencil. "Let's go back a bit. Why would she run to her brother if she'd murdered the parents?"

"Why indeed? That was also one of the points that helped to clear her. Apparently she always runs to her brother when she's in trouble."

"Why was the will changed? Does anyone know?"

"There was no evidence on that point. Miss Tindall said she didn't know the will had been changed, but when she heard, she said that was probably what her mother was upset about on the phone."

Oliver swung his feet to the floor, went restlessly over to the big plate-glass window, and looked down into the street. "Living the way she lives, I'd say the parents had had enough of her. Also, the father had a big manufacturing business. He'd want his son to carry on. There's Alec-damn-Godfrey coming down the street like he owns the whole of London and the Home Counties. Useless bastard! I'm going to get him transferred."

"And did he?"

"What?" Oliver swung around belligerently.

"Carry on the business?"

"I suppose so."

"Was he in the clear? The brother? I'd have thought of him as the first suspect, since he inherited the money."

Oliver came back toward his desk, head down, scowling. "Of course he was investigated. And yes, he was in the clear. He's a very different character from his sister. Pillar of the church and all that. Generous with his money, too. Supports underprivileged kids in India. Helps with charities. Very well thought of. No problem there. He clearly doesn't approve of his sister's lifestyle. Who would?"

Pointon gave him a quizzical look. "Perhaps, with respect, Chief, you haven't quite caught up with the London scene. One-parent families are pretty common these days."

"And very smart they are, too," Oliver retorted sarcastically, "unless you happen to be related to the girl, who, in my view, always comes off worst. Always has, always will. It's a fundamental fact. I can tell you, Bill Pointon, I would not be amused if my daughter got herself pregnant to someone who couldn't or didn't want to marry her. Self-indulgent, that's what I call it."

The buzzer on the desk sounded. "Mr. Fortune to see you, sir."

The pop scene had been glamorous and exciting after a year as a doctor's wife sitting at home in an inadequately furnished flat while Charles worked around the clock at the hospital, but Caroline Halbert was frankly bored now, had been bored for a month or more. Jerry Fontainville—real name Joe Martin—three years younger than herself, had taken her in twenty-five thousand pounds' worth of Rolls Royce to an air-conditioned penthouse in Mayfair that was very adequately furnished indeed, and there had been no turning back. The sunken Roman bath, the circular water bed, the stereo in every room had been a delirious experience, but she had never succumbed to the wealth of temptation that ebbed and flowed through the pop world, and so she found herself almost as alone (though certainly more comfortably so) as she had been as the wife of a hard-working young doctor.

Jerry's album was the serious thing in his life at the moment. Ironically, it had turned out to be quite as absorbing as Charles's work at the hospital. There was a limit to the amount of time Caroline could spend lying around reading glossy magazines, trying on clothes, telephoning women in the same situation as herself. She was tiring, too, of her new friends. The old ones had slid away one by one. She didn't blame them, but she was beginning to miss them now that the novelty of expensive restaurants and nightclubs was fading. Only the clothes still enthralled, but she couldn't wear them all. There were simply not enough waking hours.

She shrugged into the Harrods negligee with the crepe de chine frills and strolled elegantly through to the Harrods kitchen, her long bronze-colored hair sweeping silkily over her shoulders. Jerry Fontainville was standing at a window that was screened by an armada of tropical fish. He was eating cornflakes out of a Wedgewood bowl and reading the morning paper. His blond hair had been permed into a frizzy halo and he wore his silk shirt open to the waist. His jeans were so tight that his already too narrow hips had a corsetted look. Caroline found herself eyeing him with faint distaste for the first time. What's wrong, she asked herself, suddenly depressed. Am I outgrowing him?

"Hey," he exclaimed, glancing up, flinging his mop of hair back, jumping from one light foot to the other like a robin watching the starlings take the crumbs. It meant he had not yet had his morning dose of Librium. He was always calmer after that. "Sara Tindall's in trouble again. Isn't she a friend of yours?"

"A friend of Charles's." Caroline came forward and looked down at the paper with interest.

Jerry passed her the newspaper, then slid his cornflakes bowl carelessly along the Formica bench. "Gotta go. Gotta be at the studio in twenty minutes. See ya, Caro." He jerked the enormous, diamond-studded safety pin that dangled from his right ear. "You'll have to amuse yourself today. Could be working till midnight. Okay?" Without waiting for a reply he flipped up her chin, gave her a sugary, milky kiss, and danced long-leggedly through the drawing room, picking up his velvet jacket and his teddy bear as he went.

Caroline took the paper into the drawing room, where she curled up like a cat in a corner of the lime-green velvet sofa, feet tucked beneath her. She was leggy and elegant in the way Raine was elegant, but without Raine's zest and ready humor, softer than Raine. Baked in the same batch, Charles's devoted housekeeper would have said in despair—but she would have been wrong.

So Sara Tindall was in trouble again! And Charles was once more involved! Dr. Halbert, in reply, said the child was unharmed but there were signs of disorder and a great deal of blood. Caroline knew that the Tindall girl and her actress friend were living in a flat Charles had found for them just across Osbon Square from her old home. The long, long day stretched interminably before her. She glanced uncertainly at the golden reproduction-period telephone. Whatever was going on in her old stamping ground, at least it offered potential excitement. And Charles might be glad to see her. Their marriage had been breaking up when that other man—Guy Fortune—had been shot. She remembered it all vividly: Charles coming in from seeing some patient and she, Caroline, saying, "Somebody's been killed. That actress friend of yours was on the phone. It's her fiancé, she says. She wants you to go over to Notting Hill."

Charles had not gone right away. He had sat down looking strangely upset. She thought he might have had a bad day. He drank the brandy she brought him, downing it almost at a gulp. She remembered wondering if he was in love with Sara, and thinking, Well, that's a way out. And after he had gone, bored and lonely once more, she had picked up the morning paper and seen Sara Tindall's engagement to the man called Guy Fortune, who was now dead.

Caroline stared unseeingly at the purple and gold wall opposite the sofa. She stared at it for a long time. Then, with fluid elegance, she unfolded her long limbs, crossed the lushly carpeted floor, and went into the kitchen. She had better have some breakfast—she glanced at the clock—make it brunch, while she thought about this. She could pretend she hadn't seen the morning paper. Couldn't she simply walk in saying, "I was passing and thought I'd run up and say hello"?

16

SARA rocked the child in her arms. Primmy was calm, enjoying the attention. Raine had said, critically, that she ought to be back in bed for her morning nap, but Sara couldn't let her go. Remembering that Raine had said the police would now find the writer of the anonymous letters, Sara shuddered. It had to happen. It had to end. She shuddered again, and, as though she knew, the child gave a whimpering little sigh.

If only she could crawl with Primmy into a hole in the ground, emerge for performances, then crawl back again. That would do for the present, until some miracle occurred to protect her from the agony that would come from exposure of the facts. She had prayed that the persecution would stop of its own accord, burn itself out. She had prayed for the strength to endure what was happening, what seemed as though it had to happen. She had endured it, while it was aimed at her. Even Guy's death she had endured, because she knew he hadn't been afraid to die.

Guy had believed in a term of life on earth. Early or late, he had said, he would accept death knowing his moment had arrived. He had gone, perhaps, knowing that his destruction was part of her endurance. Thinking like that had brought Sara a feeling of resignation that filtered through the agony. But now it happened again, and resignation dissolved. For Max was no fatalist. Max believed in survival, believed his life, and the quality of his life, lay in his own hands. Max would die, if he had to die, cursing his killer and turning a cold shoulder to the Promised Land.

"If St. Peter wants me through those pearly gates before I reckon it's time, he'll have to drag me through backward, kicking all the way." And he had laughed, looking strong. Stronger than Fate.

Sara glanced down at the sleeping child. Primmy has a right to live, she thought fiercely. And living, she has a right to my love. Sara laid her gently on the bed and drew the covers over her.

The doorbell rang. "I'll go," she called to Raine. "Jamie!" Sara put one hand to her heart in an automatic theatrical gesture that looked phony, but wasn't.

James Fortune stood there looking incredibly like Guy, and yet not looking like him. Tall, with chestnut hair, and there the resemblance came to an abrupt end. Beaky, she thought now, with his lips drawn into a thin line and his pale face dragged into shape around cold, narrow, haunted eyes that looked at her coldly. The inner man, the discovery of which had sent Sara from one twin to the other, had taken over. Guy had loved people, loved good and found it everywhere. James hated the bad, despised the mediocre, judged, and consequently found himself to be judged in return; the one twin constructive, the other destructive; two attractive shells with very different cores. James's shell was cracked now, the core exposed. He said stiffly, "I'd like to talk to you, Sara. May I come in?"

Raine looked up as they entered the living room. Hiding her surprise, she greeted James. Apart from a distant glimpse of him once with his wife (she had hurried in the opposite direction), she hadn't seen James Fortune for eighteen months. She had hoped not to see him again. She rose and said to Sara, "I'll run down to the shop and get some salt. I can't find any in the kitchen. Won't be long." She took her handbag from the bedroom, pausing to look in it for the key. It wasn't there. Where had she left it when she came back this morning with the basketful of food from the square? "Ah! Now she knew how that wretched reporter from the Dispatch had gotten in. She had been certain she had heard the lock click when she kicked the outer door shut behind her. She must have left the key in it. She hurried down the hallway. But the key wasn't in the lock. James's and Sara's voices filtered through from the living room.

But of course! Charles had come back to collect his gear and take it to old Mrs. Cavelley's house in the lane. If he had seen the key in the lock, he would certainly have removed it. She glanced down at the hall table. No key there. He could have slipped it into his pocket. Never mind. Sara would be here to let her in. Raine slammed the door behind her and crossed the landing. As she ran down the stairs, it struck her that Max's disappearance was really no concern of Guy's brother. She stopped, frowning, half turned, took a hesitant step backward. No. She had said she would get the salt. She had better do it, now.

James was saying, "Deirdre and I have talked it over at length, Sara. We feel very strongly about the child's involvement. At least until this matter is cleared up to everyone's satisfaction, we think she should be away from you. Deirdre's prepared to take leave from her job. She's prepared to resign, in fact. As she said, it's the least we can do for Guy's child."

Sara's face was still. She hadn't heard much of what James was saying. Some sort of trap door had closed in her brain, keeping his words out, and her own feverish thoughts had taken over. They wanted the child, too. First Elliott and Lil. Now James and Deirdre. Patrick Delvaney had said the child must be given to someone for safekeeping. Even Raine had agreed. Had the police suggested, or had even Charles suggested, that Primmy be taken from her? The threats crushed in from every side. She cleared her throat and asked in a polite voice, "Jamie, could you loan me a thousand pounds?"

For a moment he was too shocked to reply.

"You must have it," she said urgently.

"What do you mean?"

"Guy's money," she said. "Guy left everything he had to you." It was to be expected. He hadn't married Sara yet and he had died without knowing about the child.

"Guy's money is being held for the baby."

"I want it for her. I want to take her away."

James blinked. "Take her away?" he echoed. "I've just offered to take her away."

"No, James. No. I want to take her away. A long way away where she'll be safe."

He was silent for a moment, staring at her with a haunted look. "You can't leave. You're acting in a play."

She said in a panicky rush. "There's nothing to stop me from getting away. I've got a passport."

"Sara," said Guy's brother, in a voice that was almost brutal in its certainty, "you're not going anywhere. I've been talking to Superintendent Oliver, and I know."

In the first moment of shock her hand came up to her mouth. "Why were you talking to him? What has this to do with you?"

"It has a lot to do with me," he replied calmly. "It's not just that my niece is involved. Guy's death has never been cleared up." And then it came again, what everyone knew. "You didn't have an alibi." He leaned forward, his voice low, as though conscious wickedness might with decency be subdued. "Nor for the night your parents died," he added.

He saw the shock, the disbelief settling, saw

the panic in her eyes as she took in the fact that he hated her beyond reason. "It's all going to come out again, Sara. And Primmy is our niece. She's our flesh and blood, like it or not. She's an innocent child, and we think she ought to be protected."

Sara felt the ground crumbling away beneath her feet. "They don't suspect me! They can't!" She didn't have to point out that she had been with Raine when Max disappeared. Everyone knew.

James rose from his chair and went to the window. He looked down into the square because he couldn't look at her, remembering how he had loved her and aware that his love, rejected, had poisoned itself in returning. It came back as venom, inflamed and inflaming, and slapped him in the face, blinding him. He knew he was behaving stupidly, overemotionally, and knew he couldn't help it. What he saw in Sara's eyes, the fear, the shock, the sheer blind panic, gave him a kind of vicious relief. He turned half around and, without looking at her, said, "He knows you didn't do it on your own."

They stood in silence, half the width of the room between them, neither knowing what their emotions were going to make them do next. At last he said truculently, "Where's the child now?"

Sara didn't answer. She was thinking. He's held it against me all these years. All through his own marriage. The fact that I went from him to Guy. It isn't in him to forgive. I'm alone in the flat. He can take the child if he wants to, just as Elliott would have taken her if Charles hadn't been here to stop him.

The telephone rang. Sara, walking backward, her eyes alive with terror on James's face, went to answer it.

A woman's voice, speaking brightly, said, "It's Caroline Halbert here—"

James had moved toward the door. Sara dropped the receiver and leaped forward, leaving it clanking and clattering against the table leg. If he went near Primmy she would kill him, though she didn't yet know how.

Some sixth sense seemed to have conveyed the message to him. He stopped, an uncertain expression on his face. Across the room an irritated voice spoke distantly, "Is someone there? Is Doctor Halbert there?"

"Get out of here." Sara's words were scarcely more than a low hiss. "Get out of—"

"Sara," James said. "I've never even seen the child."

"No," she replied in a low, breathless voice that didn't sound like hers. "You never cared. You could have seen her, but you didn't care, until you found a way to punish me."

"I didn't need to interfere before, but things are different now."

She said, "Give me a thousand pounds of Guy's money. For her. You said the money was for her. Give it to me now." She held out a hand, palm up. She came closer to him. Closer, without seeming to move her feet.

"No." His eyes narrowed, hardened. "You're being stupid, Sara." She went on staring at him, still holding out her hand.

He said, "You're mad. Look at your face in the mirror. You're mad. It's in your eyes."

Yes, she thought, I believe I am. I believe I'm going mad. I can't stand much more of this without going out of my mind. But if I go out of my mind they—someone—will take Primmy. So I have to keep calm. In the distance she could hear Caroline's voice demanding to know if anyone was there. It brought a touch of reason. She said in a trembling voice that nonetheless exuded a power that was numbing in its ferocity, "When this is all over, when the murderer is caught and she's safe, you can see the child, but leave the flat now, James, and don't come back. Don't, under any circumstances, return."

Without taking his eyes off her, he backed toward the door. She watched him with eyes like blue steel. He went out, slammed the door, and she collapsed against the table, weeping with terror and despair.

17

SUPERINTENDENT Oliver said, "I won't keep her long . . . Yes, I realize she's bound to be overwrought under the circumstances, Miss Mathieson . . . Yes, I know she has to go onstage tonight . . . I do assure you, it's not in my interests to upset her, either, but I do have a job to do."

From the sitting room doorway Sara could see Raine's aggressively stiffened back, hear the sibilant whisper of her replies. She came forward, saying quietly, "Let the Superintendent in, Raine."

He grinned, and looked less sharp-eyed, less flinty and tough than he had seemed the night before. Her heart lifted a little and she wondered fleetingly if something had happened to lighten his suspicions of her. Last night she had recoiled from his ruthlessness. She smiled gratefully at Raine, a new Raine, ragged and tense. Neither of them was helped by this all-pervading heat. Ever since lunch the thermometer had been climbing. It was nearing the nineties now. They needed a thunderstorm to clear the air.

"Mind if I take off my jacket?"

"Please do."

The Superintendent threw it across the television set, ran a finger around the inside of his collar, loosened his tie. He was bulky without his coat, solid as an ox beneath the thin shirt. He drew up a chair to the gate-legged table and sat down without being asked. Sara seated herself on a low stool facing him. He allowed himself a moment to take a good look at her. White face. Orange dress. Blue eyes. White, orange, blue. All that fair hair. You wouldn't think she would have it dragged back and held with a rubber band. You'd think she would make the best of it. Yet, the funny thing was that it didn't make her look any less attractive. Only different. More dignified, perhaps. He wished he could read something in her face. There didn't seem to be anything other than anxiety and a willingness to cooperate.

"There's one question I didn't get around to last night. It's personal and I hope you don't mind. I need to know the names of men you've been—er—in any way involved with." He looked at her hard, trying to read through the extraordinary innocence that made him feel guilty for asking the questions it was necessary for him to ask, trying to persuade himself that the dewy, untouched look was put there deliberately, for she was, they said, an actress of very high caliber. At the same time he had to try desperately to be fair because she was less than half his age and, as Pointon had reminded him, lived in a world of very different standards from his own.

"I've only ever been seriously involved with two men," she said.

Cool as you please. But what did she mean by seriously involved? He glanced away. Listened to the purr of traffic down below. Frowned. Eyed the bouquets on the mantelpiece. Took his time. He'd known young chaps who were badly thrown by a girl's kissing them passionately one night, then going out with another chap the next. But he didn't suppose kissing meant much these days. The fact remained that hurt pride could be the very devil.

"Ritchie and Fortune?" She nodded. "But you have had plenty of boyfriends." It was a statement rather than a question.

"No, I don't think so. If you mean friends who are boys, or men, then yes. But you don't mean that, do you." Hers was a statement, too.

He said with a flash of quickly concealed irritation, "I am trying to establish the possibility of someone getting at you because you left him. Someone who might have hoped you would marry him. Someone who was feeling very serious about you when you left him for another man." She was silent, wondering how much Jamie had told him. With an abrupt gesture he encompassed the room, the entire flat. "For instance, how long have you known Dr. Halbert? Tell me about him."

She was so surprised that she laughed. "I met him accidentally," she said. "Years ago. He saved my life."

"Yes. Go on. You were ill?"

"No. My brother and I were canoeing on a river near my—er—" She faltered and her long dark lashes drooped against her cheek as she touched upon one of the subjects she so desperately needed to avoid. "—My parents' cottage in Carmarthen. It was the year they bought it, and we weren't familiar with the river. There was a bend, and beyond it a waterfall, but we didn't know about the waterfall. There was a sign marked DANGER, but it had been knocked down. Charles found it in the bushes afterward and put it back. That day my canoe got caught up in the rough water above the fall, a sort of rapids, and got out of control. Charles—Dr. Halbert—was fishing from the bank. He yelled a warning and tried to stop the canoe with a pole. He couldn't, but I leaped out and managed to grab the pole, and he pulled me out."

"The canoe went over?"

She shuddered, remembering. "Yes. I'd have been drowned, for sure. There were rocks at the bottom and a whirlpool."

"What about your brother?"

"He'd got out just before the bend. We had his fishing gear in the canoe. He took it and climbed up on the bank. He was lucky because Charles wouldn't have been able to save both of us. That was how Charles and I met, and we've been friends ever since. He found Raine and me the flat when we had to leave the one in Notting Hill after—you know—after Guy . . ."

The Superintendent nodded. "You never had a romantic relationship with the Doctor?" He watched her closely.

"Good heavens, no. Nothing. There's never been anything between us. He got married, actually, while we were out of touch. While I was away in Rep. I never even met his wife. By the time I came back to London he and his wife had parted.''

''I get the impression he's interested in Miss Mathieson.''

Sara smiled. He found himself feeling unsuitably gentle toward her, and fought it. No wonder she got into trouble, a girl with looks like that. ''Everyone who meets her is interested in Miss Mathieson,'' Sara said warmly. ''My brother wanted to marry her once.''

''What happened there?''

She glanced away. ''You must know, Superintendent, as sister on one side and friend on the other, I'd be the last to hear.''

''Mr. Fortune, your late fiancé's brother. Could we talk about him?'' He saw her stiffen. Well, there was a reaction at last. ''Twins tend to be alike in more than looks. I've heard they sometimes have the same taste in women.'' He watched her shrewdly, saw the faint flush rise in her cheeks. ''I talked at length with Mr. Fortune when his brother died, and again this morning.''

''He blames me.''

''I beg your pardon. I didn't catch what you said.''

Sara cleared her throat. "He blames me."

"Yes. He got that anonymous letter accusing you. But there's one thing that puzzles me. He gives the impression of having been very close to his brother, but so far as we can ascertain they didn't see each other for quite a long time before the tragedy. Neither you nor your—er—fiancé, Guy, went to his wedding."

"It's true they were estranged for a while."

"Could you say why?" She had removed the band from the nape of her neck. She shook her head and the bright fair hair fell forward, whether deliberately or not he couldn't tell, onto her face, partially obscuring it. "Could it be that you were in love with James first? You've said you've only been in love with two men. Was James—" The break was deliberate. He waited.

"I met James first," Sara admitted, not meeting Oliver's eyes, wishing she had brought the subject up herself. She might have known a man of his type, in his job, would do his homework meticulously. "But it wasn't serious. Not on my part, anyway."

"Would you say that James had hoped to marry you?" the Superintendent asked bluntly. "That he never got over losing you to his brother?"

"I can't answer those questions, Superintendent. You've interviewed him. Couldn't you make up your mind for yourself?"

"Yes," he replied quite straightforwardly. "I've made up my mind." He stared at the wall, at the big seascape painted by Charles's father, re-crossed his ankles, then began again. "Fortune told me he and his wife would like to look after the baby. They're childless, it seems."

She jerked erect with a suddenness so startling his sharply honed mind went uncharacteristically blank. Blazing blue eyes, a white face, a rigid body strung halfway between terror and uncompromising obdurateness. "My brother and sister-in-law would like to look after the baby too, Superintendent. They're childless, too. I love my child. And she's mine. Nobody is going to take my child away. Nobody."

There was a long silence. He was stunned by her reaction. He had known of the power of the maternal instinct, but there was something purely animal here that was outside of his experience. They could hear Raine moving about in her bedroom, the sound of the radio turned low, again the muted purr of cars moving about the square. The Superintendent rose, shook himself mentally. "Are you on good terms with your brother, Miss Tindall?" he asked.

She glanced aside in that way she had, drooping as though the reaction that had shaken him had affected her, too. "He is my only relative."

"That wasn't exactly the answer I wanted."

"I love him very much."

"And your sister-in-law?"

"We haven't a great deal in common."

"We've covered the men in your immediate circle. What about these 'friends who were boys, or men'? You haven't given me any information about them. Can you name anyone you would admit to having treated badly?"

"I don't think I've ever treated anyone badly, Superintendent. Not deliberately."

"Perhaps young Fortune would disagree with you on that point." She didn't answer. "It's the sort of thing I mean," he said pointedly. There was that inexplicable innocence in her face again. It was unlikely, with her looks, that she'd ever had to fight for a man. She would have spent her time sending them away. How would one develop normal sensitivity, he asked himself, grudgingly merciful. If you did anything, however unpleasant, often enough you were bound to become numbed to the feelings of your victims. You can't cry for everyone all the time. "Well, I must go," he said, rising. "Thank you for being so helpful." He moved toward the door. Sara relaxed. Her shoulders lifted on a faint sigh. Then the Superintendent swung around sharply. "When I talked to you last night I formed a very definite impression you knew who the culprit was, had always known."

There was a startled silence. Then Sara said, "No. How could I?"

"How indeed." He waited. Her face was very pale, very still. His eyes were on hers, searching. "You haven't been entirely honest with me, Miss Tindall, but perhaps we have made a little headway. Don't show me out. I can very well do it myself."

18

AT the Knightsbridge branch of the Leisure and Languor interior decorators, James Fortune collapsed into a swivel chair behind his wife's desk, which was littered with samples of furnishing materials and sales slips. Leisure and Languor was one of those exclusive little places where everything cost a great deal and the customers were happy to be seen carrying their purchases in the shop's heavily imprinted plastic bags. The floor was split-level, the lighting elegant, and the pictures original watercolors either on loan or for sale.

"Don't you think you ought to go back to work?" Deirdre spoke crisply with a confidence she didn't feel. Within the frame of copper hair, the pallor of her face gave her feelings away. James's head was thrust forward and down. His face had a new sharpness, almost a new dimension, as though something had happened at Scotland Yard to change him into a different man. Ludicrously, he might have lost pounds in weight in just a few hours.

He wore his expensive clothes thinly and badly today as if he wanted to hide in their folds. "I told them I'd be here all afternoon," he said. "I didn't fancy having them turn up at the office."

"Who? Who are you talking about?" She seemed very small this morning, very young and vulnerable in her pinafore dress with the frills, her slim bare brown legs in flat-heeled sandals.

"The police." He saw her eyes dilate and added sullenly, "They told me to hang around. They suspect everybody. I didn't have an alibi for last night."

"An alibi?" She swallowed. "Why should you want an alibi?"

"I told you." His impatience lay thin and ragged on his words. "They suspect everybody."

"But you said you were at the office." She didn't look at him. She took the frayed end of a length of cotton curtaining patterned with hyacinths and twisted it in her fingers, winding it, tightening it, letting it go.

"So I was," James returned, sullen again. "But I can't prove it. No one else was there."

She thought fiercely. You fool, you fool. Why did you have to go to Scotland Yard this morning? She should have told him that. Oh Jamie! Why can't you let Sara go? She said aloud, in a low, tense voice, "The world is a circle, Jamie. What you send out comes back to you."

He gave her a bitter look. "Did you get that at your Opendamn-University?" She didn't answer, but she felt the corrosion of his sarcasm, the hurt, the fear because he wouldn't see. "Philosophy, eh?"

"No. I read it somewhere. You'd no right to talk to the Inspector this morning."

"I only told him the truth. That Sara's not a fit person to bring up our niece."

"And he decided you're still in love with her? Was that it?"

He said gruffly, not meeting her eyes, "I might as well have saved myself the trouble."

"Are you, Jamie?"

"Am I what?"

"Still in love with Sara?"

"Sara's buggered up my life. You know that."

"You've got to stop thinking she took Guy away. Guy went because his love for Sara was stronger than his love for you. You've got to believe it, Jamie."

"He didn't have to die for it," James exploded. There were tears in his eyes.

"You said yourself he was a fatalist, so if he believed he died because his life was over, then you must believe it, too." James seemed to shrink further away from her. Compassion took over. "Oh, Jamie, I'm so sorry." Deirdre had neither brothers nor sisters. Her mother and father had parted when she was two years old, and after that there was only a succession of schools and holiday homes because her mother had to work to support them. Marriage was supposed to end all that. Marriage was to charge her world with a warm glow, fill it with children and their children's friends. With happiness and comfort and laughter. But like breeds like, she now knew. Her life was going on as it had always been, except that she had a certificate to say she was not alone, being legally tied to a man who was in love with another woman and walking arm in arm with a ghost.

The little bell on the door tinkled and a customer came in, a well-groomed woman in honey-colored high heels and an Italian designer dress. A perfect specimen of the kind of client the Leisure and Languor shops courted. Jamie receded behind a screen, a fan of Granny-prints designed for the new Edwardian bathrooms, and Deirdre went down the double step to the shop floor. James watched her through a gap in the curtaining that Deirdre had draped so artistically over a rod screwed into the wall. His wife was good at her job, and B.J. Sail, who owned the chain of Leisure and Languar shops, was going to be upset if she said she had to leave to look after her niece. Sail would try to talk her out of it, or into putting the child in a nursery, but James was confident Deirdre would not do that. Not after the kind of childhood she had endured. James brooded on Primmy's growing up. Balm for Guy's loss. He had loved Guy until . . . That love would grow again between Guy's child and himself.

"It's true, isn't it, that you and your brother never spoke again after he took Miss Tindall from you?" Superintendent Oliver, with his hard eyes and his rough talk, could twist a man inside out. "Isn't it less for the child's benefit than to satisfy your own feelings of vindictiveness that you want to take your brother's child, Mr. Fortune?" No, no, no. Inside of him he was screaming that he had to make up for what he had done to Guy. He'd given Guy hell for taking Sara. He'd sworn never to forgive, and he hadn't. He could make it up to the child, if only they would allow him. Assuage the guilt, the nightmare of what had happened that last day when he had seen the announcement of their engagement in the paper. He'd rushed to Guy at Sara's flat. "You'll never marry her. Never, while I live."

Guy had looked at him with compassion of a kind. "I've got her, Jamie. She's mine. It's how things have worked out . . ." Guy had died with compassion for him, with sorrow for him in his heart, and that was what Jamie couldn't live with. That was the knife that twisted and kept on twisting in him. Compassion on the lips of a man about to die.

And that evening Superintendent Oliver had said, "Where were you at seven o'clock tonight, Mr. Fortune, when your brother died?"

"Jamie! Jamie!" At the soft, insistent repetition he looked up, his eyes bloodshot, his face haggard. The client was gone and Deirdre was standing there with a newspaper in her hands. He hadn't heard her go out, or heard anyone else come in. "It's all in here," she said, tapping the rolled paper, holding it away from herself as though it were red hot.

"I don't want to read it," he said.

"No." She stood there, looking down at him with a white face and enormous eyes. "They mention the anonymous letters," she said. He nodded vaguely. She turned away, one hand to either side of her head. Would you write them, Jamie? Would you do that vile and wicked thing? Surely I would know if I were married to a man who was capable of that! You're not a wicked man. You're dangerously disturbed, but not wicked, or surely I would know. And yet, she swung around, looked down at him again, looked to find out if there was something she hadn't seen in him, for there was a kind of wickedness about wanting Sara's child.

"I think I'll go around to the flat again."

"No, Jamie." She tried to take his hands but he pulled them away. "Don't do that."

"Why not?"

"You haven't told me what happened this morning. What did Sara say when you offered to take the child?" He didn't answer, and she was glad that he evidently was not prepared to lie to her. "Go back to work. You should be doing something to take your mind off it."

He looked up, his eyes burning. "Deirdre, come with me. You could convince her the child would be safe and happy with us. Come with me," he urged her, jumping to his feet, grasping her by the shoulders, gripping so hard with his fingers that they hurt. "Let's go together. Let's make her give us the child."

"No, no, Jamie."

"Somebody's got to look after her when Sara goes to the theatre. Why shouldn't that somebody be her uncle and aunt?"

"I won't do it." She broke away from him. "I'll have the child if it works out that way, but I won't harass Sara. I won't."

He could see she wouldn't. He said angrily, "You've got to ring up and make an offer. It won't hurt you to do that." He reached across the desk, picked up the receiver, and held it at arm's length toward her. "There you are. Hold it while I dial. Say we'll come and collect the child when she goes onstage tonight. Or if she says no, offer to baby-sit." He was already dialing.

"Jamie . . ." And then she heard the sweet, sad voice saying tentatively, hopefully, fearfully, "Hello."

Raine, coming out of the bedroom and crossing the hallway, heard Sara say in a flat, hopeless voice, "That's awfully kind of you, but

I'm not going onstage tonight . . . No . . . I have an understudy." And then, sharply, "It's kind of you, but—yes—but—but—" There was silence for a moment, then she cried explosively, "Jamie! No!" and trembling, replaced the receiver.

Raine asked mildly, "What was all that about?"

Sara put a hand across her eyes. "I'm going to leave," she said in a half whisper.

"No, Sara."

"I've got to go. I'm going now. I can't take any more of this. I'm sorry, Raine."

"Where to? For heaven's sake, where would you go?"

"Anywhere."

Raine said sharply, "We've been through all that. You can't run away."

Sara's hand came down from eyes that looked a little wild. "Don't tell me I owe it to Patrick to appear onstage. Don't say it again," she cried, distraught. "I don't owe Primmy's life to anybody." She ran out of the room.

Already regretting her outburst, Raine collapsed into a chair. What can I do? she thought. And then, because when all was said and done she truly loved Sara, What should I do?

Raine had hoed a harder row than Sara, running from school after a failed examination to make tea for a young theatrical company touring the halls of the West Country with a puppet show. To be in the right place at the right time, she knew with humility, was a gift, and that gift had come to her when influenza swept through a Repertory company in Tiverton. She had taken the upward step and had not looked back.

She heard the dull flop of Sara's suitcase lid, then a thump as it was flung on the bed. In the distance there was a slow roll of thunder. Stage effects, Raine thought nervously, dead on cue. Sara's name up in lights. The West End crowds flocking in. "We're going to see Raine Mathieson and Sara Tindall in Two's a Risk, while some train rushed Sara away to an unknown destination and Patrick Delvaney tore his hair.

Sara appeared in the doorway, her face flushed, her eyes bright. "I'll have to go over to the flat to get some more clothes for Primmy and me."

"Sara, you can't do this. You can't," Raine wailed.

"Don't make it harder for me," Sara beseeched her. "I'll never forgive myself, but I've got to do it. Please, Raine. Where's the door key?"

"The police won't like your going over there. They didn't like my getting that basketful of stuff this morning. Sara, you can't do this to Patrick. We'll find a complete stranger to look after Primmy. Someone utterly trustwor—"

"Raine! Stop it!" Sara's tightly clenched hand came up to her mouth, the knuckles white. "Please, darling, where's the door key?"

Raine saw the beginnings of hysteria coming again. She rose, flapped her arms helplessly. "I don't know. I had it this morning and now I can't find it." She went into the small hall and looked down at the narrow table beneath the mirror, at the single shelf, at the carpet, not thinking of the key, thinking of the theatre audience. Marion French was a good enough actress, but sensitive, excessively sensitive. Caught up in the whirlpool of circumstances surrounding Sara's part tonight, she would be a disaster. Feeling the audience's disappointment, she would be thrown off-balance. "I know I used the key to get back in," Raine said, "because you were with Primmy at the time, but it's not here. Maybe Charles found it and picked it up. Anyway, don't worry, I'll be here to let you in." She grasped Sara's hands. "And think, Sara, dear. For heaven's sake, think."

Sara put her arms around her friend and they stood clasping each other for a long moment. "Raine, do you know what I'm going through?" They were both tremulous, both close to breakdown. Sara pulled away, saying brokenly, "Don't think I don't know what I'm doing. One way or another, it's the end of everything today." She went out the door, closing it quietly behind her.

The telephone shrilled. Dear God, Mahomet, Vishnu, Angel Gabriel, St. Peter, and anyone else with influence, if you've a heart at all make this be Max! Raine picked up the receiver.

"Raine," said Patrick Delvaney carefully, "how's Sara?"

"She's about to run away, so if you've any idea of getting her onstage tonight, forget it." Raine burst into tears.

Patrick waited a moment until she had calmed a little, then replied, still in that curiously careful voice, "Pull yourself together, Raine. You're not going to believe this. Nor is Sara. But Marion French fell down the stairs. She's waiting for an ambulance at this moment. We think she may have broken her ankle. Raine, are you there? Raine?" Raine was staring into space. She felt suspended. Out of touch with reality. "Raine?"

She laughed. A light, rather hoarse laugh, faintly hysterical. "You're lying, of course."

"Raine," Patrick exploded. "I am not lying."

No. "I'm sorry. I'm terribly sorry, Patrick. I'm not in my right mind. Sara isn't here at the moment. She's gone back to our flat to gather up some clothes. She's running away, Patrick."

"Then stop her, for God's sake."

"I can't stop her," Raine said, feeling numb. "Sara's convinced that if she lets the child out of her sight Primmy will be kidnapped. Her fear of losing Primmy is very strong, Patrick. I can't stop her. I think I believe it, too." She put the receiver down, rested her elbows on the table, cupped her chin in her hands, and closed her eyes.

"Please God, do something. I promise I'll never ask for anything else if only you'll do something now."

19

THE old lady's frail body already had an opaque, about to be discarded look, like a chrysalis from which the butterfly has begun to emerge. To follow the Hippocratic Oath to the letter, he should put the patient into the hospital, feed her with drugs, and hold the fleeing spirit a week or two; but Charles believed there was a time to die, a time when it could be done as nature intended, with dignity. Though he had lost the battle, he felt no sense of failure, only of impending loss. He told the family he expected their mother to go this afternoon, or evening. The relations were converging on the house in a flurry of movement. There was a kindly, efficient nurse in charge, and no reason for him to stay.

The heat came down like a suffocating blanket. Charles's mouth was parched, his footsteps lagging as he came down the lane. The nurse had offered him a cup of tea, but he had declined. She was going to be busy enough. Out in front of the pub, The Jolly Fox, small tables were set on the pavement beneath striped umbrellas. A dozen or so girls, bare-shouldered in drooping, stylish cottons, and young men with naked torsos rising out of snake-hipped jeans, wilted in the heat as they waited for the pub to open. If that distant thunder came to anything, they were going to look a little less debonair. He glanced across in the direction of his own flat. He must go and see Sara.

And there she was, crossing the square with a suitcase in one hand. He sprinted forward. "Sara!" She dropped the case and spun around, the golden hair swirling, glinting in the sun. Charles jerked his head in the direction of her flat. "How are they getting on over there?" Two police cars were parked outside and the young policeman was still on guard.

"Who knows. The man on duty escorted me to my room and escorted me out again."

"Nothing about Max?"

She shook her head. She couldn't talk about Max. She locked his name and his memory behind a great thick wall she had built in her mind. Max was gone. She had killed him.

They fell into step together. Charles said, "Superintendent Oliver seems to think you might know more about the culprit than you're saying. Can we—er—talk a bit about that?"

"How could I know?"

"Psychiatrically speaking," he replied mildly, "but as you know I'm no psychiatrist, it is possible to bury something so deeply in the subconscious that one doesn't recognize it. Could this be true of you, Sara?"

She didn't answer. She was surprised that he should ask such a question. It was unworthy of him. He knew she was an intelligent person.

Enid made her way warily back through the hole in the hedge. She didn't want Willie to know she was returning to Wild Hatch. He would call it trespassing or busy-bodying since they weren't even on nodding terms with the present tenants. But just suppose that cry she heard had been someone calling for help? Dreadful acts were being committed these days, and not merely in the back streets of London either. Fact had overtaken fiction and the newspapers were twice as lurid as the flashiest paperback. She would feel a fool standing up in court. "You mean to say you heard a cry for help and didn't investigate?" She stood with her back to the hedge looking for the third time at the walls of the silent house. She heard the muted sound of tires and motor as a car passed the open driveway and shot away behind the hedge once more. Across by the pond fat bees hovered over some golden flower and a frog sat popeyed on a water lily leaf. Of course there was nobody there. She must have imagined that cry because it certainly hadn't been a bird.

Gaining confidence, she crossed the lawn and came around the corner of the house. Odd about that pile of clippings. It wouldn't take more than a couple of moments' work to pick them up and deposit them out of sight under the hedge. And then she stopped, blinked, walked nearer, separated the twigs with her foot. Now, what on earth! The strip of gold glinting in the sunlight extended to show a curve of copper. A pot? Filled with stones? She knelt down, put both hands in and pushed a little of the brush aside. A copper pot! And then the apparent truth clicked in. She smiled and carefully, very carefully replaced the greenery as it had been before. Of course, the house must have been re-let to a family with children. She was glad. She liked having young people around. As she reached the hedge again a big black car came crunching up the driveway. She melted into the gap, then, holding aside a twig, peered around. It was a youngish man at the wheel. She didn't see anyone else, but there could be small children in the back of such a large car without her seeing them. She had better not be caught here prying. She went back to her own house with a spring in her step. Tomorrow, or the next day, she would think about making a decent entrance from the front gate to introduce herself. And it was a Mercedes! She felt very proud about spotting the make of car correctly. Children! Now wasn't that nice! Willie would be pleased, too.

Sara, packing. Charles on the sofa, looking worried as he drank a cup of tea. Raine flipping over the pages of a magazine, back, forth, back, forth.

"What do you propose to do if she's ready to go before Patrick gets here?" Charles looked across at Raine, saw the flash of panic in her eyes.

"What could I do? In her present state of mind, if I told her about Marion's accident she might go out of that door like a shot from a gun. Just cross your fingers, Charles, and pray that Patrick arrives before she's ready to leave.

And then," she added, "pray Patrick can convince her Marion's broken ankle is genuine."

"Is it genuine? I mean, are you certain?"

"Yes."

"There has to be someone Sara would trust. Someone she could leave Primmy with."

"Sara doesn't trust anyone. You know that."

"Why can't she go to the theatre? If Patrick is that keen, surely he would waive the rules."

"It's not up to Patrick," Raine explained. "The management wouldn't allow it. If they won't have an adult who knows how to behave, how can they possibly allow in a child who doesn't? She only has to let out one yell and the whole performance is at risk. Sounds from backstage can't be kept out of the auditorium when the curtain's up. No management of any theatre in the West End would have Primmy there. Forget it, Charles. If only you were free. But sure as fate, if we left Primmy with you there would be a car accident right outside and you'd have to go. Besides, you're on call to Mrs. Cavelley." Raine wrung her hands.

The doorbell rang and he went to answer it. Raine leaped up and followed him, knowing there was no way Patrick Delvaney could have gotten there so soon without wings.

Long legs, slender curves, a drooping, luxurious dress the color of Carrara marble. High-heeled strappy shoes, glinting mahogany hair.

Charles turned and Raine saw his heightened color, his bewildered eyes. He said faintly, "Raine, this is Caroline." Raine nodded, then swung around abruptly and went into Sara's room, closing the door. The baby was on the carpet making baby sounds. She looked up at Raine with an engaging grin.

"Who was that?" Sara paused in the act of folding a dress.

"Just what we need for a little lighthearted diversion. Charles's wife."

Sara saw the desperation in Raine's eyes and misread it. "Charles lost interest in Caroline a long time ago," she said consolingly. "I should think she's here to have a ghoulish look at me."

Raine noted with a surge of panic that the suitcase was almost full. "Come and meet her, Sara."

"No, no, I must get away."

"Oh come, Sara. Don't spoil the girl's fun," Raine said in a whipping voice. "It's worth fifty pence just to have a look at her clothes." Raine moved toward the door, head high, electric with passion and fear. "Come on," she said.

How strange, Sara thought as Charles made the introductions. They could be sisters, Raine and Caroline. Not really alike, for Raine was dark and mercurial, while Caroline had a gentle, pampered air, but they were enormously similar. Were Max and Guy alike? And why is Charles looking so desperate? Does he love them both?

Caroline said with the indifferent, casually sophisticated air of the uncaring, "If I'd known you were so busy, I wouldn't have come."

Raine went out into the hallway and stood looking uselessly across the goatskin rugs to the outer door. While Charles talked to Caroline at least he wasn't free to drive Sara to the station. Hurry, Patrick! There was a patter of baby talk from Sara's bedroom, a wail. Raine returned, picked Primmy up, cuddled her.

Sara came back into the room. "So that's Caroline!"

"Isn't she awful! What nerve!"

Sara asked gently, "Do you love Charles? Really love him?"

Raine tossed the child onto the bed. Primmy gave a small squeal of alarm followed by a yell of delight as she bounced. "Dear Sara, there's more to life than love at the moment. There's more to life than Charles. Or Caroline."

Sara gave her an affectionate, wan look. "Yes, well. I'll go now."

"Where? Where will you go?" Raine was clasping and unclasping her hands.

"To one of the railway stations." Sara, avoiding Raine's eyes, bent over the suitcase and began to close it. "Perhaps I'll let the taxi driver decide." She took a key from her handbag and turned it in the suitcase lock.

"And what about news of Max?"

"I'll read it in the papers, won't I? Or hear it on the news. I'm sorry, Raine."

"Sorry? Oh, yes." Raine said it detachedly, as though she had moved beyond despair. There was a peal of thunder, nearer this time. The room darkened. That's all we need, Raine thought, her nerves in knots, a cloudburst. Traffic coming to a standstill. Patrick stuck on the road.

Sara glanced up at the window. Outside, the world was ominously still. "It's going to pour," she said. "I'd better hurry or I won't get a taxi."

"Charles will drive you to the station."

"I'd rather go alone."

"Just because he puts you down at Victoria or Paddington or Waterloo or even some Underground, it doesn't mean he's going to know where you go, Sara," Raine burst out angrily. The doorbell rang. She turned quickly and ran into the hall.

Sara had already lifted Primmy when she heard Raine say in a voice of breathless relief, "Patrick! Oh, Patrick!" She picked up her handbag, put the child in the curve of her left arm, and took the suitcase in her right. She went with outward composure into the hall.

They turned to look at her. Patrick's clever, neat-featured face was flushed, his forehead damp with sweat. There were large patches of sweat on his shirt. He was out of breath, as though he had been running hard. Sara looked at him apparently calmly, emptily.

"Sara!"

She moved forward, impregnable. He held out an arm to stop her. The little pointed beard tilted upward. His eyes glinted.

Sara looked past him to the door. He wanted to hit her. He wanted to shout, to abuse her. With immense control he put a hand on her arm and said, "Sara, your understudy has broken her ankle. Don't doubt what I say. She has—broken—her—ankle. She is already in the casualty department of St. George's Hospital and about to undergo an operation." There was a long pause. Nobody moved. Nobody spoke. Then Patrick shouted, "Sara, are you listening, are you bloody listening, because I am telling you that you are holding the destiny of other people in your hands. I am asking you, I am bloody asking you, to go onstage."

Sara cried shrilly, "Please let me past, Patrick. I want to get a taxi before the rain starts." Charles gently took the case out of her hand.

Caroline exclaimed, "Oh, what a dear little baby!"

Primmy began to scream and Patrick shouted, "Are you bloody deaf, Sara? Are you out to ruin us all? For Christ's sake, do I have to shake some sense into you?"

Someone took the screaming child, Sara never remembered who, nor much about what happened after that. She seemed to be standing in a vacuum trying to remember what she was supposed to be doing. Charles led her back into the living room and made her sit down beside him on the sofa. He held her hand, saying gently, "You have to go onstage." Somebody brought her a brandy. She took it mutely, obediently. Charles said, "Whoever your enemy is, it's someone you know, Sara. You don't know Caroline. If Caroline were to stay here with Primmy, you would be certain she was safe. I'll stay, too. But Primmy will be Caroline's responsibility." Sara looked up. It was as though, Raine said afterward, Sara knew that that was the beginning of what was to happen, a chain of events that now nothing could stop.

Caroline, head raised, beautiful face glowing, said, "I'd really love to look after her, Sara. I may not appear to be the motherly type, but I really do love babies. I really, truly do." The words seemed to sit on an outer perimeter of Sara's mind, not making much sense. She was aware only that she had tried to run away, that she had been stopped because it was right and proper that she should be stopped, but because of this the wheels of fate were set in motion and would remorselessly, relentlessly, grind on.

20

THEY would have to leave for the theatre very soon. The storm hadn't broken but it could at any time, so they'd have to be prepared for traffic holdups. Superintendent Oliver had called again. There was no news of Max, no lead. He repeated what he had said, that he thought Sara was holding something back. He wondered if the full force of Max's disappearance had really hit her. Charles said he felt she was in a state of suspended shock. They both wondered if it was wise to force her to go onstage—would she remember her lines?

Patrick, delighted at having captured Sara, was full of confidence. Raine said that if Oliver was right, if Sara's love for her child was stronger than her desire to keep her alleged secret, then she would tell. Besides, Raine didn't believe she had a secret. She had lived with Sara long enough to know her.

Sara bathed and fed the child with Caroline's assistance. Everyone—except Raine—said, Wasn't Caroline wonderful? At a quarter to six, a quarter to deadline, Sara suddenly announced, "Charles, I'll leave Primmy with Elliott after all. I've been thinking, and it does seem to be the best solution. I should have sent her off with him when he came this morning. I would feel she was safe with him."

They stared at her in open-mouthed astonishment. Raine was the first to recover. "Sara, dear," she said carefully, "you know how Elliott upsets you. Do you think it's wise to see him just now?"

There was a strange disquiet about Sara, a frail, ashen look. "I think I'd like to leave Primmy with him."

"Sara," Raine said entreatingly, "Primmy will be perfectly all right with—" She balked at Caroline's name and replaced it with "Charles".

They were all looking bewilderedly at Sara. She said, "Yes, really. I'm sorry, but I do feel strongly about this. Since I have to leave Primmy, I'd feel better if she was with my brother. She won't come to any harm," Sara added with inexplicable conviction, "if I leave her with my brother."

The room was silent, the telephone line clear. They heard the purr-rr-rr, purr-rr-rr and then faintly a woman's voice. "Lil? . . .

It's Sara. Could I speak to Elliott, please?" And then, flatly, "Oh. Will he be long? . . . If he comes in during the next ten minutes, will you ask him to ring me, please? I have to go in ten minutes." She replaced the receiver. The calm acceptance had gone. As she crossed the room to sit in a chair, they all noticed that her legs were trembling.

Raine went to her. "Why didn't you ask Lil if you could take Primmy to her?" Sara didn't reply. The room was oddly still for one that held five beating hearts. Caroline wished someone would turn the light on. It was incredibly dark for not quite six o'clock on a summer evening. Thunder rolled. It sounded closer this time. "Why didn't you say before that you would leave Primmy with Elliott?" Raine asked in a puzzled voice. "Why did you leave it until this late?"

"I didn't want to leave her at all. I was going to take her away." Sara seemed to have receded from them.

The clock in the hall chimed six and Patrick said, "We've got to go."

Sara rose, went to the telephone, and dialed. "Lil, is Elliott home yet? . . . No, thank you. There is no message." Sara put the telephone down, picked up the child from Caroline's knee, and held her tightly in her arms, face buried in the soft neck. She kissed her child lingeringly, handed the little bundle to Caroline, and taking her handbag went without a word or backward glance to the door. Raine saw her face and never forgot it.

Caroline had taken off her shoes and stretched her long legs out on the sofa. Her hair fell into an enchanting state of disorder around her face, and a tousled Primmy was bouncing happily up and down on her thighs. "You two seem to be hitting it off very well," said Charles.

"Darling," Caroline raised a glowing face, tossed a dislodged curl behind her ear, "you know I love babies. I've always loved them."

"Actually," returned Charles dryly, "it seems to be one of the facts that escaped me during our too short time together. I seem to remember suggesting a family and your turning it down. Or perhaps my memory misleads me?"

"Not at all, dear Charles. Weren't you talking about *me* having babies?"

"Who else? You were my wife."

Caroline laughed softly. "I think it's other people's babies I like. The kind one picks up in a moment of enthusiasm, you understand, and drops when they're sick down their little fronts."

"Ah."

Caroline smiled. She looked gloriously naked in that droopy dress, which was so soft and feminine, so figure-clinging, "Which one are you sleeping with?" Caroline asked, veering piquantly off the subject.

There was a faint tightening of Charles's lips. "Have you ever thought of coming back to me, Caroline?"

She raised a beautifully sculptured eyebrow. "Obviously, darling. Otherwise why would I be here?"

"I could think of reasons." Charles, battling with temptation, tried very hard to steel himself against her. "There is a bit of excitement here. Dare I suggest you're getting bored with the pop scene?"

"Bored? Do you remember how bored I was here? Nothing happened. Nothing. There was no money, and all those hysterical people on the telephone who had you at their beck and call."

"I'm sorry."

She released one hand and blew him a featherweight kiss. "You, darling, I could still take, and happily, but I wasn't cut out for the wife of a hard-working, conscientious doctor."

He sighed, flopped down into a chair, loosened his tie, took it off, and threw it on the table. "That storm must have passed over, missed us. A pity. Rain would clear the air. Things have improved, Caro. I don't get the phone calls here at the flat now. They all go to Surgery. We've got a string of receptionists in the partnership and a telephone answering service, but that's the only improvement, I'm afraid. I still couldn't supply you with the bewitching rags you're wearing. And I still need a wife who can live with my work, and respect it."

She pouted. "You say that very much as though you don't wish to be tempted, darling."

"Once bitten, twice shy."

She concentrated on bumping the delighted child up and down. Primmy crowed. "Oh dear, this is a hot job." Caroline turned back to Charles. "But are you so shy, darling? Could you perhaps make do with a wife who had a career of her own? You still haven't answered my original question. Which girl are you sleeping with? Not Sara, I hope, or . . .

Well, now tell me. What happened to these men of hers? What's it all about, Charles?"

Her velvety neck lay slim across the brocade cushion, her nineteenth-century waist and provocative breasts brought back erotic and delicious memories. He put a hand over his eyes. "You've known Sara a jolly long time," she said. "Much longer than you've known me. Why is it that you always happen to be around when she loses her lovers?"

The telephone shrilled and Charles went to it wearily. "Doctor Halbert speaking. I'll come right over." He turned. "I've got to go and see Mrs. Cavelley."

"Is she worse?"

"Worse? Er—yes. Yes, she's—worse." He stood there looking troubled and vague. Old Mrs. Cavelley, his long-time patient and friend, friend first and patient afterward by an accident of proximity, had chosen a very inconvenient moment to die. "I've got to go out."

Caroline looked resigned. "I thought you said things were better now." He seemed not to have heard. "If you're wanting your little black bag, it's over there."

"Thanks." Charles went to his desk, rifled through some papers, and extracted one of them. He put it carefully into his bag. "I won't be long."

"I think it would be an idea if we had a long, long heart to heart. While you're away I'll put the child to bed. She's starting to yawn anyway, aren't you, sweetheart?" Caroline asked, bending over Primmy and allowing the child to tug at her long hair. She swung her feet to the floor and stood there barefoot, her toenails a rich rose that went well with the soft pinks and creams of her dress. She put Primmy down onto the carpet.

Charles was still looking troubled. His glance went several times from the child to Caroline and back. "I haven't got a key," he said, making the least of his problems sound important while his mind hazed over the rest. "I had to give it to the girls."

"I'll let you in, darling."

"Yes." He frowned, rubbed his hands together, eyed her worriedly. "Now, Caroline, you're in charge here. Can I ask you not to let anyone in."

She gave a little trill of a laugh. "Darling, you've just told me I have to let you in."

"I'll call through the letter flap. I won't ring the bell. So if anyone knocks or rings the bell, don't answer."

Caroline gave an exaggerated little squeal of delight. "It's terribly cloak and dagger, isn't it?"

"It's just that Sara has this obsessional worry over Primmy. She did leave her in our care. And she's very worried about the fact that the child will come to harm. So you'll do as I ask, won't you?"

"It's all in her mind, isn't it?"

"Yes. It's all in her mind. But nevertheless, we are reponsible. So you'll do as I say, won't you? I want you to promise. This is important to me."

She came a little closer to him, looking up into his face, eyes narrowed, mouth faintly smiling. "Yes, it is important to you, isn't it, dear Charles? You are involved, aren't you?"

He picked up his bag. "I'm deeply concerned with all my patients," he said briefly. "That's what you never came to understand."

She held out her hands to him, lifted her face. "Kiss?"

Charles took her outstretched hands and looked into her eyes. "Is that what we're going to talk about afterward?" Looking faintly scared, she pulled her hands away. He saw the look and said quietly, "Do some serious thinking while I'm gone, Caroline. I'm not playing games. I'd like you to be quite certain in your mind as to why you came here today." He turned abruptly and, picking up his bag, went out of the room. She heard the door slam.

Caroline looked down at Primmy. She was so sweet and cuddly and cute. What would it be like to have one of her own? Would she really grow tired of it? Would she? She lifted her arms above her head, stretched languidly. She really didn't know. Life was such hell. Charles was sweet, so terribly sweet, and yet such an enigma. What about that Sara Tindall? There was some sort of tie, she knew, and it had begun with Charles's saving her life. If I had saved someone's life, she said to herself, I'd think I had a stake . . . She looked down at the child, and Primmy grinned, almost toothlessly except for the one white pearl, up at her, waved her arms, kicked the plump little legs, writhed in a sort of ecstasy like a dog anticipating its walk. Caroline went down on her knees, burying her face in the little front, allowing Primmy to pull her hair. "Yes," she said out loud. "I would like you. I could go for something like you very easily."

Only if she came back to Charles there

would be no money for luxuries, no night-clubs, no excitement. Just babies. And this tiny, airless flat with its ordinary furniture, its smallness, its complete absence of the sort of luxury Jerry could provide. Her eyes rested unhappily on the wooden-backed chairs, the carpet she had so laboriously mended, the desk that was neither glossily new nor interestingly antique. She thought of Charles coming in for meals tired and sometimes worried, and even having to go out again in the middle of the night. She went into the bedroom and looked around vaguely for Primmy's night clothes, not seeing them because her mind was elsewhere. Her back was to the window. She shivered, glanced over her shoulder. She had a creepy premonition, as though someone was watching her, as though something were no longer quite right here. She drew the curtains swiftly. Primmy squealed for attention. Caroline hurried back to the living room and picked her up.

Charles went up the steps of the elegant Georgian house, a replica of the other half dozen Georgian houses running the length of Kettle Lane that connected the square with Montrose Road—the busy thoroughfare that ran toward the Embankment. He rang the bell, then stood in a vacuum, waiting.

Nurse Anderson answered the door. She was a kind woman and normally calm, but emotionally disturbed now that it was her patient who had died. "Oh, Doctor, it was good of you to come so quickly," she gabbled. "The dear thing went quite peacefully and without warning. I was in the room. I had my back turned, tidying up the washbasin. I thought I heard a little sigh and turned round and she was gone."

Charles said gravely, "I'm glad she went like that. It was for the best." As they climbed the stairs he said, "I won't stay tonight."

"But where will you go, Doctor? Oh dear, you have your troubles too. I'm so sorry. I'll speak to Mrs. Cavelley's daughter. I don't see why—"

"No, really, Nurse. Don't give it another thought."

"Oh, but I must, Doctor."

"I'd rather you didn't. I'll find a bed without any trouble at all."

When he came back downstairs the relatives were there. A middle-aged woman with shaggy gray hair was waiting for him in the hall. She came forward looking distressed and saying, "I am Alice Sims, another daughter, Doctor. Perhaps if you're not in too much of a hurry you would come into the sitting room. The family's there. We would very much like to talk to you about this—about this—" Tears filled her eyes.

"Of course." He could see them all through the open door. He thought raggedly of Caroline waiting for him at the flat. This contact with a different kind of disaster brought her sharply into focus. He must be mad to even consider discussing Caroline's return. It hadn't worked before. It wouldn't work again. Primmy was where he wanted her. The door was locked. He ran a finger around the inside of his collar. There was a rattle of teacups somewhere. The heat was stifling. These poor people needed him in the first sad moments of shock and loss.

"Doctor?"

"Yes. Yes, of course." He went into the oppressive room. Five men and five women, all looking up at him. One of the women was crying. He wished someone would open a window.

21

CAROLINE did not put Primmy to bed after all. She lay back on the sofa, the child in her arms. The creepiness faded, and the flat seemed gradually to fill itself with their presence. Perhaps this was what she needed. A baby of her own to complete a life grown disappointingly empty. She wondered, with what seemed like a brilliant little burst of insight, if in denying her own maternal function she had done this to herself.

Closing her eyes, she imagined herself wandering into Maternity Dresses in Harrods, floating dreamily across thickly carpeted floors. Primmy was growing sleepy. The pink eyelids were drooping, flicking up as though the child were reluctant to drop off, then drooping again. Looking down at the firm pink curve of the baby cheek, Caroline wandered on in imagination past Maternity Dresses to the Baby Department. Such soft, pretty things. Little cot bells that jingled. "I'll have that, and that, and that." A fleecy shawl; an enormous pink bunny rabbit appliquéd on a pram cover. Pink rosebuds. Ribbons and bows. Of course the child would be a girl. The telephone rang. She lowered Primmy to the cushions, hurried across the room, and picked up the receiver. "Dr. Halbert's residence."

"Caro!"

"Oh, Jerry." The soft, fleecy world spun out of focus, the almost real one of bright lights and music snapped in. She could hear the hi-fi in the background. "I thought you weren't coming back until midnight."

"So I came home early! Maybe it's as well I did. What gives, kid?"

Caroline, balanced on one foot, ran the other one up and down her calf. Her voice was breathless. "I was bored, darling. I decided to come over and see what was going on—I mean, to see how Sara was getting on."

Jerry's voice was like marbles on a tin plate. "I thought you didn't know her."

"Now, darling one, don't sound like that." She was wheedling nervously, spinning between two worlds.

"Like what, Caro? What do I sound like?"

"Cross, darling."

"And I shouldn't be cross if I come home and find a note from my bird saying she's going back to her husband? She's got jealous on account of he seems to have taken up with his old bird? I shouldn't get cross? I should just sit down alone and . . . I'll tell you what, Caro. If you're not back here in the time it takes to get from Kensington to Mayfair, I'm going to put both your effing mink coats in the Rolls and drop them into the effing Thames. Take it or leave it, Caro. You just make up your mind which side your cake's iced on, sugar, and make it up p.d.q."

"Oh, Jerry!" No! Not her lovely minks. She looked around wildly, saw the child, and wanted to scream. "Jerry," she gasped breathlessly. "I can't come right now. I'm looking after Sara's baby."

"Baby!"

"Yes. Sara has gone to the theatre, darling. I can't leave the baby alone in the flat. I offered to look after the child."

There was a stunned silence. Then, "Why?"

"I like babies." She looked down at Primmy with desperation, hating the child for upsetting her life.

"Why didn't you say so, Caro?" Jerry asked softly. "If it's a baby you want, have one. You don't have to look after someone else's child,

Bird. I'll come and get you and we'll make a baby tonight."

Excited, confused, torn in two directions, Caroline wailed, "What shall I do with her now?"

"That's your problem, Caro love. What's the number of the building?"

"Twenty-two," she replied weakly. "Across Osbon Square from the pub."

"Okay. I'll pull up outside and you come down."

Caroline replaced the receiver and stood looking blankly down at the sleeping child, switched off as she always was when things got too much for her. Primmy lay sleeping peacefully among the tapestry cushions, head bent toward one shoulder, arms sprawled, her lashes silkily fringing her cheeks.

In an inspirational flash she knew what to do. Charles wasn't far away. She knew where Mrs. Cavelley lived. At number two Kettle Lane. And there was a carrycot in Sara's bedroom. She had seen it when she was in there with Primmy.

She dashed across the hallway into the room she had once shared with Charles, picked up the carrycot, ran back into the sitting room, lifted the sleeping Primmy carefully, and tucked her in among the blankets, pulled the plastic cover across and zipped it shut. But what if she missed Charles? She hurried over to the desk, picked up a pen, and scribbled on the blotting pad. When the horn sounded outside she was ready.

She didn't see the Mercedes because it was parked at the Portleigh Place entrance, or hear the quiet footsteps on the stairway. The lift was stationary on the landing. She stepped inside and pressed the button.

Jerry, sitting behind the wheel, looked at her from beneath beetled brows as she struggled with the door. He made no attempt to help her as she slid the carrycot onto the seat and climbed in after it. He was dressed in his wine-red satin outfit with the sequins on the lapels. He looked tense.

"I'm dropping the baby at the house Charles has gone to just off the square. I'll show you where to stop. It will only take a moment." She readjusted the carrycot across the seat. The car moved silkily forward. Jerry still hadn't spoken. "Turn right now," she said. "See that narrow lane? There's nowhere to park but you can probably put the wheels up on the footpath."

It was at that moment that she saw Charles.

He was striding out of the lane and into the square. Oh hell! She could have left the child at the flat. Automatically, she lifted a hand to stop Jerry, then dropped it. Must she risk these two meeting? Not in Jerry's present mood. He was like tinder all ready to flare. The car was turning into the lane. Why not leave the child here? Charles would see the note and come straight back. She glanced behind, expecting that Charles would be crossing the square toward his flat. She could no longer see him. Where was he? She screwed anxiously around in her seat. There he was, turning in at the door of The Jolly Fox!

"I can't get through here." Jerry was uptight, explosive. "What the hell's that? A hearse?" He braked sharply. "It is a hearse! What number did you say? Two? That's two. There's a hearse outside! Look, they're bringing out a stiff! Jesus, Caro. It's a damn mortuary." Caroline had a panicky vision of a shifting crowd in the hall beyond the open door, two tall men in formal black holding something like a box, a long box made of light-colored wood. It certainly might be a coffin. A nurse in uniform. "Somebody's dead here." The car window was down and Jerry was staring. "Better take the kid back to the flat."

"I can't get in," Caroline wailed. "I haven't got a key."

Between one emotional pocket and another, Charles felt the need to pause, to unburden himself of death, to prepare himself for facing up to the talk with Caroline. He decided to buy Arthur Masterton, the publican, a cool ale and spend ten minutes sorting himself out. There were six tables set along the pavement edged with groups of young people drooping beneath Martini umbrellas, languidly sipping their drinks. He quickened his footsteps, nodded to a pretty girl whose name escaped him but whose predilection for abortions was etched sharply on his brain, and went through the swing doors. The Fox was an early Georgian pub, spacious and attractively paneled in dark wood. Inside, the atmosphere was heavily oppressive and smelled of stale beer. Masterton, a big, friendly, expansive man with soft sandy hair and ruddy cheeks, was leaning on the bar, mustache drooping. He brightened as Charles came through the door.

"Afternoon, Doctor. Hot enough for you?"

Charles nodded wryly. "Have one on me, Arthur. Is the beer cold?"

"Cold enough." He reached for a bottle of

Charles's favorite brand while Charles looked around the empty bar and loosened his tie.

"Couldn't we prop the swing doors open? Where are the stone lions?"

Masterton placed Charles's bottle of beer on the bar and a glass beside it. "My wife never liked them. She said they were—"

There was a deafening crash of thunder overhead, the sudden beating of rain on the windows and on the road outside.

"What?"

"Sinister." Arthur Masterton looked up with astonishment at the flooded windows, at the babbling, dripping, pushing crowd of young people bursting rowdily through the door to sanctuary. "She thought they were spooky. Look at that rain!"

Charles stared in dismay at the sheets of water falling against the windows, wishing he had gone straight back to the flat. "So what did you do with the lions?"

"Gave them to my brother-in-law down at the Off-License."

Masterton's wife was wiping down the end of the bar. Blond, fresh-faced, and pretty with enormous breasts, she sailed down toward the two men. She flicked a plump hand towards the windows. "Don't look at that. It'll cool the air."

Charles was saying with useless regret and disappointment, "I'd have bought those door-stops from you if I had known. I've always admired them."

"They weren't for sale, you know. It's just that, as I said, Gladys never liked them and just lately she took against them, didn't you, dear? So when Jeff was in the other day I suggested he might like to have them." Thunder burst through the ceiling and filled the room. One of the young girls, attempting to dry her bare shoulders with an inadequate handkerchief, screamed. Everyone looked apprehensive.

"It's directly overhead."

"I hope the pub doesn't get struck."

"We might have known. It's been coming for hours."

"How are we going to get out now? We'll never get a taxi."

"Relax. It will blow over."

Masterton said, when he could make himself heard. "That swing door down at the Off-License can be pretty diabolical when you're going through with a load. Jeff thought he could use the doorstops. I'm sorry you missed them, Doctor, if you really liked them. I wouldn't be surprised, though, if Jeff would let you have them anyway. Why don't you inquire next time you're in?" The door swung open and a man came in with a rush, bringing the rain with him, splashing it from his head and shoulders, shaking himself like a dog. Charles glanced at his watch again and thought about Caroline alone in the flat with the child. If only the storm would let up just a bit.

Standing outside the door he pulled on the nylon mask, then slid the key into the lock. The gun was in his right hand. He opened the door quietly and stepped inside, closing it softly behind him. He crossed the goatskin rugs in silence, then tiptoed down the hallway. Lights were on. He held the gun cocked, ready. The first door on his left stood open. He crept warily forward. The bedroom he had seen from across the light well was here, and empty. He moved stealthily on. Raising the gun, holding it steady, he took a swift step forward into the living room, then turned his head around, holding the weapon out in front. But the room was empty. Empty! He felt a physical shock. A sense of deprivation.

He backed out and went on down the hallway. Another bedroom and it was in darkness. Something screeched inside him. There was no one here! No one! Roughly, angrily, he fumbled for light switches. Click. Empty. He swung across the hallway. The stealth became heavy-footed, choking anger. Click, and the bathroom was flooded emptily with light. He looked this way and that. Where was the child? His hands became sweaty, his breath came in jerky, furious gasps. They had beaten him. Beaten him. But they were not to be allowed to beat him! He pounded back in a blind rage. Blinking around the living room, he was owlish in his disbelief. Where had they gone? He sobbed, choked, gave out little gasping sounds like an animal in distress. Some large black writing on a white pad on the desk caught his eye. He rushed over, trembling. Charles. Sorry. Had to go. In case we pass in midstream I've taken Primmy to Mrs. Cavelley's. Love Caroline.

Mrs. Cavelley's! And he had seen Charles disappear into the pub! Who was Mrs. Cavelley? There was an address list on the desk. He flicked over the sheets. C. Cavelley. 2 Kettle Lane. And he knew where Kettle Lane was. Off the corner of the square on the same side as the pub. He opened the outer door carefully, listened. The lift was still. There was no sound on the stairs. The landing was empty. Leaving the mask in place, he slipped out of the door, pulling it shut behind him. Now he was safe.

As he crossed the landing with leopard-swift strides, he pulled off the mask and gloves. He took the stairs two at a time, crashing into the wall, gasping with emotional excitement. He reached the doorway. He could scarcely see through the bafflingly un-English, tropical sheets of rain. He pushed the outer door open. Rain swept into the doorway, reaching around him like a ragged cloak. He receded, pushed the mask and gloves into his pocket, and pulled out the cap. Jerking it well down over his forehead, he ran across the pavement and, flinging open the door of the Mercedes, jumped in.

Water was everywhere, blinding his windshield, sheeting up from the tires. He swept from the side street into the square, then across and down Kettle Lane. He peered out through the watery mask that defied the wipers. He could just see No Parking signs on either side of the road and already in front of him, the off-side tires up on the pavement, was a big car. He crept up behind it and braked. The rain eased, then lightened, and he could see that the car in front was a Rolls. In front of that was a long, black, shiny limousine that looked oddly like a hearse. Rolling down his windows, he peered out at the house numbers. One, then three. Two was opposite, its front door open.

A crowd of people in the hall. Two men blocked a window, looking out. There was a slender young woman with long hair and a pinkish dress arguing with someone in a nurse's uniform. The nurse seemed to be pushing her toward the door. And then he saw the carrycot. The girl was holding it, looking upset, and pushing her way further into the house. He leaped out of the car and ran up the steps.

Such a noisy hullabaloo. Everyone talking. Some men in black. Dismayed people looking at a box that must surely be a coffin. Yes, it was. A woman crying. A flash of lightning came right in at the door. Shrieks of consternation. The girl in pink, wet hair and wet face, looking anguished, casting around as though for help. She reached the stairs and the nurse was trying to make her go back. He slid through the crowd, listened, heard her cry hysterically, "I'm sorry, Nurse, but I've got to leave her. Charles—Dr. Halbert—will be back."

He waited. The nurse was saying very firmly, ". . . left moments ago." He closed in so that he could hear. "It's a wonder you didn't run into him," the nurse added. "Please take the baby back to the doctor's flat, my dear. You really cannot leave her here. It's not suitable. Not in a house of mourning."

Caroline knew she was growing hysterical, but she couldn't help herself. She had to leave the baby and she would leave the baby, even if it meant setting the cot down among the feet on the floor. She couldn't let Charles and Jerry meet. She couldn't take Primmy to the pub. She couldn't re-enter the flat without a key. Her voice rose and the words raced one after the other. "Please let me leave the child here for just a few moments. I'll ring the doctor. I know where he is. I'll ring—" She felt a hand on her arm. A voice said, "You're the one I'm looking for. Caroline? Charles sent me to get the child." He was already bending down, taking the handle of the carrycot from her.

He heard her gasp of relief, felt the weight of the cot in his hand as she relinquished it. He averted his head so they couldn't see his face too clearly. The girl pushed through the crowd ahead of him, then stopped because the coffin had reached the door. Someone shut the door against the splashing rain. "Excuse me," the girl said, "I want to get out." There was an ear-splitting crack of thunder and a simultaneous flash of lightning. The voices rose. Everyone talking, no one listening. He kept his head down. The girl said again, "Please let me through. I want to get out."

"Not into that, surely." But the men carrying the coffin moved aside. The girl opened the door and, with head down and shoulders hunched, fled through. He followed her.

Someone shouted, "Shut the door." Someone else cried, "Lunatic! He's taken a baby out into that!" The carrycot had a waterproof cover and a little hood. He couldn't even see the child, but knew with a satisfaction that absorbed him, warmed him, that she was there. Primmy was there. He pulled the door closed and ran down the steps into the blinding rain.

A traffic warden hunched in dark plastic from head to heel asked, "Are you going, sir? The lane is blocked. The car in front can't get forward or back."

"Yes," he replied, averting his face. "I'll

back out." Damn her. But under the circumstances, surely she was unlikely to take his number? He put the carrycot on the seat, and slid behind the wheel. The warden stood back watching, directing him. She led him into the square, watched the car speed away, then slipped back to the shelter of her doorway.

22

THE storm was passing over, taking the thunder with it. The pavements were flooded, the gutters overflowing. As Charles ran, the water splashed up his trouser legs, soaking them. They flapped wetly against his ankles. He reached the building where he lived and hurried into the hall. He paused to wring out his trouser bottoms, then took the steps two at a time. The heat hung heavy and oppressive.

He crossed the landing, slid his fingers through the letter slot, and lifted the metal flap. Bending down, he put his mouth to the gap.

"Caroline, it's Charles." He straightened, wiped away the perspiration that had already formed on his forehead, raised each knee in turn, and flipped his trouser legs with his open palm, sending little sprays of water onto the floor. Whew! It was hot! He hoped Caroline had opened the windows to let in the freshly washed air. Where the devil was she? Asleep? He hadn't been gone that long. He bent down again, calling loudly this time, "Caroline, open up. It's Charles." He turned his head with an ear against the hole. Silence. At first there was no apprehension, only puzzlement. He put his mouth to the gap once more. "Caroline! Caroline! It's Charles." Nothing. He went down on his knees and, still holding the flap up with one finger, looked through. The lights were on in the hall. He put his mouth back to the gap. "Caroline!" he shouted. And again. "Caroline! Are you there?" Silence. He stared down the empty hall, stared in disbelief. With a sinking heart, he shouted, "Is anyone there?"

A moment later he was on his feet, swinging away across the landing to take the staircase in leaps, three stairs at a time. He crossed the ground floor hall and went down to the basement without a break in speed. He stopped at the janitor's door and pressed his thumb down on the bell. The janitor, a small stocky man with tousled hair, a startled face, and a mouth full of food, came running.

He saw the anguish on Charles's face, the torment in his eyes, and swallowed convulsively. "Doctor! What can—"

Charles burst in, "My key's missing. Please

let me have yours. Quickly, if you don't mind. It's terribly urgent."

The man swallowed again, getting rid of the last of the overlarge mouthful, his eyes starting with surprise and embarrassment. "I'm sorry, Doctor. I have to come with—"

Charles brushed his words aside. "I'll return the key. I'm in a great hurry, Mr. Williams. Please understand and give it to me. Please!"

The janitor said with more confidence, "It's the rule, Doctor, that's the trouble."

Charles was explosive. "Come up after me if you like, but please let me have the key now. Now!"

Williams turned hesitantly and took the key from the wall behind him. "I should really come up with you myself, but since—"

Charles didn't even hear him. He snatched the key from the janitor's hand. The lift was waiting. He was in it in a flash and the doors closed. He shut his eyes and stood with nerves strung tight as the lift climbed, too slowly, to the first floor. He leaped out, fumbled the key clumsily into the lock, and thrust the door open. "Caroline!" He strode down the hallway and swung around the door into the living room. Only then did he stop. Somewhere in the corner of his mind there was a sense of relief that there was no body, no bloodstains as there had been at the flat across the square. The fact noted, relief fled. He spun around, ran into one bedroom, then the other. Nothing. The bathroom was empty, the light on. Back to the living room. The kitchen door was open, the room in darkness. He saw the hastily scribbled note on the desk. He grabbed the receiver in one hand, his own telephone list in the other. He flicked over the pages until he came to C. Cavelley. Swiftly, he dialed.

A woman's voice, speaking slowly, courteously, and with a gravity becoming the presence of death, began, "Three sev—"

He cut in. "Charles Halbert speaking. Have you got the baby there?"

She answered, "Your friend is on his way, Doctor. He left a few moments ago."

He? Momentarily, Charles was bewildered. He? Then he froze.

"Who left?" he asked quietly.

"Your friend, Doctor."

"She," he corrected the woman. "You mean 'she'. Caroline. Where has she gone?"

An uncertain pause, then, "It's Nurse here, Doctor. A girl—a woman—came with the baby in a carrycot asking if she could leave it here for you. But under the circumstances—"

"Where is the baby?"

"I am telling you, Doctor." The nurse was patient, pained by his abruptness. "Your friend has taken it."

"Caroline? The girl? Caroline Halbert. A tallish girl with long reddish hair and a—er—pinkish dress?"

"No, Doctor. The man took the child."

"What man?" He was rigid. "For God's sake, Nurse, what man?"

He knew he had confused her, upset her by his urgency. He asked quietly, "Nurse, what man took the child?"

"To tell you the truth, Doctor. I don't know who he was. I heard him tell the girl—"

"The one I described?"

"Yes. Yes, a very pretty girl. I didn't honestly notice her clothes, there was such confusion at the time, what with the rain and the men trying to get poor Mrs. Cavelley to the hearse. I heard him tell her that he had been sent for the baby."

Charles felt the shock physically, like a blow, yet unbelievably he managed to remain calm. "What did the man look like?"

"To tell you the truth, Doctor," she said again, "I didn't see him properly. I think he was wearing some sort of cap or hat and I didn't really see his face. It was raining, you understand. You'd have to ask the girl. She must know him. She seemed relieved to see him. She said she couldn't look after the baby because she had to go somewhere. She wanted us to—"

Charles slammed down the receiver. "Sorry, Nurse," he said to the wall as he fell into the swivel chair, pulled out a desk drawer, and picked up a telephone book. F. Fon. Fontainville? Nothing. He dialed Directory Inquiries. "London. Fontainville, J. Mayfair. I don't know the address. Surely you can find . . . But he must be on the telephone. Perhaps he's unlisted. Can you find out?"

Charles closed his eyes as the moments fled by. He was aware of physical discomfort. In the wetness of his clothes. In the oppressive, breathless heat of the room. In the heart of him a sickness, and too much anger for him to support physically and remain calm. "Hello . . . Yes, that's right. Jerry Fontainville. The pop star. He's unlisted? This is Dr. Halbert. I want to get hold of him urgently. I must get hold of him. Please. It's a matter of . . . I tell you . . ." And then with sheer physical anger, "Right. Put me through to your supervisor."

Don't panic. Think. There has to be a way. Keep calm. Be polite. It will take longer if you have to call in the police. "Hello, Supervisor? It's Dr. Halbert speaking. I am the doctor who is concerned in the Sara Tindall case, which you've no doubt read about in this morning's paper. Her baby has disappeared. I have reason to suspect that Mr. Jerry Fontainville the pop star may know something of the child's whereabouts, but his number is ex-Directory and your operator has no authority to put me through even in an emergency. I could get the police to order you to do it, but time is short and this could be a matter of life and death. I understand you can't break rules—disobey instructions—but would you be willing to ring him and explain . . .? You're very kind."

He waited for what seemed to be hours, then Caroline's voice came over the wire, shrill with guilt. "Charles, I handed Primmy over to the man—"

"What man?"

"The man you sent for her."

"What did he look like?"

"Look like?" Caroline's voice rose. "I don't know what he looked like. You should know if you . . ." Her voice trailed off and he heard her quick intake of breath.

"I didn't send anyone, Caroline," said Charles quietly.

"What!" The exclamation rose as a scream.

"Keep calm. What did this man look like?"

"Charles," she cried shrilly, not keeping calm at all, "how was I to know you didn't send him? He said you did. He said—he said—"

"Caroline!" All the strength in him could no longer keep his voice calm. It blistered down the line. "What—did—this—man—look—like?"

She was weeping noisily. There was a sharp crack and then another as of the receiver dropping on a hard surface. The line went dead.

The door bell was ringing. Charles flung himself out of the chair, raced along the hallway, and threw the door open.

The little janitor asked meekly, "Could I have the key back please, Doctor?"

Charles said, "I am very sorry to have to come like this, Nurse. Very sorry indeed, under the circumstances, but I had to. Somebody here must have seen the man who collected the child.''

The woman said starchily, ''But surely, Doctor, the girl knows him. She gave the child up without a murmur.''

''The police are on their way to interview her, but I doubt very much if she will be of much help and that's why I've come to you. Think hard. Please try to remember. You must have some idea of what the man looked like.''

The coarse skin of her cheeks had reddened. She was unaccustomed to being chastised. She pursed her lips. ''I'll do my best, Doctor. But I really didn't look closely at him. There must have been a dozen or more people in here and we were all looking at the rain, and terribly, terribly aware of poor Mrs. Cavelley in her coffin and the undertakers' men trying to get the body to the vehicle outside. I didn't even see the man come in. People were going backward and forward to the windows and the door and—'' She gestured, her hand encompassing the jutting staircase, the hall area that was not so large as to contain a crowd casually. ''I was explaining to this girl who brought the baby that it was impossible for us to take it, and she was arguing, quite excitably, you understand.

And then suddenly a man said . . . What did he say now?" she asked herself, tapping her forehead, closing her eyes in concentration. "Something like, 'I've come to take the child.' I wouldn't be quite certain about that, Doctor, but he said something to that effect. He may even had said, 'Doctor Halbert sent me.' You see, everyone was talking about the storm and the hearse blocking the street, and Mrs. Cavelley's sister was very upset. It was not a moment to—"

"Nurse," Charles interrupted patiently. "Would you be so good as to try to remember what the man looked like?"

"I believe he was tall. Quite tall."

"Big as well? Or thin?"

She sucked in her lips. "He could have been a large man. Could have been. I really am not sure, Doctor. He must have been wearing a coat. But then I'm not sure about that, either."

"Was he wearing a hat?" Charles asked patiently.

"A hat?" She pursed her lips again, concentrating. "Yes, I believe he might have had a hat. No, I think he wore a cap." She brightened, "Yes, I believe he was wearing a cap and that's probably why I don't really know what he looked like. He may have had it low over his face because of the rain."

"Didn't it occur to you," Charles asked, quietly exasperated, "that it was rather odd for a man to come in with a cap pulled down over his eyes and take the baby?"

"No, Doctor," she replied with a return of spirit. "I can't say it did. Anyone coming in out of that deluge would have had his cap or hat pulled down. It was frightful outside. You must know because you were somewhere near. You had left only a few moments before."

Charles nodded, "Yes, I know."

"And really, as far as taking the baby was concerned, nobody here knew whose baby it was. How could we know? The girl didn't say it belonged to Miss Tindall."

There was a sound of someone clearing his throat. "Excuse me." They both looked up. Mrs. Cavelley's younger son was standing in the doorway. "I was there when the girl was arguing with Nurse," he said. "Perhaps I can help. The man came up and said, 'Charles sent me.' And he said something like, 'You're the one I'm looking for.'"

"What did he look like?"

"He was well covered up. He had a cap. And a coat, or perhaps a tweed suit."

"A tweed suit?"

Cavelley answered wryly, "Yes, it does seem unlikely in this heat, I agree. It was probably a coat. I really didn't see what he looked like. Sorry. What's the trouble?"

"I was simply concerned with the impossibility of having a baby here in a house full of mourners and undertakers' men," the nurse broke in, justifying herself. "I was most anxious to get rid of the child. You must see, Doctor."

Charles slumped a little against the banister. How had this happened? Someone had been watching the flat, had seen Caroline leave. "The police will be here soon," he said dully. "Please be good enough to ask everyone to go into the drawing room for questioning."

"Really, Doctor. And dear Mrs. Cavelley not co—"

"I'm sorry, Nurse," he retorted, coming to life again, his voice sharp. "I do understand this is a most unfortunate situation. But Mrs. Cavelley is dead and nothing will bring her back. By inconveniencing yourselves you may be able to save the life of a child."

The nurse wrung her hands. "It's a matter of respect, Doctor. Respect for the dead."

"Please do as I say." He glanced at his

watch. At least time was on his side. The play wouldn't finish until ten-thirty.

"There's one thing we've established, at any rate," said Oliver as they left the house in the lane. "If this johnny came by car he rode in a hearse, a Rolls Royce, or a Mercedes. Thank the good Lord for a well-lit street and the deceased's observant son. Unfortunately, the traffic warden has gone off duty and we can't contact her."

"The Rolls Royce would belong to Jerry Fontainville."

"Do you know anyone with a Mercedes?"

Something pricked at the back of Charles's mind, then lay still. "Nobody specifically connected with Sara. Nothing that I can put a finger on. Anyway, it's not a certainty that the Mercedes was involved, is it? They have said the lane was blocked by the hearse. The Mercedes might have belonged to an innocent bystander who came in behind the Rolls, found there was no way through, and backed off minding his own business. Whoever collected the child might easily have gone on foot."

"All the same, we've got to eliminate the

Mercedes. I'll get a request put out over the air."

The rain had stopped. Charles sucked in great gulps of the clean air and felt his tiredness ease a little. Superintendent Oliver opened the car door, settled his tough, nuggety form in behind the wheel, and looked up at Charles on the pavement. "This girl, she's your ex-wife?"

"She is still my wife. The divorce isn't final."

"I wonder if you should come over with me to talk to her. Pointon's there, but he's not getting far. She's hysterical and Fontainville is uncooperative." Oliver was rubbing the back of his short thick neck with two fingers, staring at the wet pavement, ruminating aloud.

"I'd rather not," Charles replied. As he saw it, apart from the embarrassment of the situation, his presence could only make things more difficult.

Oliver gave him a shrewd look. He had great respect for the medical profession and he had come to like this good-looking young doctor, but he was disturbed about the complexity of Charles's involvement in this case. He had learned a long time ago that nobody was either pure black or pure white, that human beings ranged rather through various shades of gray. But he liked to exempt the medicos. He liked to think that their professional, orderly image extended into their private lives. Yet this wife of the doctor's, from what Pointon had told him over the wireless, was a right bit of crumpet. Was Halbert's friendship with these two actresses really as straightforward as he made out? "You go back to your flat," he said finally. "So long as I know you're there and can get in touch with you, that's okay. You're not on duty or anything?"

"One of my partners is standing in. Has been all day. I was only available for Mrs. Cavelley because she is a very old friend. I'll stay at home, but remember I shall have to leave for the theatre before ten. I must be there to break the news when Sara comes off-stage."

"Mmm." Oliver rubbed his chin, looked up into Charles's face, saw how tired he looked. "What about that brother of hers? Isn't it his job to break the news?"

"I'd rather do it myself. She's going to take the child's disappearance very badly, Superintendent. I think it had better be me."

Oliver nodded. "And there's this affair of the key to your flat." He reached for the starter. "I'll send one of our chaps around to watch the door."

"Thanks. Thanks very much."

"You know, I still think Miss Tindall could tell us something if she would." Charles didn't reply. "Is she going to stay with you tonight?"

"You won't let her back into her own flat, I suppose? She's going to be in a pretty bad state. If we could get her into her own bed, it might make a difference. I would be grateful."

The Superintendent went on rubbing his chin. "I'll nip over now and see if my chaps have finished at her flat." He turned on the ignition. "I'll be in touch."

Charles walked back across the square thinking of Caroline in bed with Jerry Fontainville. It was something to grind his teeth on, and considerably more palatable than the thought of having to tell Sara he had trusted Caroline with her precious child and been let down. He should have known. Hadn't he trusted Caroline with his own future and been let down?

His mind was a storehouse of knowledge about people, their weaknesses, their reactions under strain, the good and the bad in them.

Theoretically, he knew all the pitfalls. Why was it that when the problems came his own way he was no wiser than the next man?

23

THE back of a stairway formed a sloping, stepped ceiling above the stone stairs where Max was perched. Though he might hear nothing through the heavy door, he felt certain that he would be aware of footsteps if anyone climbed to the upper floor. And by the same token, anyone going upstairs would hear him call. But who was likely to come in except his captor, who would either own or rent the building anyway? He had already decided what to do when the man returned. He would be waiting inside the door. Weak as he was and with only one arm, he was a fighter. He surmised his captor was not. He had judged by the puffing and panting as he was dragged from the car down to the cellar that the man was not in good condition. Until a couple of days ago, Max had been in fine fettle. And he was desperate. If he could catch his opponent by surprise, he reckoned he had a chance. But how to effect a surprise when there was little possibility of hearing the man's approach?

He would have to be ready, and in darkness, when the door opened. But the fellow might not return for another hour, six hours, twelve hours. Could he leave the light on? No. One chink would tell his captor that he was free. Max regretfully turned the switch and settled awkwardly on the hard stone step, his head resting against the closely fitting door edge, a piece of firewood at his feet. It was an awkward, chunky piece of wood, perhaps useless, but there was nothing in the cellar that in any way resembled a weapon.

He dozed fitfully, wakened stiff and cold, settled himself into another position, and dozed off again. This time he wakened screaming, toppled off his perch, and found himself falling head first down the steps. The pain from his arm set his head swimming. He stayed where he landed, fighting back the waves of pain, telling himself to straighten his back, lift his head, keep going. He focused on Sara's beautiful face, Primmy's rosy round baby face, and held onto the vision until the pain went, then he climbed the steps and switched on the light again. There was a fresh wetness in the dark, red-caked blood of his sleeve.

He stared up at the inverted board staircase

above his head. He had already tried yelling, knowing there was no chance of the sound escaping through all that wood, through the inner and then the outer walls of the house. He tried again. "Help! Help!" The sound seemed to hit the ceiling and cling like a dead thing. "Help!" He was wasting his strength. The stairs could be thickly carpeted. He could be down a lane, in the middle of a field, in an abandoned building miles from anywhere. Bleakly, he went back down the stone steps and picked up the cord that had bound his feet and hands. He wished he knew what time it was, whether it was night or day. He returned to the top step with the cord. It was some sort of weapon, he supposed, though he didn't know how he would use it with only one hand. He turned off the light, put the cord on the step beside the piece of firewood, and settled down once more to wait.

An hour later, perhaps two (who could tell in this black void), there came a soft sound of footsteps above. Max jerked himself clumsily forward, staggered to his feet, and felt his way back into the cellar. Better not chance yelling from the steps just in case the sound could be pinpointed from above. "Who's there?" he shouted, and again, "Who's there?" The footsteps slowed, halted, then went hurriedly on into silence. Max crouched down on the floor of the cellar shouting at the top of his voice. "Help! I'm in the cellar. Help! Help!" Silence. He shouted intermittently for perhaps half an hour, and then the footsteps came again, descending, "Who's there? Who's there?"

A voice replied, muffled by the staircase but familiar, "Don't waste your breath. No one can hear you except me. And you might wake the child."

"You've brought Primmy!"

"What?"

"You've brought Primmy?" shouted Max in anguish.

"She's asleep upstairs." He laughed.

Keep calm. Don't let this awful thing tear you to ribbons. Think constructively. "Come and talk to me," shouted Max.

"What? I can't hear you. That cellar of yours is pretty soundproof." He laughed derisively.

"Come down and talk to me, there's a good chap."

"Sorry."

"Please."

"Sorry."

"What time is it?"

"Don't worry about time. Enjoy what you've got left. Tomorrow you are both going into the Thames with a couple of stone weights around your necks."

Keep sane. Keep calm. "I might be able to help you if you'd only—" Max broke off as a muted scatter of footsetps sounded above, then stopped, leaving the blackness and silence with him. He felt his way along the wall, stumbled up the steps, and pressed himself close against the door, breath held, waiting. After about ten minues he knew his captor was not going to come, knew he was alone in the house with the child. He crumpled hopelessly on the step, head on his knees. "Oh God, how can you let this happen? Aren't you supposed to be a wise, compassionate God if you exist, if you bloody exist at all! Oh God, if you exist show me how to save that child."

She felt sick and she was shaking, shaking as though she had been wrapped in electric wires and a weak current had been turned on. Someone was holding her. She could see the navy-blue sleeve and, drawing a warm cloak of deceit about her, thought it might belong to Max. The arm in the blue sleeve lifted her gently into an upright position. She allowed herself to know it was not Max's arm. Somebody asked, "Is she all right?" Hannah, her dresser, was dreadfully upset. Sara felt guilty for staying out of reach, for wanting to die. That would upset Hannah even more.

"Wrap her in the blanket. Turn on the radiator, Raine. She's shocked. We've got to keep her warm."

It was the sort of shock that killed all response. Sara was aware only of cold. She was in a sea of ice, rocking and shivering as it moved, slowly freezing to death. It was easier, even less painful, to think fancifully about the cold than about what had caused it. Someone held a cup of hot liquid to her lips, and the aroma of coffee brought her marginally nearer to reality. She sipped, realized Charles was speaking to her, and clicked her mind shut. Ice. Ice that numbed. Hold it to your heart and die in it. Someone was rubbing her hands. Someone else flung words abrasively against her frozen senses. "Sara. Sara, answer me." Perhaps if she kept out of reach they would go away and leave her to die. She blocked out the smell of coffee and the warmth.

"Sara." Let somebody else deal with what they wanted of Sara. Pain and terror were out there with the voices. Carefully, deliberately, she drew her cold cloak of impenetrable silence around herself.

They took her back to her own flat. The police had removed the drawing room carpet and the loose cover from the sofa. The shaking had stopped now; she was walking, fairly steadily, on her own two feet. She stood in the doorway to the sitting room and looked bleakly at the bare wood floor, at a shabby sofa that she didn't recognize. At a memory of blood. Max was dead. "I'll help you into bed, dear. Sara, don't stand there like that. Come on, dear. Come to bed. I'll get you a hot water bottle and a drink. In here, Sara." She was being led, gently but firmly. Here, in her own room, there was sanctuary of a kind. She became aware then of the helpless despair around her. Raine had said it at the theatre and it came up now out of memory: "It seems like the end of the world."

She thought, At the end of the world there will be Primmy and Max and Guy. So, it isn't the end. There's hell first, but if I stay switched off I won't become a part of it.

She sat on the end of the bed with her legs curled up under her, staring into space, and stayed that way until the fear in Raine's voice penetrated.

"Sara. Talk to us. What can we do?"

They sounded so helpless and she couldn't help them. An age passed and then she was in bed, moaning quietly. "Why didn't I give Primmy to Elliott! She would have been safe with Elliott."

They stood in a silent little ring around her bed, charged with guilt. Raine because she had insulted Elliott. Charles because he had sent Elliott packing. Patrick the most conscience-stricken of all because it was he who had insisted that Sara go onstage.

Somebody whispered, "Shall we get Elliott?" and someone else replied, "Sshh."

Sara sat up. "Elliott's here?" A voice quietly said, "No, I'll ring him."

Raine sat on the bed, touched Sara's wrist. "It's very late."

"I want him."

Charles said, "We'll get him if you really think he could help, Sara."

She looked up into Charles's kind, tortured face.

"I should have left Primmy with him," she said pathetically, and crumpled.

"Yes, dear. As it turns out, you should. But it's too late for regrets."

"Elliott! Elliott!" she moaned, then unexpectedly flung herself over the side of the bed.

"Christ! Grab her."

"Here, help me." Charles had his arms tightly around her.

"Sara, dear, relax. Lie down."

"Get Elliott," screamed Sara. "He's my brother. He must come."

Charles said shortly, "Get him, Raine." Raine went into the sitting room and dialed.

"Is that Mrs. Tindall? Lil, it's Raine Mathieson here. Could I speak to Elliott, please?" Her face changed. The eyes became bleak. "Then tell him, please, that Primmy has disappeared and Sara is very upset. She needs him. I'm sorry, Lil. I am truly sorry. Yes, I know we were rather . . . Yes, all right, I do admit we were a bit blunt with him. She was very upset . . . Because she wants him. She needs him. Yes, of course she should have given him the child. I don't know. I don't know. She has simply disappeared. Yes, I know she would have been safe with you, but it's too late now. Yes, I am truly sorry. We all are. But it's too late, Lil. Please, Lil, please ask him to get out of bed and—"

Charles, entering the room, saw the startled expression on Raine's face as she held the handpiece out, looking at it, heard the empty buzz on the line. He closed the door carefully. "He won't come?"

She replaced the receiver, looked up at him. "Elliott has gone to bed. He won't even speak to me. He's sulking because of what happened this morning." Raine's temper flared. "Elliott is an insensitive, self-indulgent clot, Charles. We're better off without him. If you've got lousy relations, you just have to rely on your friends. And one thing Sara has got plenty of is friends."

Charles said quietly, "I think you had better get over whatever happened between you and Elliott, Raine. Sara needs him. I'll give her a jab," he added, opening the door behind him. "I'll put her out."

Later Raine and Charles sat up talking, drinking coffee, worrying. They were awkward with each other now because everything they needed to talk about concerned Caroline. Charles said, "Mercedes. Mercedes. Mercedes. There's something in the back of my mind."

"Who do you know, or what's more to the point, who do we know who owns a Mercedes? Who does Sara know with one?"

Charles shook his head. "They're common enough around this part of London. I don't think there's anyone I am in the habit of seeing who has one. But—"

"But what?"

The sharpness of her voice jolted his memory. "Got it," Charles said. "Booby-prize stuff, though. I saw some fellow in a Mercedes outside the Off-License yesterday evening. I wonder if it's worth following up?" He would have to go to the Off-License anyway if he wanted the lion doorstops. He had forgotten about them, wanted to forget about them. If he had gone directly back to the flat instead of to the pub, if he hadn't stayed talking about the doorstops and been cut off by the rain, he might have been in time to prevent the child's disappearance.

"I'm still puzzled about how that reporter got into your flat yesterday morning," Raine said. "I'll swear I shut the door behind me when I came back from here. I've thought and thought about it and I'm sure it's not imagination when I say I heard the latch click."

"The mind does funny things."

"I still think I shut that door."

"Didn't you ask what's his name how he got in?"

"Ossie Mount of the Morning Dispatch? He said the door was open, but the more I think about it the more certain I am that he was lying. Somebody could have gotten in and seen Caroline's note on the pad."

"Why don't we telephone him?" Charles reached for the book. "Morning Dispatch?" He flipped the pages over. "Here it is."

They told Raine that the man called Ossie Mount was off duty. "Who wants him?"

"Just a friend." Charles flicked the pages over rapidly. Mount, O.J. He put a finger under the insertion, and Raine said into the receiver, "He lives in Fulham, doesn't he?"

"That's right."

"I'll ring him there." She put the receiver down, lifted it again, and dialed. A sleepy voice answered. "A simple question, Mr. Mount. How did you get into Dr. Halbert's flat yesterday morning? It is terribly important that I should know, now. It's Raine Mathieson speaking."

He was no longer sleepy. "Has there been some new development?"

"No," she lied. "Please tell me how you got in."

"The key was in the door, love. You must have left it there yourself. Are you sure there's nothing new?" he asked suspiciously.

"If there were, I am sure a sharp reporter like you would know even before it happened." She replaced the receiver and slumped down into a chair. "I left it in the door." They were both guilty now, both of them causes to the diabolical effect.

Charles rose. "I think I had better turn in," he said. "Nothing is to be gained by our sitting up all night. The police are doing everything possible." He put a hand on her wrist. She left it there for a moment, then jerked her arm away. "Nothing is to be gained either by our hating each other," he said quietly.

She stood up, her beautiful face haggard. "Let's just settle for hating ourselves, shall we, Charles?" She looked at him with glittering eyes and chin lifted. "Perhaps Sara would have been better off staying with Elliott. Perhaps he knows that. Perhaps he's not sulking. Perhaps he's suffering, too. We have made a rotten mess of things." She began to cry.

Charles put his arms around her, holding her close against him until she calmed. "I'll bring Elliott over first thing in the morning," he said.

She nodded, wiping her eyes. He kissed her gently, then left without another word.

24

ELLIOTT and Lil Tindall lived in a Georgian house with a considerable amount of garden beautifully tended, an ideal setting for the church garden parties that were held there once a year. Charles turned his car in at the open driveway. The woman who answered the bell was large with mousy hair, light eyes, a reddish complexion, and a jutting, meaty chin. She smiled faintly in greeting, exposing the neatest and most unreal looking set of dentures he had ever seen. Charles thought she must be Lil Tindall's housekeeper, but there was something about her clothes that made him hesitate. Housekeepers did not usually answer the front door in expensive-looking, chocolate-colored velvet house gowns.

"Mrs. Tindall?"

"Yes."

Raine had said Sara's sister-in-law was ugly. Yet this total contrast to Sara was a shock. Lil Tindall was excessively plain, with ugliness manifest in something dark that showed through. Resentment? Sadness? Evil? No. None of that, he thought. He said, "I am Charles Halbert, Sara's doctor. May I come in and see your husband?"

"I'm sorry. He's not at home."

Charles glanced at his watch. It was eight-thirty. "Where might I find him?"

"If he were here he wouldn't talk to you," Lil Tindall said, "so I'm sure he doesn't want you chasing after him." One hand rested on the door handle, tentatively.

"May I come in?" Charles stepped forward, very close to her so that she could not close the door without appearing to be excessively rude.

She hesitated. "There's really no point, under the circumstances, is there?" She looked uncertain now.

Charles replied, "I'd like to have a talk with you, Mrs. Tindall, and I'd rather do it inside."

She hesitated again. "It's very early."

"Yes. I'm sorry to turn up at such an hour." He gestured to her to precede him into the hall, an authoritative movement that she automatically if reluctantly obeyed. The hall was bare except for a Sheraton mahogany sofa table and a wing tapestry chair. A narrow but beautifully proportioned staircase curved upward, and from where he stood Charles could see an enormous Chinese enameled porcelain pot on another table on the landing. There were exotic Chinese porcelain plates, too, on the walls.

"Come into the library." Lil led him through a doorway on the left into a medium-sized and very elegantly designed room furnished with total disregard for style. There was a bright Spanish looped pile carpet side-by-side with soft, velvety Persian prayer rugs; a William and Mary chair, high-backed and austere; some over-decorated Chippendale and, incongruously, a modern three-piece suite, low-backed, wide-armed, and upholstered in gray checked cotton. A library? Charles glanced around curiously but didn't see any books.

Lil went over to the elegant Adam fireplace and took down a champagne-colored glass with enameled decoration that was doubling as a cigarette container. "Do you smoke?"

"No, thank you." Charles seated himself in one of the modern armchairs while Elliott's wife lit a cigarette for herself. He had been in Sara's home only once before her parents died. It had been tastefully furnished with good carpets, good furniture that gave the big rooms a lived-in look. This so-called library without books had an air of having been filled with the chance contents of an auction sale. Except for the small bowls of roses and carnations set here and there, it could have been the interior of a spacious furniture shop. He said, "I was there when Raine Mathieson spoke to you last night."

"I didn't hear from Raine Mathieson last night."

He looked at her sharply. "About midnight. She telephoned you about midnight."

"I wasn't here. Neither of us was here. We went out to dinner. Elliott was upset. I didn't want him bothered by any more of Sara's problems. We didn't get home until after one this morning."

Charles blinked. "Then who was here?"

"Nobody."

"But Raine spoke to someone. I was there, standing beside her. She said, 'Mrs. Tindall.' and 'Lil'." Lil Tindall shook her head. Strange, Charles thought, she did not appear to be lying. "She spoke to someone. She dialed your number and spoke to someone."

Lil shook her head again. "It's easy enough to pretend there's a person on the other end of a line. She's an actress, don't forget. Raine hates my husband. What was she ringing about?"

"Sara wanted your husband to come over."

"And Raine didn't want him to?"

Charles was silent. After a moment he asked, "I suppose you've seen the morning papers?"

Lil went to sit down in a high-backed chair. "No, I'm afraid I haven't. I haven't had time."

"Have you heard the news on the radio?" She shook her head. "Then you don't know that Primmy is missing?" He was immediately sorry he had said it like that, so badly. Lil's jaw dropped and the peas-in-a-pod teeth seemed to sit up and look at him.

"Missing?" she repeated, then sharply, "What do you mean, missing?" She jerked forward in her seat like a runner at the start, her colorless eyes popping.

Charles thought then that the dark behind her face came from a deadness inside. Lil Tindall could have been a better looking woman if things had turned her way. It flashed through his mind that somehow, in spite of the trappings of wealth, life had gone wrong for her.

"Perhaps you'll call your husband now," he

said more gently. "I would like to talk to you both."

"He isn't here." She rose abruptly and strode to the fireplace, threw the unsmoked cigarette into the grate, and, with shoulders hunched, neck somehow withdrawn, she turned on him. "He left early because he didn't want Sara and her friends getting at him. It was dreadful, the way you treated him yesterday. He went over to your flat all set to do anything he could for Sara, just as he always does when she's in trouble, and you threw him out. What do you expect of him? Do you think he would be sitting here waiting to run back just as soon as Sara crooked her little finger? How do you think he felt on Wednesday night? How do you think we both felt, standing there outside the theatre? Treated like lepers."

"Mrs. Tindall—"

"I'm sorry, Doctor Halbert, but I've got to say this. I don't know what you are to Sara."

"A good friend."

"All right. Elliott and I have always done our best for Sara. We've really tried, but we've come to the end of the road now. Elliott doesn't want his life disrupted anymore. You can only take a certain amount before you have to give up. We offered to adopt that illegitimate child when we first knew Sara was having it. We were willing to take the child and bring it up in a decent Christian household. We offered to cover up for her, too." She hesitated, reddened, then went on in some embarrassment. "I'll tell you this, Doctor, I even offered to pad out my clothes for months on end and pretend the child was mine. It could have been so easy. There would have been no scandal—" As though the suppressed horror, amusement, and disbelief in Charles had somehow slipped through to show on his face, she broke off, then added viciously, "But Sara's such an exhibitionist! She loved all the publicity, didn't she? She thrived on it."

Charles sat mesmerized, never for a moment doubting that her emotion was genuine. He shook himself mentally, blinked the unreality away. He felt a need to be gentle with this woman, but one part of him sat in judgement of her, revolted. "I don't believe there is such a thing as an illegitimate child," he said at last. "I think little Primmy is quite legitimate and has a very legitimate right to a normal life with her mother, whom I respect and who is greatly respected by those who know her. She chose to have that child because she was deeply in love with Guy."

"Yes," snapped Elliott's wife bitterly, "and now she's 'deeply in love' it seems, with some other man."

Charles shifted uncomfortably on his very comfortable seat. "I didn't come here to talk about morals. I came because I believe your husband might be able to help his sister if he could only bring himself to take a charitable view of her. She is very, very unhappy."

"She's brought it on herself."

"That may well be so, but if your husband is in the house, I'd be very grateful if you would produce him. Sara needs her family at this time, and Elliott is all she has."

"I've told you he's not here."

"Then tell me where I can find him."

"I've already said I don't know."

"When did he go?"

"About half an hour ago."

"Why didn't he tell you where he was going?"

"Can't you see? So that people like you couldn't get it out of me, of course."

"Has he a car radio?"

"Yes."

"Do you think he would return if he hears the news of Primmy's disappearance?"

"Why should he, after being thrown out of the flat yesterday? Would you, if you were in his shoes?"

Charles rose. "I'd like you to ask him to get in touch with Sara when he returns. She's back in her own flat."

"I'll tell him what you said."

At the door he turned. "Are you fond of children, Mrs. Tindall?"

"I've never had anything to do with them."

"I just wondered why you were so anxious to have Primmy when you don't seem to have had anything to do with her and haven't any of your own."

Her face was still, cold, and suddenly incredibly ugly, with all that was wrong accented by the emotions behind it, the awful false teeth, the unreadable darkness beyond her eyes. He understood why Raine viewed Lil Tindall as a very unlovely woman. Raine might, because of the passions involved, tend always to see her like this.

"Perhaps they didn't tell you about infertility in your training hospital, Doctor."

"They did, actually, and a lot about people. I just wondered why you and Elliott hadn't learned to laugh about your sister-in-law's irregular situation, hardly even irregular in big, sophisticated cities like London." They faced each other for a long moment, then Charles turned abruptly and strode into the hall. As he stepped through the front doorway, he said with a noticeable lack of his normal gentleness, "If you would care to have your infertility investigated, Mrs. Tindall, I would be only too glad to put you in touch with—" The door into the library was still open. She had turned in silence and was walking back inside. He waited a moment, then with a quick sigh drew the front door closed behind him.

25

CHARLES drove by the Off-License. There was no one around. Traffic wardens didn't bother much with this stretch of road. They were normally good-natured about the need to pick up heavy boxes of liquor. He parked on the double yellow line and pushed the door open, noting in passing and without much interest now that there were no doorstops standing inside.

"Morning, Doctor." Jeff McGarry, brother-in-law of the host at The Jolly Fox, came forward, looking concerned. "How are things around there? Is there any word of the baby?"

Charles shook his head. "The police are looking for a Mercedes."

"Yes. We heard it on the radio."

"I saw a Mercedes parked outside here two days ago," Charles said. "The man who was driving it was tallish and he wore a rather heavy suit—you will remember it was a hot day. I saw him putting a crate in the boot."

McGarry's wife, who had been listening in

the doorway at the back of the shop, came to join him. "He's the one who took the doorstops," she reminded her husband. "That man had a Mercedes."

"The lion doorstops from The Fox?" Charles asked wryly. So he had missed them again! "Tell me about this man. What did he look like? I saw him in the distance, but I didn't look very hard."

"What did he look like?" she repeated, and shook her head. "He came in for a bottle of gin. Jeff here and me, we were having a heated argument about those doorstops at the time. My brother-in-law up at The Fox wished them on us. Gladys didn't like them. Thought they were evil, and so did I, but I hadn't said so to Jeff. Jeff brought them along here and I nearly had a fit. I was telling Jeff here to put the lions into an empty champagne crate when the man came in. I was going to get rid of them somehow. And this man, he looked at them and he laughed and said he'd like to buy them. So I says, 'Right,' I says, 'two pounds each.' They were worth a great deal more than that, I can tell you, but I wanted to see the back of them. And he laughed again, gave me four pounds, and carried the lot out to his car."

"What did he look like?" Charles repeated

the question. "He was tall, I know. What color was his hair?"

They both shook their heads blankly. "He might have been wearing a hat." Charles thought, Now I remember. He wore a cap. McGarry was leaning on the counter scratching his head, puzzling. "He looked familiar. Vaguely. I might have had him in before. Maybe he's a regular at The Fox. I might have seen him there. But I couldn't say that for certain either."

"You didn't happen to notice the number of the Mercedes, I suppose?"

"No. Sorry I can't help you more."

There was a traffic warden standing by his car when he came out of the Off-License. She was busy writing out a ticket. She smiled, her eyes steely, unforgiving. "Yes, I know you're a doctor, Sir," she said, "but don't tell me you were in there buying brandy for medicinal purposes."

A faint flicker of irritation showed on Charles's face. "I don't suppose you were on duty last night?"

"Yes, as a matter of fact I was."

"Have the police contacted you?"

"No. I didn't go home last night. What's the matter?"

"You know about Miss Tindall's baby being missing?" At her blank look he added, "Surely they told you when you clocked in this morning? Surely they asked you if you saw—" He could see they had not. He asked patiently, "Did you know Sara Tindall's baby has disappeared?"

"The actress?" Charles nodded. "No, I didn't know. Someone was attacked in her flat."

"Yes. Now her baby has disappeared from a house in Kettle Lane. Possibly taken by a man driving a black Mercedes."

She put a hand to her forehead. She was a pretty girl under that masculine uniform, that terrible hat. "I didn't listen to the news. I saw the Mercedes. A man came out of a house carrying a baby—I mean a carrycot. I was just going off duty at the time. I helped him back out of the lane because it was blocked by a hearse."

"Did you take the number?"

"I didn't write it down."

"How's your memory?"

"It's good for car numbers. I'll try to remember." She closed her eyes. Her forehead was wrinkled in concentration. Charles waited. Would she remember? Hopefully, he pulled a notebook and pencil out of his pocket. The girl opened her eyes. "I'm pretty sure I've got it right." She reached for the pencil and paper. "Yes, I am certain. I'm not often wrong." She wrote the letters and figures down, staring at them. "Yes, I could almost swear that's right." She looked up brightly, anxious now to atone. "It's my job, of course."

Charles said, "I think you had better get in touch with Homicide. This is the number." He tore a sheet out of his notebook and handed it to her. Then he hurried around to the driver's door, jumped into his car, shot up the road, across the square, and parked outside his own block of flats. Without pausing to lock the car, he took the stairs at a run, let himself into his flat, and, slamming the door behind him, hurried through to the living room. He picked up the telephone list, flicked it through to O, the new entry for Oliver, and dialed. "Superintendent? It's Charles Halbert here. Have you got a pencil? Here's the number of that Mercedes that was parked in Kettle Lane last night. I got it from the traffic warden. Yes, she slept out and didn't listen to the news. Well, it seems she wasn't questioned. Don't ask me. She appears to have slipped through your net. I'd be glad, anyway, if you would let me know when you trace the owner. I might not be here. I might go over to the girls' flat." Charles put the receiver down and stretched back in his chair, trying to ease the tenseness in his muscles. He closed his eyes. Stop chastising yourself. It won't do any good. Work on the unacceptable. But he couldn't. He found himself going back uselessly over the facts, just as he had last night as he lay awake with his guilt long into the early hours.

He knew—who better?—that Caroline was unreliable. He could even have asked the janitor to keep an eye on her. Williams could have stationed himself outside the door under orders to allow no one to come and go. Then there were the police, only too willing to cooperate. He could have called for someone to stand by. Hindsight! Punishing hindsight. Yet deep down in the self-chastisement a root of common sense told him quite categorically that you couldn't go through life expecting people to betray you. He had had to trust Caroline. But if he had returned directly to the flat, he would have seen the Rolls and Caroline would have seen him. It was his fault the child was gone, and it was up to him to find her. He stared at the bouquets still standing in their flat bowls on the mantelpiece. He should have taken them over before to relieve the starkness of the girls' denuded sitting room.

Go back to the beginning, to that first day when he met Sara. He had been standing on the bank with his fishing rod when her canoe came whirling downstream toward the waterfall. It was a miracle he had been able to save her, immensely helped by her own presence of mind in jumping out and grabbing the branch he pushed far out into the stream. He had been angry, he remembered. He had said, "There are notices on the bank. Can't you read?" And poor Sara, shaken, had only looked at him blankly. Afterward, on his way home, he had searched for the notices but they weren't there. Elliott had said it was their first time on the river. Work on the unacceptable. He could have been speaking the truth, using the plural. The police had found the warning Danger signs in the bushes later. "Vandalism," they had said.

Charles stared into space. His mind was buzzing from point to point, lifting ideas, discarding them. Sara said she loved her brother, yet there were discrepancies. Why had he and his wife been forgotten the night the play opened when the other guests were told the party was off? Because Elliot and Lil were not sitting in the block Sara had booked for her friends. Why had she chosen two seats for them apart? If she didn't want them to meet her friends, why had she invited them to the party?

Work on the unacceptable. He picked up the telephone book, looked up a number, and dialed. "Mrs. Tindall, it's Charles Halbert here again. Sorry to bother you. I just wanted to ask about those stone doorstops your husband bought the other day. Really? I mean, are you certain? He didn't mention them? Well, they came from a pub near here. Off-License, actually. They told me your husband bought them. Oh well. Sorry to bother you. No, it doesn't matter. I'll explain another time." He replaced the receiver and stared into space.

The death of Mr. and Mrs. Tindall. Mrs. Tindall had been a sweet person. Sweet and loving. The police had not been inclined to believe Sara's story about getting a phone call from her mother on the afternoon before they died in the fire, but Charles did because he knew Sara to be truthful. She was also essentially nonviolent. He didn't believe that she was capable of setting a house on fire, with or without anyone in it. Could her mother have had a call that day from someone who knew Sara? Could she have telephoned because she was worried or frightened?

Sara's troubles began at about the time she started her R.A.D.A. training, shortly after she met both Charles and James. He picked up the telephone book again. F. Fortune. He jotted down the address, looked up Dry Cleaners in the Yellow pages, found one in the same block as James Fortune's flat. Dialed. "Is that Mrs. Fortune? It's the Westway Cleaners here. Remember that tweed suit we cleaned for your husband? No? But surely, at the end of the winter . . . Doesn't possess a tweed suit? Are you absolutely certain? Well, perhaps we have . . . If you say so. But I seem to remember him bringing it in. He was driving a black Mercedes. He has got a Mercedes, hasn't he?" The line went dead. Charles put the receiver back on the stand. He sighed, conceding that Deirdre's hanging up in his ear meant only that she was quick on the uptake. He hadn't proved anything.

Whom else had Sara met about the time she began her theatrical career? Some queer, introverted freak, as Raine had suggested, who thought so little of his chances with her that he never came forward? Who followed her career and made her suffer because he knew he could never have her? Murders are not often committed by people who are strangers to the victim, he reminded himself. His fingers drummed on the table. Think. Think. Think.

Max had fallen asleep and once more toppled off the top step. Weak from hunger and loss of blood, he slid hopelessly back down to the cellar floor and allowed himself to lose consciousness. There seemed nothing to be gained now by staying awake, and sleep, in the absence of food, might give him strength. Light would cheer him but he did not dare turn it on. There was no way he could plan, for his world began here in the cellar and ended in a passageway beyond the door. He knew only that there was space for a fight and that his adversary was bigger than he was, whole as he was not now that his left arm had stiffened into uselessness, and undoubtedly well fed. Surprise was all Max had on his side, and he didn't under-estimate that. The man would be waiting for night, therefore it was now daytime. Or, was there a third arrow to his diabolical bow? Did he intend to bring

Sara here, too? He shook his head to clear it.

He must not allow himself to be confused by conjecture. After all, the whole thing was torture for Sara. Once she was dead the fun was over. Anonymous letters intended to destroy her brilliant career. The mysterious death of her parents by fire in a lonely cottage must have been meant to deprive her of background, comfort, and love. Whoever was doing this probably knew Sara's only brother was no great help or ally, but her parents, Sara had said, were loving and devoted. Then Guy, who had loved her. Now me, because I was moving into her life, giving her protection and happiness. And lastly, the epitome of success would be to take Primmy, her darling, her jewel, and her star. No, Max thought with relief, he doesn't intend to kill Sara. That would be the end of his fun. "By eight o'clock tonight," his captor had said, "you will both be drowned." Max's hope lay in the possibility that he would go upstairs first to fetch Primmy, and Max, hearing his footsteps, would then be ready when he came to the cellar door.

He rose, stretched his limbs, and settled down on the top step once more, his legs across the cold stone, at his feet the piece of firewood that was the wrong shape, without a handhold, and not heavy enough. He tried to wedge himself in so that he wouldn't fall again. Time passed once more in troubled dreams interspersed with stiff, tense wakefulness. Primmy, up there at the top of the house, alone. Primmy, terrified. Sara going out of her mind with worry. Time seemed to merge. Events drifted through clouds of apprehension. There were moments of pure shock when he dreamt a sound or thought he heard a cry, and wakened, not knowing where he was. His arm throbbed. He couldn't risk taking off his jacket and shirt to look at the wound because he must be ready. There must be a bullet lodged in his arm and it might already be festering. Sometimes he dreamt he heard footsteps and wrestled with sleep only to wake finally in a cold sweat, to silence.

He was wide awake when at last they came softly on the stairs above his head, and he knew as one sometimes knows with shock and a sense of inevitability that the moment had come. He did not call out as he had done before. He stayed where he was, listening as the footsteps ascended and faded above his head, then he pulled himself to his feet, flexed his stiff knees, his ankles, his right arm. With his right hand he tried to pull his left one straight, but it was too stiff. Every movement was a scream of agony in his mind, bringing faintness and overwhelming nausea. He bent down to pick up his clumsy piece of firewood, then tucked himself into the corner, pressing his weight against the door so that he was ready to fling it wide as soon as the catch was lifted.

Deirdre hadn't gone to work. She stood tensely beside the telephone with the receiver held to her ear. "I'm sorry, Bernie."

"Come, come. If all the ghouls 'just happen' to drop in, think how good it will be for business, darling. Besides, where am I going to get someone else at such short notice?"

"If I came down with flu," retorted Deirdre bleakly, "you'd have to find someone. Just pretend I'm dead or ill. I'm sorry, but I cannot face the public today. The radio is regurgitating the Guy story every half hour. I haven't seen a paper but—well, I'm sure you have. Are there screaming black headlines?"

"Oh, come on. It's not as bad as that, Deirdre."

"Isn't it?" she asked tersely. "I've already had a reporter here and had to slam the door in his face to get rid of him. I'd rather lose my job than go out today, Bernie, so if you want to take on someone else, do so."

He was contrite. "Sorry, old thing. I'll go down to the shop myself. I'll keep in touch. How's James?"

"He's all right."

She hadn't seen James since he walked out last night, since she lost control and told him he had a sick mind. He had gone, slamming the door behind him. Believing her own ghastly accusation, she had packed a bag, written a note, then gone down to the underground car park that was part of the Three Square garage adjacent to the flat, intending to take the car and run away to Yorkshire, where her mother lived. But James had been there first. The car was gone. Looking at the empty parking space, she had momentarily had a sense of the ridiculous. It was one thing to run off dramatically in the car that was half hers anyway; it was quite another to be beaten to the punch.

She had come back to the flat to lie awake all night. She had told James he was evil, wanting Primmy like that. Tried to make him see he had a sick mind. Humbled herself to ask him for a child, seeing that as his only route to normality.

He had looked at her as though he hated her. "I want Guy's child. And I'm going to get her."

"You're mad. You're obsessed! James, let me love you. Let me help you to forget."

He had stood before her, his face pulling thin down the cheekbones, whitening around the wickedness in his eyes. "We're going to have Primmy."

"I won't have her. I'll tell everyone you're mad, crazy. I won't take her. I won't take her, do you hear me? I—"

He slapped her hard across the face, so hard she lost her balance and fell clumsily against the big orange patchwork cushion, one hand to her numb cheek, thinking the bone broken, the skin somehow cut. She had not been able to gather herself together and rise before he was gone, slamming the door shut behind him.

She had made coffee, watching it brew through a plunging veil of tears, listening to the percolator's obscene gurgling noises within a kind of deafness. But, drinking the coffee, she had managed to see clearly, managed to find compassion within herself and work back to the twin tie that had seemed so understandable until two days ago. I am not a twin. How can I know? How can anyone who is not a twin know what happens to the surviving one when the other dies? But she, who was whole and healthy and sane and knew right from wrong, could not, would not take Sara's child.

No amount of compassion for Jamie would make her steal someone else's baby. Not unless Sara asked her, or the police asked her. She would have to take Primmy then, even knowing the child would ruin her marriage, preclude the possibility of their having their own children. But James must sort himself out alone. It was then she had decided to run away, and found the Mercedes gone.

And now, following the news that a black Mercedes was seen outside the house in Kettle Lane from which Primmy had been taken away, she had had that prying phone call asking if James owned a Mercedes. She wanted to dive under the bed, crawl into a cupboard, run away, somehow hide. She wanted to ring Sara and tell her the registration number that might have been the Mercedes parked in Kettle Lane last night, wanted her to know that Jamie was sick and he might have her child. But she had to see him first. Surely he would come back here? Perhaps even bringing the child? She had to wait. She might not be able to help him by being here, but she might be able to help the child.

26

RAINE answered Charles's soft knock at the front door. She was dressed in a flimsy blouse and her jeans were torn off at mid-calf. Her feet were bare, the toenails painted bright red. Her eyes rested momentarily on the bouquets he carried without seeming to notice them.

"There's some news. They've got the number of the car."

Raine's hand went to her mouth. "Oh, Charles!"

"Sshh. Let's go into the sitting room and shut the door. I'll tell you where I've been." He put the flowers down on the gate-legged table. He told her first about the incident outside the Off-License. "It was a pure fluke. I was trying to fit a Mercedes into Elliott's life."

Raine shook her thick hair back from her shoulders. Her head came up, the eyes startled. "What? Elliott? Are you mad?"

"Mad? No, I don't think so. The chap I saw in the tweed suit outside McGarry's putting a box in the boot was about the same size as

Elliott." Raine blinked. "Okay, it was a bulky suit. That's suspicious. Why does a man wear a heavy tweed suit on a hot day? Because," Charles answered his own question, "he's less liable to be recognized if you can't see his figure. I told you last night I was going to try to get Elliott here this morning. I went to the house, but he had already left. Certainly his Volvo wasn't there. It was after that that I went to the Off-License."

"There you are. You said yourself, Volvo. And we're looking for somebody with a Mercedes."

Charles brushed her point aside. "Oliver said he thought Sara was holding something back. It seems to me the only person she would want to shield would be Elliott."

"Oh no, Charles. He's—"

"Well." He gave her a straight look. "What is he? I've not been able to make you say."

Raine looked down at her hands. "He's just a creep. An uncaring creep. Besides, he's her brother. Who is going to attack both of her fiancés but someone who's in love with her? Or someone who's obsessed by her and knows he could never get her. Maybe someone who sits in the audience drooling while she's onstage." They were silent for a moment, then Raine said bleakly, "I daresay Elliott was in bed sulking and Lil was covering up. He's always in bed when Sara wants him. It's a sort of trademark to her troubles. I'll get you some coffee." He followed her into the kitchen. "What did you think of Lovely Lil? What about those teeth?"

"She could have had a set that didn't look like a row of peas. What happened to her teeth, do you know?"

"She had shark's teeth. Killer teeth. They stuck out and frightened people."

It was, after all, possible to laugh again. "Oh, come."

"It's true. They were awful. And really, Charles, if one had teeth like hers one would probably lie awake dreaming of having the most even teeth in the world. So I suppose when she could afford to buy some, that's what she did."

"Why do you hate them so much?"

She picked at a thread on her jeans. "I'll get the coffee first. Go and sit down." He went back into the bare-floored sitting room and seated himself on the coverless sofa. Raine followed with two cups and handed one to him. "I wouldn't have to hate them if I didn't live so close to Sara. You know how it is when you hate someone. You keep away. But I'm never able to keep away from Elliott, not only because he's Sara's brother, but because she has to see him—and I know how insufferably bad he is for her." She settled into a small chair with wooden arms, placing the cup beside her.

"In that he upsets her?"

"Yes, he upsets her, you know that."

"And . . .?"

"If you make me say it I will, but I don't want to."

"I'm making you."

"Elliott is nasty. He is revoltingly nasty with girls. I know because I've been out with him. Sara senses it, I think. Lil knows about it and that's why she is as she is."

"Is what?"

"Unhappy. Doesn't know what to do with herself. That's why, I suppose, she turned to the church. Works in the church shop. Puts on fund-raising things in her garden. Turns up at church twice on Sundays."

"But so does Elliott, I understand."

"Yes, but perhaps for different reasons. A method of getting at little girls in the Sunday school?" Suddenly she shook her mane of hair across her face and cried in a distraught voice,

"Charles, don't make me say these things."

"Is that why Sara wouldn't let him take Primmy?"

"Perhaps. I don't know. Last night you heard her say she wished she had. Would a mother rather have her child tampered with than dead?"

He knew he was tearing Raine to pieces. He didn't know how much it had to do with his own guilt for what he had done the previous night. Guilt fired him into realizing how blank a mind he had actually turned to the strange elements in Sara's life. A doctor must not get too personally involved. Well, he thought, if he had allowed himself to become more personally involved none of this might have happened.

Raine rose lifelessly from her chair. "I'd better do those flowers."

"Lil pretended she hadn't had that call from you last night." Charles watched her face. She merely shrugged. He continued to watch her as she walked to the kitchen, wondering how far Raine would go in shielding Sara and wondering, too, how much the shielding had to do with her own feelings about Elliott. He rose and paced restlessly across the room, pausing in front of the bouquets. The odd-man-out rose was still there, pink, frail, and rather bruised now. It had almost given up the struggle to survive. He hesitated. It seemed to have taken on a new familiarity that puzzled him. He took it out from where it had been tucked behind the ribbon. Raine emerged from the kitchen carrying a vase. "Shall I throw this away? It seems to have had it."

"You may as well. Poor little rose. It never had a chance."

He stared at it for a long moment, then went into the kitchen and put the rose in the dust-bin. Hearing a movement behind him he looked around to see Sara standing in the doorway. Her face was pallid, the beautiful eyes puffy from the drug he had given her the night before. She wore a bright, gold-colored kimono that starkly heightened her pallor. She said listlessly, though her eyes burned, "Is there any news?"

Charles put an arm around her. "I'm afraid not, Sara dear. Raine has got some coffee ready. Would you like me to pour you some?"

Ignoring, or bypassing his question, she asked, "Has Elliott rung? Has he been here?"

Charles's heart contracted with pity for her. "No. No, he hasn't. I'll get you a coffee."

Raine heard. Dropping the flowers, she hurried in. "Charles tried to get Elliott to come," she said. "He was out."

"He won't come." Sara's voice was small, pathetic, lost. She looked small, too, and incredibly thin. She turned.

Charles put out a hand to steady her and led her to the kitchen table. "Boiled eggs," he said to Raine, then gently to Sara, "Two boiled eggs is what the doctor orders." He picked up the coffee Raine had poured and carried it to the table. Raine poured another and brought it over to him. He and Sara sat facing each other. "We'll get Elliott as soon as we can." They sat in silence until Raine brought the eggs and two slices of toast.

Sara's eyes swam, a sea of blue in her white face, and the tears spilled over. "I can't eat."

Charles reached for her hands. They were ice cold. He held them tightly. "Come on now, you have got to eat."

"I didn't know you were such a nosy parker," said Willie Theobald. "Poking around people's gardens!"

Enid flushed. The color was only part embarrassment at his criticism. It was also a flush of warmth and excitement over what was happening next door. They had wanted children desperately when they were first married. Then somehow life settled. The arrival of children could, in a manner of speaking, have been awkward. Willie, an engineer, had been sent abroad, often staying away for months. Her mother died, and Enid did not relish raising a family without either of her nearest and dearest to hand. She would have managed, of course, if a pregnancy had occurred naturally, but to deliberately encourage one seemed, if not tempting fate, then certainly putting the ball in her court when she wasn't certain she could bat it along alone. She began to go abroad with her husband, and gradually they grew accustomed to being childless. Only now was she beginning to contemplate what she had missed. The thought of young people next door delighted her.

Willie said, "If we'd had children I daresay we would be grandparents now."

"There's a baby at Wild Hatch, too," she said, glowing. "I heard it cry."

Willie grunted. He was pleased that his wife didn't rail against fate. Their marriage was a contentment for her as well as for him. Other people's children brought no responsibilities. He said, "Turn off that damn radio, will you.

There's nothing but disasters these days. I can't be bothered. Turn it off, Enid."

She said, "You should be interested in world affairs," but her criticism was laced with indulgence because she was happy today. There were to be children next door again.

He put his heels on the low windowsill and lay back with the morning paper unfolded before him. "I can't do anything about world affairs. They give me ulcers. Turn—" He broke off, raised one hand. "It's that actress." They were silent, momentarily chilled. Then the total unreality of the world in which Sara Tindall lived fragmented their concern and they listened detachedly. ". . . disappeared last night. Anyone who saw a man in the vicinity of Osbon Square, Kensington, roughly between the hours of six-thirty and seven-thirty, carrying a baby's carrycot is asked to contact the police. The police would also like to interview the owner of a black Mercedes that was seen to be parked in Kettle Lane off Osbon Square during this time so that they can eliminate him from their enquiries."

"Funny," said Enid, "how once you're aware of something it's always there. I notice the people next door have a Mercedes, and the next moment they're talking about a Mercedes on the radio.''

Willie grinned over the top of his paper. ''We're never going to hear the end of that. You could get to know all the cars on the road if you put your mind to it, you know. Makes for variety, too,'' he added shrewdly, not wanting to be stuck with continuous repetitions of Enid's small success.

She smiled. ''I'll make an apple pie, I think. Then after we've had our elevenses I'll go down to the shops and see if my magazines have come in. If there's anything you want . . .'' Her voice trailed away as she disappeared into the kitchen.

''Peppermints.''

''What?'' She came back and stood in the doorway.

''Peppermints.''

She nodded, musing, leaning on the doorpost, letting the moment slip pleasurably by as she contemplated the new interest of the family next door. ''I'm sorry for that girl, losing her baby.''

''You stick to your cars, Enid. Actors and actresses and pop stars with rings in their noses, they're mostly riffraff. An unsavory lot.''

She laughed lightly. "Safety pins, Willie. There was a picture in the Saturday Pictorial of that fellow Jerry Fontainville with an enormous diamond safety pin in one ear." She giggled.

"What bothers me is that muck spreads," commented Willie ominously. "There's a doctor mixed up in this. If you can't trust a doctor, whom can you trust?"

"Perhaps he is the father of the child. Ah well. Where's my apron?" She went to the kitchen, humming. Her life was another world away from quick fortunes, diamond safety pins, and people who got themselves kidnapped or murdered. Eight ounces of flour, six ounces of fat. She glanced at the clock on the wall. It was already after eleven.

Bob Diarmid, who worked at the Tunstall garage, was standing in his overalls at the counter of the Chinese takeout store.

Mrs. Wong came out of the back of the shop with his bamboo shoots and spare ribs in a lidded foil container. He jerked a thumb toward the radio. "Been listening to the news, Mrs. Wong?" She nodded. "I been wondering. A shifty-looking character with a Mercedes was hanging around our garage yesterday. I never seen him before. He took off when he saw me looking at him, but he stopped about here. Tall guy. Blue shirt. D'you see him?"

The Chinese woman's eyes narrowed thoughtfully as she tried to remember. Yesterday had been a very quiet day. Only two men had ordered food and one of them had been wearing a blue shirt. "He have a Mercedes? I don't know. But he have pink rose in buttonhole. He not a bad man, Bob. He come from Colonel Roberts's house."

"The Retenmeyers? How do you know?"

"Because he wear pink rose in buttonhole. Mr. Retenmeyer always wear pink rose. Little ones. Grow in Colonel Roberts's garden."

"Does that mean he's not a criminal?" Diarmid asked logically. "Whoever took that Tindall baby has to be somewhere. Why not here?"

Mrs. Wong chuckled. "You been looking at too many TV serials, Bob."

He shrugged as he picked up his parcel. "The chap has to be somewhere. I'm only keeping my eyes open, like the police ask."

He went out of the shop feeling humiliated. You try to be public-spirited and people laugh. Wasn't that Mrs. Theobald strolling along the pavement in the pink dress? He couldn't be sure because of the sunhat she was wearing. He hurried and caught up to her. She would know who was next door to her place. She turned as he slowed beside her. "Morning, Mrs. Theobald. Lovely day."

"The storm last night did the trick, cleared the air, didn't it? How did you get on? Did you get soaked?"

"No, we were all right. People don't arrive for petrol when it's coming down cats and dogs. Tell me, do you know these neighbors of yours, the Retenmeyers?"

"I think they've left."

"Left?" he echoed in disbelief. And then, indignantly, "They can't leave. They haven't cleared up their account."

She looked at him uncertainly. "There's a new family there. Actually, we didn't know the Retenmeyers. The house has changed hands so often we got tired of always having strangers in. I know it's not neighborly, but there have been so many short lets and one has one's own life to lead."

He frowned. "I'd better nip up and see the new people. You're sure they're new?"

"Yes. Quite sure. There have been children

playing in the garden. The Retenmeyers didn't have children."

Bob Diarmid went back to the garage with more on his mind that a doubtful-looking man with a Mercedes. If Hans Retenmeyer had shot off back to the States owing him money, at least he knew where to go. Retenmeyer worked for the Flier Oil Company. Or said he did. Diarmid frowned again. He had better investigate. He'd have said Retenmeyer was as honest as the day was long. And that blond wife of his, too.

Patrick Delvaney climbed out of the taxi and stood on the footpath looking across at the windows of the flat. He had never been in a mess like this. All his innate cleverness, his shrewdness had come to bear on his problem and left him defeated. If Sara would not go onstage tonight, and in all conscience he could not ask her to appear, then he would have to withdraw the play. He walked past the house, hands in pockets, then back again. What should he do? His heart told him that Sara as a person was more important than his career. But Patrick Delvaney would never have climbed so high if he had been a man to retire in adversity. It was the devil of hope that had driven him here this afternoon. If the play had to be withdrawn, then something of his reputation would be lost with it. People who criticized only remembered that a show had run for one, two, four days. They forgot the whys and wherefores.

"Can I help you?" Delvaney looked up into the face of the young policeman he had seen standing on the sidewalk a dozen yards away.

Patrick identified himself. "Have there been any developments?" The policeman shook his head. "Can I go in?"

"We're just keeping an eye on the place." The officer turned and strolled away.

Patrick saw little groups of women standing under the trees by the railings, gossiping and staring. Another couple watched from the corner opposite the pub. Ghouls!

It was Raine who opened the door. Even her frayed jeans and see-through blouse, her bare feet and red toenails, did nothing to brighten the dismal picture. "How is she?"

"What do you expect? Rock bottom, of course."

"The police will find the child."

"Will they? They haven't found Max."

"Give them time."

"Time? How much time does a ten-month-old child need to die? Why have you come, Patrick? As if I didn't know."

He glanced aside so that he didn't have to meet her eyes. "I had to go somewhere. Do something."

"If you could persuade her to go onstage it would be the best possible thing for her. She'll go mad, in the end, sitting around here. Either that or give up and die. I'm not just saying this for my own sake, although of course I don't want the play taken off. Sara's alive when she's acting, and I believe she could do it. Come on in."

They went into the carpetless sitting room. Charles was seated with his legs straddling the arms of the shabby sofa, Sara standing with her back to the window. She, too, had changed into jeans, a very respectable pair in comparison with those worn by Raine, and she wore a blue cotton T-shirt and rope sandals. She looked small, broken. Her face was pale, the eyes swollen, the dark lashes matted thickly by tears. "Don't make me go onstage, Patrick," she pleaded.

He held her hands, increasing the pressure on her fingers with his own. "Could you do it?"

"She could do it," said Charles. He rose and went into the kitchen carrying his ashtray. He put it down on the counter, then on second thought took it over to the dustbin in the corner. He put his foot on the lever and the lid came up, exposing some crumpled plastic with the dying rosebud lying on top. He hesitated, then bent down and picked up the flower. He tipped the ash and butts in, then, holding the rosebud between finger and thumb, absently put the ashtray on the counter. He was still staring at the flower when Raine came in. He held the bud up for her to see. "This damn thing is worrying me. Where did it come from?"

"I found it on the floor. I told you that," Raine replied. "Throw it away. It won't come around now."

"Listen a moment, Raine. What floor did you find it on, and when?"

She looked at him as if he had gone mad. "Here. When I came for our stuff the night Max disappeared, or maybe the next morning. Yes, it was the next morning. I found it just outside the sitting room door, I thought it belonged to the bouquets, but apparently it didn't."

Charles slipped the bud into his pocket.

"I'm going to skip out for a while. Don't say anything to Sara. If the police come back to question her and she gets upset, give her this capsule."

He slipped out the back door, bent double as he passed the sitting room windows, and hurried across the square. He unlocked the door of his car, jumped in, and drove as fast as he dared toward the Boltons.

27

"YOU again!" Lil Tindall said ungraciously. "Elliott hasn't come back." She was dressed in an unbecoming cotton dress with a shirt collar, short sleeves, and buttons down the front.

"May I come in?"

"I can't help you."

"Aren't you concerned about the disappearance of your little niece?" asked Charles.

"Of course we're concerned. But—"

"We?" asked Charles. "So you have spoken to your husband? Is he coming to see his sister?"

Lil's face settled into sullen lines. "If that's what you've come for, you're wasting your time. We've been through this before."

"May I come in?"

"I've told you, there's no point."

"I'd like to come in, Mrs. Tindall. Please."

Reluctantly, she backed into the hall, then indicated an open door on the right. Ignoring her gesture, he hurried toward the room in which they had talked that morning. "I may have left something . . ." He was through the doorway and into the room, too engrossed in what he wanted to do to finish his sentence. A woman was dragging a vacuum cleaner across the floor. She glanced up at him in surprise. As he looked around, his face tightened. "There was a vase of flowers here this morning."

"Yes. They was fading. I threw them out."

Behind him Lil asked sharply, "What on earth are you doing, Doctor?"

He swung around to face her. "Where are the roses that were in that vase this morning, the blue one over there on that table?"

The two women looked at each other in puzzled silence. "I told him I threw them out," said the cleaning woman.

"Then they're somewhere around? In the rubbish bin, perhaps?" asked Charles. The woman nodded. "Could you possibly get them and bring them back?"

The woman looked timidly past him to Lil, who asked, "What on earth do you want them for?"

"I'll explain later. I'd be grateful if you would ask this lady to bring the flowers from the dustbin. Or perhaps you would show me where the dustbin is and I could get them myself."

She said angrily, "Look here, Doctor. You can't walk into my house and order me and my staff around like that. I'll call the police."

"Please do. It might be simpler in the long run."

Lil looked bewildered. The woman said placatingly, "I could get the flowers, Mrs. Tindall. They've only just gone out."

"Oh, all right. Bring them back."

Charles seated himself awkwardly on a chair arm, hands on his knees. Lil stood silently, looking out a window. The cleaning woman returned, carrying the flowers in a roll of newspaper. He hurried over to meet her. She spread out the untidy bundle and he picked up a handful of the pink buttonhole roses. "I'll take these," he said.

"But why?" Lil was standing beside him, puzzled.

"Let's go into that other room. Sorry to disturb you," he apologized, speaking to the cleaning woman. Then to Lil, "You might be able to clear up a little matter for me. Where did these roses come from? Out of your garden?"

"No. We've got a cutting in now. My husband brought it home the other day."

"So where did this bunch come from?"

"From the friend who gave us the cutting. Why are you asking these questions, Dr. Halbert?" They were entering the room on the right-hand side of the door. It was a sitting room, smaller than the so-called library and decorated expensively in the same haphazard manner.

Charles turned to face her. He said coolly, "I would like the name of the people who grow these roses."

"I'll ask my husband if he could get you a cutting."

He said, looking at her levelly, "I would like the name of the people."

"Retenmeyer. Actually, he only rents the house. I don't know the owner's name. I doubt very much, now I come to think of it, if Elliott would feel inclined to get a cutting off someone else's tree for a—a stranger."

"He won't have to. I propose to ask the owner myself. What is their address?"

"I don't know. I don't really know them myself. They're Elliott's friends. Americans."

"What is their telephone number?" Lil sighed, then with resignation went to a desk and opened an address book. Charles took out a pen. She read the phone number off and he wrote it down in his notebook. "Would you mind if I rang them now?" She pointed to the telephone, then went to stand by the window while he dialed. "There's no reply."

She said stiffly, "I hope you don't mind if I ask you to ring from your own place, Doctor. I am really very busy."

Charles eyed her thoughtfully but didn't move. "I should have thought that if you cared enough about Primmy to offer to adopt her, you would consider her disappearance your affair."

"You're not talking about the child," Lil burst out. "You're talking about roses. I think you've got a cheek to come bursting in here at this time to talk about roses. And anyway, I don't give a damn about Primmy. I don't even know her. Of course I'd like to have a baby of my own. I don't want Sara's. We offered to take her to avoid the scandal and embarrassment. I never wanted her."

"Tell me the truth, Mrs. Tindall," Charles said quietly. "Why haven't you got any children of your own?"

She looked away, over into the corner where there was nothing to see. He waited. She spoke quickly, as though the words were bursting through a barrier that had been held there too long. "We don't sleep together. That's why."

Charles said gently, "If you'd like to tell me about it, perhaps I could help."

"A psychiatrist might help," she burst out bitterly, "but he wouldn't go to one. I'll tell you why Elliott wants Primmy. Because she's going to be beautiful like her mother. That's what my husband likes, Dr. Halbert. Beautiful women. He isn't going to get a beautiful child from me."

"Then if you'll forgive me for what may sound like a personal criticism, but which I assure you is meant kindly, why didn't he marry a beautiful woman?"

"Because he couldn't get one, that's why. They don't want him. Don't think I don't know all about it. Don't I see him sitting in front of the box drooling over the beauty contests? Miss World! You should see his face. It's quite disgusting to see Elliott looking at beautiful women. I tell you this because you're a doctor and it's in confidence." She put a trembling hand over her mouth as though that was the only way to stop the spate of bitterness and disgust that had burst through.

Charles stood before her in silence, one part of him excited, another part appalled. "Has he never . . . . touched you?" he asked gently.

"He's revolted by me. Just as I am revolted by his—by this—" She was beside herself, half crying, her chest heaving, "—by his obsession with beautiful girls. One day, unless he's cured of it, I am afraid—" She seemed unable to go on. Her face screwed up and she closed her eyes.

"Is that why you didn't want Primmy?"

Lil said in a frightened, uncertain voice, "She's only a baby. I don't think . . . I mean, if she was ours . . ."

Charles didn't help her out.

Lil shook her head. "I don't understand you, Doctor. Going on like this—today—about roses."

"It's not entirely about roses," he said. "Look here, Mrs. Tindall, I know your husband has a Volvo, but has he by any chance a second car?"

"We have a Rover 2000. You know that. I saw you creeping around to the garage this morning. Spying, weren't you? You didn't believe me when I said my husband was out, did you?"

"Frankly, no."

"Well, he wasn't out. He was in bed. When Sara's in trouble, he always gets into bed and stays there."

Charles started. "He's there now?"

She shook her head. "He is out now."

"Since we're being so honest with each other, I went around to the garage because I did wonder if he also owned a Mercedes." He expected a gasp of horror, astonishment, disbelief, anger. Nothing happened. Then her face grew slowly ugly, twisted, a readable book of the darkness of her life.

"Get out."

He picked up the roses and left. As he went down the steps he wondered if the telephone exchange, or the police, could get an address from a phone number.

Enid walked past Wild Hatch and peered through the hedge, seeing nothing but the heavy summer foliage. She turned back, hesitating at the driveway. There were no signs of life. She returned to her own place. Her husband met her at the kitchen door. "Where on earth have you been?"

"Down to the shops. I told you I had to do some shopping."

"You've been a helluva long time. I thought

you must have gone next door. I went through the hedge to see if you were talking to the new neighbors. I think you're mistaken. I don't think there is anyone there."

Enid put her packages on the table. "Down at the shops they're all talking about this actress's child being missing."

"You could worry yourself silly about other people's problems."

She turned to him gravely. "Willie, I was wondering about next door. Bob from the garage says he doesn't think the tenants could have gone, but I'm sure they have. And I did hear a baby crying there. I told you, didn't I? And yesterday, I thought I heard someone calling for help."

"A baby?"

"Don't be silly. I thought it was a man calling for help. It was rather faint. And the baby's cry was faint, too, but of course there are a lot of trees. And the windows are all closed. I can't understand that. If there are people in residence, the windows should be open."

"Not necessarily. Don't you remember when we were in Kuwait we never opened our windows. Or in Sydney during the summer. Keep the heat out, that's the rule. We ought to do it ourselves." Suddenly he grinned mischievously. "So you reckon we've got the Ritchie man tied up next door, and the actress's baby? All I can say is," he commented, stretching and yawning, "that everyone is susceptible to suggestion and p'raps you more than most."

"Don't make fun of me, Willie. These two people have disappeared. They have to be next door to someone."

"Sure. But I've just been in there looking for you. I don't think there's anyone there."

"Let's ring the police."

"Now come on, Enid. The police have got enough on their hands without us spreading false alarms." He saw her mouth tighten, and added, humoring her. "All right, let's go in together and have a look."

They went through the hole in the hedge and looked up at the mullioned windows. The sun was directly overhead and the glass was shadowed by overhanging eaves. The dark red hanging tiles glowed in the light. The garage door was shut, the garden empty. "There are signs of children having been playing in the garden," she said stubbornly. She led him across the lawn toward the front of the building. "Look," she said. "See that pile of greenery? It's not just hedge clippings." She pulled some of the pieces away and they looked down in silence at a large copper preserving pan piled up with stones and full to the brim with rainwater. "Who would put that there but children?"

Her husband bent down, picked some of the smaller stones off the top, pushed the remainder of the fading lilac and yew away, and stared thoughtfully at the pot. "It would take a mighty strong child to carry those," he said.

"Who else would put them there but children?"

"It's over the coal hole, isn't it? Perhaps the tenants have taken the iron trap to be repaired and this lot is to keep the rain out."

"What?" Her face was wrinkled up in disbelief.

Willie grinned. "There's nothing so funny as people."

With a flash of mild indignation, Enid recognized the pot. "It belongs to Mary Roberts. I've seen it hanging in the kitchen. They've got a nerve. The stones will scratch it."

"Maybe they're using it to disguise the hole.

A small burglar could get down a coal hole, I should think," Willie suggested.

Minding their own business, they piled the greenery roughly over the stones and went back toward their own house. As they came abreast of the hole in the hedge Enid stiffened, grasped her husband's arm. "That was the sound I heard before. Isn't it a child's cry?"

"A bird, I think." They stood quietly listening, but the sound didn't come again. Only the noise of an engine, a crunching of tires and a black car came down the driveway. They drew back into the hedge, watching its approach. The driver's face was hidden under a cap he had pulled low down on his forehead. They watched him drive around by the buttonhole rose tree, then turn the car to face the way he had come. He jumped out, a tall man dressed in a denim jacket that matched the denim cap. He went straight to the back door and opened it. From where they stood they could not see whether he had used a key or not. The sound that was like a child's cry came again. Willie and Enid looked at each other, then Willie went back through the hole in the hedge. "Mercedes is a pretty common car," Willie said, making excuses uncomfortably. "Let's not make fools of ourselves." It was all too ordinary to be suspicious. A man in a car going into a family house. If they had bothered to get to know the Retenmeyers, that would be another matter. They would have some rights. But they hadn't. You couldn't go up to people and ask them their business.

They would have a perfect right to bump you on the nose.

But Enid made a mental note of the registration number, and when she went into the kitchen she wrote it down on her order pad. There would be another news flash soon. She would make a point of listening.

28

HE unlocked the door of the box room and turned on the light. The big, bath-like linen cot he had bought was just the thing for imprisoning a ten-month-old child. He had tested her when he set it up. Primmy couldn't walk, but she could pull herself to her feet if there was anything she could use as a lever. Even then, the top of her head was only level with the top of the strong cotton walls. He withdrew the layers of blankets he used as a ceiling and muffler across the top of the cot. She looked up at him dazedly, blinking in the light, and her little face, plastered with the banana and biscuit he had left for her to find, crumpled. "Sshh, Primmy. Sshh." He bent down to pick her up, then withdrew. She smelled foul. He couldn't take her along with him in that state. Could he risk moving her to the bathroom? Anyway, the Retenmeyers might have turned the hot water off. She opened her mouth and began to scream, long drawn-out cries of fear and despair. He leaped at the door, banged it shut. He looked into the carrycot and found some diapers. This was woman's work. He felt angry at having to cope.

Trembling with repressed disgust, sweating in the heat of the enclosed room, he laid the child on the floor and pulled off her plastic panties. He wiped her with one of the diapers. She stopped screaming and looked up at him hopefully, looking like Sara. Then her beautiful blue eyes swam with tears and she opened her mouth to scream again. Losing his head, he jammed a diaper against her face. She writhed and kicked. He took the cloth away and looked down at her, silent with shock. He said, "Be a good girl, Primmy, and I'll wash you." The banana and biscuit had dried. He must get her to water. He didn't want to hold her close to comfort her. He didn't feel anything for her. She was a hostage. A punishment. A tool. Carrying her, he went out into the passage and looked around. There was one small window, firmly shut and made of small, diamond-shaped leaded panes. He hurried to the bathroom and, still holding the now silent child, turned on the bath tap. To his astonishment hot water gushed out. Of course, there was a gas multipoint water heater in the kitchen. Be bent down and put the plug in.

As the bath began to fill he thought, Why not drown her here? It would do away with the complication of noise. But it would also take away some of the excitement and that exultant moment when he tipped the two of them into the river together and watched them disappear. He had it all planned so perfectly. He had the doorstops. The boat was ready beneath the willows. It wasn't dark, but he couldn't wait for night because the hunt was on and the excitement in him was rising high. He already felt the heady thrill of success. Time, he had already learned, was not often on one's side. Move fast while the police were still baffled. Finish it before they began to put two and two together. He'd heard the latest news flash. They now had the number of the Mercedes. He would have to get rid of it, fast.

Primmy liked the warm water. He held her skirt and vest up around her neck while she sat in it. She looked up at him trustfully and asked, "Mum, Mum, Mum?" With a cloth he had found lying on the basin he washed her face, then her legs and bottom. He took a towel from the rail, sat down on the stool, and dried her, then carried her back to the box room. Holding her on his hip, he looked helplessly at the diaper. But what did it matter?

She was only going to be lying in the carrycot until he got her onto the boat. He wound the diaper clumsily around her and pinned it down.

Primmy began to cry again. He was tempted to slap her, but common sense told him that would only make things worse. He should talk to her, but he didn't know how. He picked her up and held her for a moment against his shoulder, looking at her. He felt nothing. Nothing at all. She was a beautiful possession. Something to take from Sara. Getting down to basics, she was rather a smelly little mess. He put her in the carrycot. She protested, trying to sit up. He pulled up the waterproof cover, pressed down the studs. There was nothing she could do but yell now and the plastic hood would mute the noise. On second thought, he folded up one of the blankets and laid it on top. He would slip it across her face if necessary. She wouldn't suffocate. He hoped not, anyway. He looked around at the scatter of baby things. The Retenmeyers were not due to return for another week. He had plenty of time to come back here and clean the place up.

He carried the cot down the stairs, through the back of the house, and out to the car. Movement seemed to calm the child. She was making little gurgling noises as she tugged at the plastic cover, grunting with the effort to push it away. He opened the front door of the car and put the cot on the seat. Primmy was crying again because she couldn't get out, but without spirit, without noise. The big eyes looked up at him despairingly, the big tears rolled down her cheeks. She hiccupped. He pushed the blanket against the hood so that she was in darkness. No need, after all, to put it over her face, where she could push it away. The tweed suit he used for his town disguise was on the back seat.

He had better hurry. He ran back into the kitchen, hoisted one of the stone lions clumsily up from the floor, and, holding it in his arms, reached for the gun on the kitchen table. He went out to the car, put the gun on the front seat and the doorstop on the floor. Then he went back inside, picked up the other doorstop, and dumped it on the gravel beside the car. Better put Max in first. He went back into the house, and as he crossed the kitchen he pulled the nylon stocking over his face.

Down at Tunstall's garage Bob Diarmid was saying, "Now that I've finished the job on the mini I think I'll run up to Wild Hatch."

"I've rung them three times now," the girl said. "Of course the phone might be out of order. What's the matter?"

"I met Mrs. Theobald. She was quite certain the Retenmeyers had left and new people had come in." He pulled off his overalls as he spoke. "If the Retenmeyers have gone, then the sooner we get on to his company the better. I can't afford to lose money that way."

"He seemed such a nice man," remarked the girl.

"Yeah. Crooks always are. That's part of their stock-in-trade. Maybe he doesn't even work for the Flier Oil Company. I won't be long."

The latch went up with a knocking of wood against wood and the door moved outward. Max lunged forward. The door swung back, catching the man off balance and momentarily at a disadvantage. He uttered a cry of alarm as Max leaped at him, his piece of firewood held high. He aimed for the strange, distorted face in its nylon mask. The face ducked. The wood caught his shoulder, the impact wrenching it from Max's awkward grasp. He made a swift dive, caught the man with a strong right to the stomach, then staggered off balance, his left arm putting him at a hopeless disadvantage.

The masked man lunged forward, grunting with surprise. Max evaded the lunge and, with his assailant now off balance, swung a hard right to his face. His opponent, Max realized, knew little or nothing about fighting, and with a burst of wild confidence he swiftly landed a blow to his stomach followed by a right to the head. The other man fell back, gasping. Max leaped forward raining blow after blow, his feet nimble, his one good fist punching like a machine. The man swung around, leaped through a doorway into the kitchen, grabbed a small table as he went, and swung it into Max's path. It hit Max in the groin as he tried to fend it off with his bad arm. He lost his footing, fell, scrambled up clumsily from the floor in what seemed like a forest of table legs, and dashed in pursuit. Over the doorstep and onto the gravel. The car was not more than twenty feet from the back door.

The man in the mask was already behind the wheel. Max leaped across the intervening distance and, unable to grasp the door handle, flung himself across the bonnet, spread-eagle and face downward with nothing to grip and only one arm with which to hang on. The engine roared, the car swerved. Max was sliding. He managed to fling himself up as the car leaped forward again, but it swerved once more and this time Max felt himself sliding hopelessly over the side. He was going to fall. He pulled up one knee, kicked himself sideways with the help of the rubber sole of one shoe. Faintly, he seemed to hear a screeching horn over the sound of the engine, a man's excited shout, and then the car seemed to dive from beneath him and he was sliding clumsily, landing with a crash on his shoulder and one side of his head in a scatter of gravel and small stones.

Someone was bending over him. "Are you all right?" He looked up into the startled face of a young man with dark hair falling over his forehead. "Are you all right? Don't move," as Max tried to unravel himself. Half stunned, he could feel no pain. He moved his feet, fell weakly over onto his back, and an agonizing pain shot through his arm. "What happened?' What's going on?" asked the concerned stranger.

Max tried to prop himself up on his good elbow. "Did you get the number?" he asked. He tried feebly to wave the man away. "Get the car number.'' The young man disappeared. Max blinked, shook his head, and tried to sit up again. He saw that he was lying directly in front of the wheels of an old Austin. He pulled himself up to his knees, then staggered to his feet. He stood dazedly, supporting himself with one hand on the bonnet of the car, trying to work out why the car was the wrong way around. He closed his eyes against the pain in his left arm.

A woman's voice close behind him asked urgently, "What happened? What happened?'' Max turned slowly and looked groggily into a face framed with white hair. "I'm Enid Theobald from next door.'' There were running footsteps. The woman said, "Oh, it's you, Bob. This poor man. What's happened?''

"I didn't get the number,'' he said breathlessly. Max's head fell forward. He shook it dazedly. He heard the woman say, "We'd better get a doctor.''

The man said, "As I came up the drive a Mercedes came roaring out with this chap floundering across the bonnet. I couldn't get out of the way. Then the Mercedes went up over those bushes and off. I managed to stop just in time. Who is he?''

Max tried to walk. He had to get to a telephone. Faintly, as from a great distance, Max heard the woman say doubtfully, "Maybe he's the new tenant," and then the car's bonnet seemed to come up and hit him in the face.

It was afternoon but Deirdre hadn't moved from the tub chair by the radio when the key slid into the outer lock and Jamie appeared. He came and stood in the doorway, looking at her. He wore a thin, short-sleeved shirt, jeans, and sandals. "You're not dressed," he said.

"No." He was haggard, but not strained, wild, and mad as he had been last night. He looked tired, desperately tired. "Where is she?" Deirdre asked without moving. There was an incredible stillness in the room. A presentiment of earthquakes, or thunder, or death.

"Who?" he asked. There seemed to be ham acting in the thinness of his voice.

"What have you done with Primmy?"

He didn't answer. Instead, he went across the room with a dragging step and fell into a chair. "I'm sorry about last night." He ran both hands through his dark chestnut hair, then across his unshaven face. With a feeling of shock she saw that the wickedness had left him and he looked quite suddenly the image of Guy—with his hair ruffled, his wide mouth relaxed in a tired gentleness, the brown eyes ready to smile. As though all were now well in his world.

Deirdre felt outrage, fear, and anger. "Where is she?"

He said, "Make me a coffee, there's a good girl. I'm done in. We'll talk."

She stayed where she was in the blue tub chair, her bare feet and ankles showing beneath the white, tailored robe. "Where is she? What have you done with her?"

He muttered something under his breath, pulled himself up, and went into the kitchen. She watched him across the dividing bar, looking around for coffee that was right in front of him. Deirdre could see it from where she sat. She said, "James, answer me. I want to know what you've done with the child."

He had found the coffee jar and picked it up with a sigh. "It's been on the news." She rose and went toward him, her face still. "They're looking for our car," she said. "The garage will tell them it was out all night." There was in her that same strange awareness of storm and disaster. He said, holding the coffee jar in one hand, "I've been walking. All night I've been walking. And thinking."

"No," she replied in a still, cold voice. "I know where you've been because I was going to run away. I packed a bag and went for the car. It wasn't there. And on the radio I heard that the police want to interview the driver of our Mercedes. What have you done with Primmy, James?" She was not in the habit of calling him James. He shook his head, as if he didn't understand. Some self-protective instinct told her to be careful, but the rage and horror were too strong. She said, "I am going to ring the police." She spun around suddenly and picked up the receiver. She already had written down the Scotland Yard number the moment she heard the radio news. She had known she would do this, ring the police just as soon as he came home. She had her forefinger in the dial at the first figure when he gripped her wrist hard and painfully. She gasped, jerked away, and the phone crashed to the floor. She could see the violence in his eyes as he came at her.

"You bitch!"

She opened her mouth to scream and felt his palm slap across her lips, saw him toppling toward her as he tripped on the small table that stood between them. He fell against her before she could back away, and as she felt the weight of his body she lunged, pushing him sideways. But he had grabbed her arms and pulled her with him. They both fell, he against the corner of the big table, she more gently against him. His fingers released their hold on her. She scrambled to her feet. He was lying there, awkwardly, his rump raised over the frail little table that had broken beneath his weight, his head tilted back against the onyx lamp stand with its metal roses that were filling up with his blood.

"Jamie!" She wasn't certain if she said it out loud, or even if she said it at all. Perhaps the name was only in her heart from the time before things went wrong. Before she found out he couldn't live without Sara, without Sara's child, without Guy, his more-than brother. She looked down at him while the terror froze inside her. Two human beings had slipped off the plane of reason, two people crazed with disappointment, with fear, and with greed.

I killed him because I couldn't let him have Primmy. She stared down at the still face, still herself beneath the weight of guilt. Then she thought he seemed to be smiling faintly and she remembered the silence when he came into the room. Part of her knew, fatalistically, that there had been a death waiting for Jamie in that strangeness as he entered the flat and that nothing she could have done would have changed it. She looked back at him. His face was still, expressionless as a face always is in death, and she knew she had only wanted to believe he smiled.

She went into the bedroom and began to dress. There was a photograph of Guy on the chest of drawers. Guy certainly smiling as Jamie had seemed to be in death. Smiling at her. She wondered with a little shiver if that weird, unearthly silence had come with Guy's return to get his twin. Well, he was gone, they were both gone, whatever the way, and it was all over. Methodically, she packed her bag. Before leaving the flat, she knelt down and kissed the dead face. Leaving the door ajar so that someone could come and find the body, she went quietly down the stairs. They would come after her, of course, but not immediately. Not before she had had time to herself, to think. If there had been anything she could have done for the child she would have done it, but there wasn't so she might as well go. She had a feeling of having taken part in these people's lives without having touched them. Sara had left one twin for the other, taking both of their hearts so that there had been nothing for her. Fate had merely used her to end James's intolerable life. She walked to Sloane Square and took the Underground to Paddington.

29

"WHO is it you're ringing?" Raine asked.

Charles replaced the receiver. "It's just a hunch. Anyway, there's no one there. Do you, by any chance, know if a name and address can be found from a telephone number?"

"I shouldn't think so. Not without going right through the telephone book. What are you onto?"

"It's the number of a man who grows the sort of rose you picked up on the floor of this flat the night Max disappeared."

Raine said incredulously, "I should think a million people grow it."

"It was a very old-fashioned rose. Very uncommon."

"And how did you get the number?"

"Lil Tindall had them in a vase at her house."

"You're saying Elliott took Max away?"

"I'm not saying anything of the kind. I am

following up every possible lead, however apparently futile."

Patrick and Raine looked at him with disbelief. "He's her brother," Patrick said.

They were still staring at him when the telephone rang. Charles answered. It was Oliver.

"I'll tell you what's happened and leave it to you to decide whether or not to tell Miss Tindall. James Fortune owns that Mercedes." Charles didn't reply, but Raine heard his sharp intake of breath and moved closer. Patrick stood up.

"Go on," said Charles.

"I'm ringing from his flat now. He is dead and there are signs that his wife left in a hurry."

"Murder?"

"We don't know."

"The child?"

"Nothing. We're going to have to interview Miss Tindall again. I told you, didn't I, that I thought she was holding something back. Now, this is the problem. If it is Fortune and she has always known, then she isn't going to want to be questioned about it. We don't want her leaving, too. So if you want to tell her because you think you might get something out of her, you've got a responsibility not to let her get away."

"I understand. But—"

"I'll be along as soon as I've finished here."

Charles looked down at the telephone number written in his notebook, hesitated, then closed it resignedly. "Okay." He replaced the receiver.

Raine and Patrick moved toward him. "What's happened?"

Charles glanced around at the closed door, listened for footsteps, then told them. They listened to the news in stunned silence. After a while Raine whispered, "Primmy must be dead, otherwise Deirdre would not have run away."

"Unless she has gone to collect the child," said Patrick.

Another long silence, then Raine remarked, "You're not surprised, Charles. Is this what you suspected?"

"No," he said reluctantly. "It's not what I suspected. I've been working on a hunch which I find difficult to drop."

"The rose? A complete stranger?" said Raine.

Charles pulled his car keys out of his pocket. His notebook was still in his hand. He looked down at the telephone number Lil had given him and memorized it. "James and Deirdre lived in Fordcombe Mansions. I know a chap who lives there. He garages his car at the Three Square, around the corner, so the chances are James kept his Mercedes there. I think I'll go around and investigate." He tore the page out of his notebook and handed it to Raine. "I meant to give this to Oliver. There's really no point, now. He wouldn't take it seriously. Raine, would you mind ringing this number whenever you've got a spare moment."

"What do I say?"

"Just find out who lives there and get the address. And don't tell Sara anything. It won't make her feel any better. Oliver will be around later. It's not going to take me long to find out what I need to know."

It was half an hour before Sara came out of her room. She looked as though she were dying inside. "Charles has gone?"

"He's coming back soon."

Sara merely nodded. She went over to the telephone and sat down, looking at it. Twice she put out a hand, then withdrew it. It rang and she jumped up, lifting the receiver. Raine and Patrick watched her face. She said,

"Oh!" It was a small, warm gasp of incredulity. They rushed to her. There was a flash of fear in her eyes and she turned her back on them, saying in a controlled voice, "Oh, I see. Tell me about it." Raine and Patrick sat down again. Sara pulled out the desk chair and seated herself with her back to them. They heard her say, "Thank you for telling me," and then, quite formally, "I'm so glad." She replaced the receiver.

Raine asked, "What was that?"

Sara smiled. "They've got a lead, at last."

"What? What happened?"

She was silent, apparently composed but with something extra. There was a vibrancy behind the stillness and on her face a look that Raine, baffled, thought she would have construed as sly on someone else. It flashed through her mind that Sara had lost her reason and just as swiftly the thought went. "I'd rather not talk about it for the moment," Sara said. "I don't want to raise your hopes, or my own. Let's wait awhile. They're going to ring again. I am going to lie down in my room."

Her handbag was on the bed. She snatched it up, quietly closed her bedroom door, and tiptoed down the hallway. At the back door of the flat she turned right and fled down the narrow alleyway between the brick wall and the house. Approaching the pavement she slowed and looked for a cruising taxi. There was none. She turned left and began to run. She was aware of footsteps behind her. Someone grasped her by the shoulder, spinning her around. She looked up into a crumpled, good-natured face framed in shaggy blond hair. "You're in a hurry," the man said. "Can I give you a lift? My car is just over there."

She hesitated. "Who are you?"

"My name is Ossie Mount." Then, as she hesitated again, frowning, he added, "I'm a friend of Raine's."

"Could you take me to Hampton Court?"

"Sure."

"Fast?"

He grinned. "I'm a fast driver. That's my car over there. That TR7. It goes like the wind." He already had a grip on her elbow and was propelling her forward at a run. "Jump in." She fell into the passenger seat and Mount revved the engine to a roar as they shot across the square past The Jolly Fox, down Tulley Street, and into the mainstream of traffic going toward the river. He glanced around. "Something has happened, then?"

"Yes."

"You'd better tell me."

"I think Primmy has been taken to Hampton Court."

"Good lord! You've told the police?" She didn't answer and, glancing at her again, he saw that her hands were twisting together on her knees. "May I ask why not? They're there to help, aren't they?"

"It's important for me to go alone."

He took several moments to digest that, then asked carefully, "I assume you believe the child to be alone? You're not by any idiotic chance expecting to tackle her kidnapper?"

"Oh no. She is alone. I've had a message. All I have to do is go and collect her."

He sped through an orange light. "How did you get the message?"

"I had a telephone call. It said I must go by myself."

Without knowing her, he knew she was lying. He also sensed that under that almost calm exterior she was near the breaking point. "I see," he said. She was sitting very still, watching the road. She didn't speak again for about ten minutes and he concentrated on the driving, trying to maintain the fastest possible speed without breaking traffic laws. Keeping an eye open for the police, he wove in and out of lanes and roared to a head start at the lights.

"Who are you? I've never heard Raine speak of you?"

"Just a friend."

She eyed him suspiciously. He smiled to put her fears at rest. "I haven't known her very long and I don't know her very well, but I assure you we're friends. And I'd like to help."

"You're not that newspaper man? The one who broke into the flat?" He took his eyes off the road again to smile at her. "What a suspicious mind you have, Miss Tindall. I told you, I'm a friend of Raine's."

She was staring at him as though he had suddenly become a monster. She clapped a hand to her mouth. "You are!" she cried. "You are! Let me out! Let me out!" They were approaching traffic lights. She had one hand on the door handle.

"Don't jump," he shouted harshly. "Don't jump, Sara. You're perfectly safe and I am going to help you." He could see she had the door partially open. He shot through the red light. "Shut that bloody door. You're not going to be much good to your daughter as a corpse. You just sit tight and I'll get you there."

She moaned.

"Jesus!" he exclaimed, with exasperation. "There's no way you're going to avoid publicity. Relax. And who the hell cares, so long as you get the child back?" She put both hands over her face and curled up in the seat like a small hunted animal. Ossie Mount shook his head and kept going.

The Three Square garage was no more than five minutes by car from Osbon Square. There were gas pumps in the front of the lot, and a young man standing in a glassed-in booth waited for customers. Charles parked the car at the far end of the lot where it wouldn't get in anyone's way and ran to the office. There was a girl behind the desk. Yes, she said, Mr. Fortune did park his Mercedes here, and then she asked shrewdly if he were a detective.

"Why should you ask that?"

"They're going to check on everyone with a black Mercedes, aren't they?"

"Are they? Yes, I suppose you could be right." He smiled. "I am sure you'll be very cooperative."

"Why not? But as it happens, Mr. Fortune's

Mercedes has a very good alibi." She said it with a smile. "It's over at Frosts in Surrey Place having a service. It's been there since before all these . . ." she gestured toward a folded newspaper on the desk, ". . . goings on."

A. P. & G. Frost weren't difficult to find. Charles knew Surrey Place. He went up one street and down the other and there they were, their big black-and-white sign announcing flamboyantly that they were agents for Fiat, Mercedes, Volvo, Renault.

Charles could see at a glance that there were several Mercedes. He went into the small untidy office, which smelled of engine oil. No one was there. He went out into the yard, then swiftly up and down the rows of parked cars, reading off the numbers of the Mercedes. There were six in all and not one with a registration that tallied with the car seen in Kettle Lane. A mechanic in a greasy dark-blue overall was crawling out from beneath a Volvo. Charles went up to him and said pleasantly, "Is that by any chance Mr. Tindall's Volvo?"

The man shook his head. "He took it this morning."

"I believe you've got Mr. Fortune's Mercedes in for a service."

The mechanic shook his head. "He brought it in but we were full up. He hadn't booked, so he had to take it—" The man broke off, scratched his head, grinned with faint embarrassment, and added, "Anyway, it's not here. What do you—" He looked inquiringly at Charles.

Trying to keep the urgency out of his voice, Charles asked, "What happened to Mr. Fortune's Mercedes?"

"Like I said, we couldn't take it."

"So he took it away?"

"Yes. Er—yes. It went away."

"Who took it away?" The mechanic reddened slightly, glanced toward the office, then back at Charles. A man in white overalls had gone into the office and was sorting through a file. Charles said, "I suppose you read the papers and hear the news. You must know a Mercedes is involved in this—"

"Oh yes, sure, I know that. Are you from the police?" The man glanced back at the office again.

"More or less. I'm working on the case. Hadn't you better tell me if something irregular has happened with a Mercedes?"

"Yes, I s'pose I shall have to, in the end. Just goes to show, you don't get away with much." He said apprehensively, "That's Mr. Kennington, the service manager in the office. There's going to be hell to pay from him when he hears. On Wednesday Mr. Fortune brought his Mercedes in for a service. I was in the office. He said he'd booked it in, but I couldn't find any note of it in the book and the girl was out to lunch. Another client came in and was talking to Mr. Fortune while I was looking through the book. Then Mr. Fortune left, leaving the car there. I came out blowing my top because I knew there was no chance of it getting a service when it wasn't booked in. Look at all those cars." He encompassed the yard with a gesture. "We're flat out all the time. Anyway, the other client said he'd brought his Volvo—"

"Mr. Tindall?"

"Yes. They were obviously friends," the young man said defensively. "He just wanted something small done to his Volvo and he said he'd leave it for half an hour while we fixed it and he'd take the Merc. to Mr. Fortune's office. He said Mr. Fortune had been in a hurry and they'd arranged it. I mean, Mr.

Tindall had told him to go on and if we couldn't fit his car in, he would bring it around to him. What could I do? That's what he told me. It sounded okay." He glanced apprehensively again toward the service manager, who was still busy in the office. "If I'd taken the Merc. in and overloaded the work, I'd have gotten hell from Mr. Kennington."

"Of course," agreed Charles bleakly. "And when did Mr. Tindall pick up his Volvo?"

"Today. He said he'd be back in an hour on Wednesday, but he didn't come. But he did come today. I couldn't very well blow my top because it's his sister that's in trouble. I guess that's why he didn't come back."

Charles nodded. "I guess that's why. Do you think your Mr. Kennington would mind if I used your office telephone?"

"No, I'm sure he wouldn't. I'll take you in."

"And while I'm ringing, could you get me the registration number of Mr. Tindall's Volvo, please?"

He dialed the number that was very familiar to him now. "Superintendent, the man who has Miss Tindall's baby is her brother, Elliott

Tindall. He was driving James Fortune's Mercedes."

"Jesus! How do you know?"

"Never mind. I'll tell you later. Now take down this number." He reeled off the one he had left with Raine.

"I've had a call from Ritchie, and he is at that number. Has been incarcerated in the cellar. I've just put the phone down."

"By Tindall? Was he held by Tindall?"

"He didn't know. The chap had a nylon stocking over his head. But the woman next door got the car number. He's off with the child in the Mercedes. We've alerted the traffic police, but we don't know what direction he's taken."

"You might have to look for a Volvo. Elliott Tindall picked up his Volvo this morning. If he's listening to the radio, he may have the Volvo planted somewhere."

"He threatened to drown Ritchie and the child using some weights Ritchie recognized as doorstops from The Jolly Fox. I think I'll get up to Osbon Square and interview Miss Tindall."

"Okay. I'll see you there."

"Thanks," said Charles to the popeyed mechanic, and ran.

He saw the police car come around the corner as he went up the steps of number seven. Raine answered his ring. "Where's Sara?" he asked as he hurried into the hall.

"In her room. She answered the phone, then went off to her room looking strange. Thank God you're back. Patrick and I were just wondering what to do. I couldn't get through to that number you gave me. First of all there was no reply. Then it was engaged. Where have you been, Charles?"

He could hear Oliver's footsteps outside. They both turned. Oliver barked, "Where's Miss Tindall?"

"In her room."

"Get her."

Raine sped down the hallway and knocked at Sara's door. When there was no reply she opened it with apprehension. "Sara." She swung around, screaming, "She's not there!"

"Perhaps she's in the bathroom?"

"Outside?"

They scattered in every direction, then came back, meeting in the kitchen.

"She's gone."

"But where?"

The Inspector said grimly, "It seems Tindall has cut his losses, taken the child, and is proposing to drown her."

Raine gulped. "James," she corrected him. "James has the baby."

"Sshh," said Charles. Raine put a hand to either side of her head and Patrick gasped, "Are you crazy? Her brother?"

Charles put an arm around Raine. "Sara's phone call could have been from Max. She could have gone to catch Elliott before the police get there. She knows something. Guess, Raine. Where would Elliott go to drown—"

"The Sally Blow," shrieked Raine.

"What?"

"Elliott has a boat called The Sally Blow. It's a forty-foot motor cruiser. He keeps it near Hampton Court."

"Do you know where it's moored?"

"Yes, I do."

Oliver was running for the car with its two-way radio. "Come on, Doctor, you may be needed."

Patrick hesitated only a moment before hurtling after the others, and fell into the back seat of Oliver's car. He was thinking they might not notice him, or rather his reasons for being there. He was also thinking, albeit shamefacedly, that with a bit of luck he still might have Sara onstage by eight o'clock.

30

ENID Theobald ran square into her husband at the gap in the hedge. "I've rung the police and they're on their way."

"They're wasting their time," Willie replied. "Mr. Ritchie has persuaded Bob to rush off after the Mercedes, though what chance they've got of finding it I can't imagine."

"They've got the number," Enid said proudly.

"So they have, my dear. So they have. And you did hear a baby's cry, and you may well have heard Ritchie shout for help, and you do know a Mercedes when you see one." He smiled down at her fondly. "You'll be able to dine out on this for the rest of your life."

Enid bridled. "You might say 'congratulations', Willie."

"I'll do more than that. If they save the child I'll take you out to dinner."

Max, hunched forward in his seat, was saying anxiously, "You're not going fast enough. What about letting me take the wheel?"

"With one arm? Sorry. I'm doing my best, but I don't want to smash the car up. This is a thirty-mile-an-hour-limit area. We're never going to catch that Mercedes, especially since we don't even know where it's going."

"If you take the shortest route to the Thames, we won't be far off. You say yourself there are no lakes or big ponds between here and the river."

They sped past a piece of common land, over a crossroad, and up a steep incline. A small wood opened out onto a golf course. They joined the main road and were swinging into a hairpin bend when Max, whose eyes were scouring every inch of the wasteland accessible from the road, shouted, "Stop!" Bob hunched over the wheel and ran the car clumsily up onto the grass. "Look! What's that under the copper beech? See? The sun is catching on a bit of chrome. It's a car! Keep the engine running." Bob, straining his eyes, could see nothing. Then a gentle breeze touched a leaf and the flash came again. Max leaped out. Halfway across the grass he turned to wave, then ran on. So it was a car!

Bob Diarmid ran after him. Max was already under the drooping branches of the tree. "It's a Mercedes all right," he shouted, and then, "It's his. It's empty, though." Max tried the trunk. "Locked." They banged on the metal with their fists, making enough noise to waken a live baby who might have dozed off. Nothing. "Come on," Max said urgently, "let's get going. We'll stop at the first phone box and ring the police. I don't think there's one chance in a million that the child is in the trunk."

They jumped into Bob's car and bumped back onto the road. There wasn't a great deal of traffic. Diarmid drove faster.

"Give me the exact location of the Mercedes. What road is this? I want to make it easy for them."

They swung off the road where a little cluster of shops and a post office lined the border of another area of common land. Max leaped out. He was no longer aware of his arm in its bloodstained sleeve. The pain was sublimated now by the tight apprehension that constricted his chest and jerked at his nerves. He slammed through the telephone box door, grasped the receiver, and dialed.

Back in the car Bob Diarmid was thinking,

"Poor sod, he must realize we've got no chance. What are we looking for now, anyway? A baby in a carrycot hidden under a rug in a Vauxhall, Morris, Austin, Daimler, Fiat, Datsun, Mini, Rover, traveler, saloon, truck, whose driver we can't recognize."

Max was taking a long time. When he finally lurched out of the box, he looked stunned. Diarmid leaned across and opened the door for him. "What did they say?" Max turned and looked at him vaguely. "What did they say?" Diarmid repeated anxiously.

"They said wait here and someone will pick us up."

Diarmid's curiosity flamed. "But what did they say?" His passenger didn't seem to hear. Max slid sideways, head against the window, eyes closed. Bob asked kindly, "Can I get you something? Something to eat?"

Max opened his eyes and sat up with a jerk. "How far are we from the bridge at Hampton Court?"

"Not far. About ten minutes."

"I've just remembered. She once pointed out the boat. I think I could find it. Get me over that bridge as fast as you can. Break the sound barrier if you have to."

"It's a built-up area." But he had already

started the engine and was rolling the car toward the road.

"I think, under the circumstances, if we're stopped it can only be to the good. A cop with a siren would surely give me a lift."

"If you'll stop over there I'll jump out and check that the boat is where it should be."

Ossie Mount obligingly pulled the car over to the curb. Sara ran down a narrow lane that skirted a warehouse and some ancient cottages. She came out near the boathouse on the bank. The Sally Blow wasn't there. Heart in mouth, she ran up to a young man in bathing trunks who was intently examining the gauges of a small motorboat. "Excuse me. Do you know where The Sally Blow has gone?"

He looked up, smiled, showing good teeth in a sunburned face. "Can't say I do. I don't belong around here. What does it look like?"

"Forty feet long. It has a white hull with a blue water line."

"Oh, yes. Yes, I saw it as I came up. It's moored under those willows over there. There's a small jetty that's scarcely ever used because it's falling to pieces." He turned and pointed across the river. Sara's face fell. He saw and asked helpfully, "Is there anything I can do for you?"

"I am going out on The Sally Blow. But I thought she would be here." Sara looked down at him in his little speedboat with as cajoling and sweet a smile as ever shone across the footlights of a stage. "I don't suppose you would run me over?"

He looked delighted. "Sure. Why not? Jump in."

She paused only to cast an apprehensive look back up the lane, then stepped gingerly aboard. He started the engine and they whisked out from the bank just as Ossie Mount appeared. He shouted, but the owner of the boat neither saw nor heard and Sara turned, pink-faced, to stare out over the bow, her back to the receding bank.

"The Sally Blow is a nice cruiser." He had to shout over the noise of the engine.

"Yes."

"Is the owner a friend of yours?"

"Yes. This is terribly kind of you. I couldn't be more grateful."

"No trouble." He cut the engine and they nosed over to the rotting jetty. Some of the wood had slumped away and fallen into the river, but The Sally Blow's mooring rope was slung over the one bollard that stood firm. The saloon curtains were drawn as if the cruiser were deserted, but the engines were turning over. There was a metal ladder reaching down from the aftdeck. Sara edged forward, stood up, and grasped one of the rungs.

"Are you all right?"

"Yes, I can make it easily. Thank you very much."

He saw her with one foot on deck, then with a cheery wave turned and sped away. Sara crept forward, her feet silent on the deck in her rope-soled sandals. She was puzzled by the silence because her taxi had been noisy in its arrival and departure and set the cruiser rocking in its wash. Then the roar of another motorboat filled the air and as it sped by The Sally Blow rocked again. Below deck, a man intent upon getting away single-handedly might not notice that one craft came closer than the other.

She climbed down the companionway. From the bottom rung of the ladder she could see through the partially closed door leading to the saloon. It was about sixteen feet long, with chintz-covered cushions on storage boxes that served as seats on either side of the narrow table. He was standing with his back to her, tying a rope around the neck of a stone lion that had a weirdly familiar look. The door leading to the forecabin was open, and she could see in. Primmy wasn't there. The aft-cabin doors were closed. She said softly, "Elliott." Sliding the doors open, she went in.

Elliott spun around, his face blazing. "Sara!" The child, perhaps recognizing Sara's voice, cried out from behind the aftcabin door. Sara's eyes filled with tears of agonizing relief. "Thank God," she breathed. Elliott was staring at her with his mouth open, standing between her and her baby. She had never seen him like this, defenseless, with the shutters open on his mind. It seemed then that part of her had always known what lay there behind the cool, patronizing shell. Sickened and horrified though she was, she said with compassion, "You had better go. I expect you've got the Volvo somewhere handy." He continued to stare at her, but now he was jerking the rope between his hands. She said nervously, "There's no way out for you now but to disappear. You can disguise yourself easily enough. You can get away."

His face twisted with a sort of despair. "Sara," he said again. The repetition of her name was hypnotic and at the same time obscene.

She said in a suddenly frightened voice, "It's up to you whether or not you escape. It's only me you have to punish, isn't it? If you never see me again you won't—I mean, it won't be necessary—I mean, everything will be all right, won't it?" He still didn't answer. He continued to jerk the rope between his hands. "Put that down. You're running out of time. They're coming after you."

"You bitch! You told them." He gave a blubbering wail of despair and momentarily the evil slid away, leaving a weak boy, hurt, defenseless.

"We will talk another time. You can get in touch if you need to and I will help you. Now that it's out in the open between us, I shall be able to help you."

"It's your fault." He flung the accusation at her like a spoiled child.

"I was lucky," she admitted. "You weren't. That's why I can't bear to see you caught."

"But you've told."

"No. They're about to find out. And they will come after you."

He came toward her, twisting the rope threateningly between his hands. "I have a job to do. I'm going to drown that shameful illegitimate child. The Lord has asked me to punish you. The Lord has been raining down curses upon you."

She caught her breath in fear, but when she spoke the words came calmly. "I always understood the Lord to be merciful."

"Not to wanton women. I'm going to drown—"

"No dear. No, you're not. What could this sort of violence lead to? Only to prison. Go away and hide, then later I'll get help for you."

"I'll drown you, too."

"You're not going to drown anyone," she said quietly. From behind the aftcabin door Primmy gave a long drawn-out cry. As if reminded, Elliott put the rope down on the saloon table and, breathing deeply, went right past Sara, deliberately not looking at her. She followed him with apprehension a little way up the companionway. Her head and shoulders were above the level of the deck. He walked slowly and in silence across the deck and looked down at the mooring rope. Then he bent down, took it in his hands, and drew it toward him until the cruiser bounced against the one remaining bollard.

Sara saw to her horror that he was about to cast off. She was up the ladder in a flash. But the deck was slippery, her sandal soles worn. She fell against the railing and Elliott's legs. Before she could clamber to her feet he had her around the waist and easily lifted her over the rail. She screamed, grabbed the wooden handrail, and hung on. Elliott grunted, swore. "Let go, you bitch." With the strength of sheer desperation she clung tighter. There was no breath for protest, for persuasion. Everything in her, all of her, went into dragging herself back over the railing. And at last she had one leg across. Her foot came in contact with an upright and she twisted her leg around it, knitting herself in, trying to push herself into the bars so that he could not extricate her. Elliott was excited, panicky. She could hear the quick, soft animal grunts of surprise and anger. He grabbed her wrist and she bit him, hard. He screamed and let go. It was the break she needed. She hurled herself back onto the deck. As she staggered to her feet, she saw that the cruiser was drifting out into the river. Elliott lunged for the controls. She raced after him, but he got there first. He grasped the steering wheel, pushed the Morse throttle forward, and the boat leaped into midstream.

31

SARA's first instinct was to bring Primmy up on deck, but Elliott could easily set the controls, take the child from her, and toss her overboard. He was at the wheel, heading the cruiser downstream. He turned his head. "You always were a bitch," he said, his voice vile with hate. "I'll enjoy throwing that bastard child overboard while you look on. Then you. I've got a weight for you. She won't need it. She'll sink in the carrycot."

Terror engulfed her. Elliott could, with his superior strength, throw the child overboard, and there was nothing she could do to stop him. She slipped down the companionway, staggered through the saloon, and opened the door of the aftcabin. The carrycot was on the floor. She peered in at the little bundle in the pink nightdress. Her baby looked up out of tearful eyes. "Mum-mum-mum." Stunned with fright and dread, Sara bent down and lifted the child into her arms.

"Whatever happens, darling," she whispered passionately, "I will keep you safe."

Dear heaven, why had she allowed her emotions to outweigh her common sense? Tears, the unspent force of the agony of the past days, spilled over and rolled down her cheeks. Elliott's spite was remorseless. She had been a fool to think she could reason with him. Primmy, as if sensing the situation, moaned. Tenderly, Sara stroked her brow. She stepped into the saloon and looked toward the companionway. Instinct told her not to go out on deck with the child. She would be at her most vulnerable there.

But it wasn't going to be all right. She heard the cutting of the engines, the predatory silence, then heavy footsteps, and she spun around to see his form filling the doorway, his mad eyes. "Elliott!"

"We've all got to die now," he said. "I've decided we'll all die together."

"Elliott!"

He bent down and picked up the rope, knotted it, and slipped it over the head of the stone lion. Then he pulled it tightly around the neck.

"Elliott! No!" Sara screamed, looking at the stone lion with its wild, wonderful eyes and the rope around its neck. She swung around and leaped through the cabin doorway.

The door latch was frail, useless against Elliott's weight. She put Primmy down on the top bunk, struggled up onto it, and wrestled with the porthole flange. Sobbing, she fought to move the wing nut that held the cover in place. If only she could get this porthole open, her screams might carry across the water. It would not budge. Elliott was banging on the door.

"Come out, you bitch. The Lord is ready to smite you down in your sin. And your shameful child. Open the door."

Sara slid down, gathered the child protectively to her, and threw her weight against the door. "Elliott! Listen to me." He rattled the door violently. Primmy began to cry again. Sara put a gentle hand across the back of the child's head, holding the little face close to her neck. Gradually, she calmed. In the silence Sara could hear Elliott's harsh breathing on the other side of the door. "Elliott," she said breathlessly. "You're ill, but I can get help for you."

There was a splintering of wood, a snap of metal, and the door gave way. She cringed back against the cabin wall. Elliott appeared, shoulders hunched, his eyes murderous, one end of the rope held in his hands, the middle tied around himself, the other end around the neck of the stone lion.

It was useless to try to rush past. He seemed content to have her where he could see her, for he backed to the end of the seat and sat down. To her horror, he began to fashion a noose at the free end of the rope.

Controlling her panic, knowing she had no chance, she sat down on the opposite seat and held the child closely. There must be some way of getting through to him. They had been friends once. They had shared the same house, the same parents. He had been a normal child. Her fear eased a bit. A calmness settled on her. "I would so like to help you. You've taken the wrong turning. You could have been an actor. You've acted a part all your life, and to what end?"

His eyes narrowed. "You had everything," he said childishly.

"Were you so twisted with jealousy, watching me, that you couldn't do anythng constructive for yourself? Did you really enjoy knocking me rather than making something of your own life?" His mouth hardened but he didn't answer. "I always knew you were behind our parents' death. I knew you sent that anonymous letter telling me to go to

Wales so I would find our parents' bodies." He lifted his head, gave her a sharp, odd look. "But Mother telephoned that Saturday afternoon. She said you had talked Father into changing his will and leaving me out. You convinced him you would look after the business and me. That you would go back into it and stay. And he was so anxious for you to carry it on he made himself believe you. But Mother didn't. She knew you were short of money. And sick.

"You never had any intention of working in the business, had you? Just as soon as you could you sold it and took the money. I think Mother knew you would do that. I believe she wanted me to stand up to our father with her and make him see sense. Oh Elliott, you could still get so much out of life if you would allow me to help you." He was looking at her with deadly rancor, the wound of his inadequacy running with blood. "Oh, what a fool I've been," said Sara in sudden despair. "I should have gone to the police in the first place."

A sly look came over his face. He straightened and, catching her unaware, flung the noose over her head. Sara screamed. In a reflex movement she thrust out her elbows and let Primmy go so that the child slid through her arms. Sara buckled at the knees to break the fall and Primmy rolled gently under the table. The noose jerked tight, pinioning Sara's arms. Then to her horror, Elliott swayed down the opposite side of the table and picked up the lion and the child. Sara screamed again. "Put her down. Put her down!" Holding the child under one arm, Elliott jerked the rope, dragging Sara on tottering steps the length of the saloon, bumping against the table, stumbling.

Elliott brought Sara up to him with a fierce jerk of the rope. Then, to her fevered imagination he seemed to lift up his hands like eagles' claws, menacing except that they had no sharpness. Only strength. Like blown-up rubber gloves. Odd that she had never noticed his thick, powerful hands, she thought, in a strange terror of detachment. He must have put the lion and the child down, for he had picked her up. She seemed to be flying through the air. Then she bumped against wood and there was noise and iron bars and a great rocking. She fought fiercely to loosen her arms, fought drunkenly to stand up without support.

She didn't see the boats. Didn't see the men—Oliver, Charles, Ossie Mount—trying to get up the side, clambering on the rails. The young man who had brought her in his motor-boat made it to the deck. But she had eyes only for Elliott emerging from the companionway with the child clutched under one arm, the lion under the other, and the rope tied around himself. Sara was aware in that last moment of terror of the strange, potent, knowing glare of the animal's eyes as Elliott, off balance, lurched out onto the deck, of the fact that the deck was heaving. Sara heard shouting. But the shouts might have been only in her mind, for out in front there was only Elliott at the rail balancing the heavy, strangely triumphant lion on the wood and holding the child with his other arm against his hip.

Everything went silent. Even the deck stilled. It was as if life itself stood suspended. A quiet voice behind her said, "Give her to me," and Sara knew it was Max, in a dream. Afterward she remembered the feeling of stretching herself beyond strength, beyond pain, and all at once the rope was over her head. Afterward her blouse was torn, her arms grazed, but at the time she only knew she had to get to Elliott while he was immobile, while somehow, miraculously, Max in this strange dream seemed to have Elliott mesmerized.

Then someone in a boat standing off, some crazy fool, she thought, shouting, "Look out, he's going to—" Sara was lunging, and at the same time flying through the air. Her arms came around Primmy, inevitably, because of the way he held her, encircling Elliott's arm. With the three of them locked together, she felt him throw himself in one violent lurch upward and backward. They were going with him. She felt the rail beneath her, felt her body see-sawing, then strong hands grasped her. Max's voice again cried out of the melee. "Let go. I've got her. I've got the child." She knew then that it was all over and she let herself fall inward, crumpling against the iron railing. She did not feel Elliott's boot, his final act of vileness as he went over. It caught her on the side of the head and she lost consciousness, drooping into one of the many helping arms as the water closed over Elliott's head and he disappeared from view.

They sped toward London with the sirens blaring. Max said, "I'll do the worrying, my darling."

Sara looked up at him, loving him with her eyes. "Max!"

He smiled and kissed her on the lips.

"It's over." He grinned. "I'm sure there are easier ways to win a woman."

Ossie Mount grinned back from the front seat. "They say you get what you pay for. The Sara Tindalls of this world come highly priced."

Perhaps he was right, Max thought. Perhaps it was arrogant of him to have assumed he could have her without paying.

"I'll make it up to you," Sara vowed.

"You do. I'll enjoy it." His arm tightened around her as they swerved to avoid the cars obligingly pulling to a stop. "You knew all the time?"

"No." She shook her head with a nervous movement. "I don't think I knew. Not really."

"The Superintendent said you knew," Max told her gently, unable to accept it himself. "He thought you had always known, since the first anonymous letter."

She was silent a moment. Sirens filled the air. "I had it inside my head. Yes, if you call that knowing, then I did know, but it wouldn't come out. It came out today when I was talking to Elliott on the boat. I said it out loud. So I suppose I did know. Odd, isn't it? The mind, I mean. I said all sorts of things, like not giving him away before because it wouldn't bring back our parents, or Guy. But I couldn't have told the police because it was—" she broke off, frowning.

They shot through red lights, and Ossie Mount said exultantly to the driver, "Gives you a great sense of power, doesn't it?" The driver smiled.

"Behind a closed door in your mind?"

"Perhaps that's it."

"And that's why you wouldn't agree to marry me, isn't it?"

"I suppose so." She shuddered. "I suppose I knew he would try to kill you, but in me there was only a sort of intuitive instinct that things would go wrong for you. And you see, I did have this very conscious problem. I always knew if I allowed him to adopt Primmy he would be satisfied. That would have been the ultimate success, to take my child. But I couldn't let Primmy go to him."

"No."

Ossie Mount, in the front passenger seat, was scribbling frantically in his notebook. Sara didn't care. He had done his share in saving her child's life and had earned his story. The publicity would be intolerable, but she was going to have to live with it. She had been trained in a hard school. She hadn't cracked yet and she wasn't going to do so now.

Sara heaved an enormous sigh, put her head down on Max's shoulder, and said in a small voice, "His mind had gone. Will you say that for me, that his poor mind had gone? He didn't have much luck in life because—because—he was not able to overcome problems."

"What problems did he have?"

"Talk, Sara darling," Max urged her kindly. "It will do you good to face up to it."

"Only the normal ones." Elliott had even resented losing his hair. "He never actually found out how the world works."

There was a long silence, then Sara said thoughtfully, "My brother was destroyed in trying to destroy others."

"So an oversimplification of your philosophy is that you get what you give?"

"Come on, Sara," Max urged her.

"I agree that would be an oversimplification," she said shakily. With Max's help, she would be able to talk freely about her brother in time, but it was too soon.

"Mr. Ritchie, has Doctor Halbert looked at your arm?"

"I'm going to the hospital after we get Sara

onstage. It has waited two days for attention. It can wait a bit longer."

They took the child to the children's hospital for a checkup. Charles was sure there was nothing wrong with her, but he wanted her properly looked after while Sara went to the theatre. Sara was happy to be parted from her, in the child's interests, now that there was no danger.

They were at the theatre with little time to spare. The dresser was waiting, and everyone helped.

Max used the stage doorkeeper's telephone to call his parents. "I'm going around to the Casualty Department at Guy's Hospital shortly after eight o'clock," he said. "I'll tell you all about it if you meet me there." He thought wryly that there was going to be a great deal of explaining for him to do. Tomorrow, he would take Sara to them. It was not perhaps the best auspices under which to meet a future daughter-in-law but . . . that's life, he thought, and hurried off down the hallway to Sara. In the dressing room Charles was gazing into Sara's eyes. "You ought not to go on," he said. "You're a bit concussed."

"I have to go on."

He nodded. "Do you think you will remember your lines?"

"Yes."

"Doctor, I'm afraid you will have to leave." That was the stage director's voice, the voice of authority. "Miss Tindall has to be dressed and made-up and on stage in twenty minutes. And you must go, Max." Max, sitting on Sara's sofa, his hair awry, his dark, unshaven face haggard, showed by neither movement nor gesture that he had heard.

A worried voice on the intercome said, "Fifteen minutes, Miss Tindall."

Hannah, with Sara's gown over her arm, shooed them all into the hallway and closed the door. All except Max, quietly smiling from the sofa, the arm in its bloodstained sleeve resting on his knees.

Sara finished her face, Hannah finished her hair. The stage director's voice said, "This is your five-minute call. Beginners please, ladies and gentlemen. Beginners please. Your calls, Miss Mathieson and Miss Tindall." Sara stood up, turned to Max.

"Your poor arm. I'll come to the hospital immediately after the show."

"Even if I'm anesthetized?"

"Especially then. I'll hold your hand until you come round."

"Thank you." He put an arm around her. "All in all, darling, you look remarkably normal."

"I have to be normal. It's nearly eight o'clock." They smiled at each other. The stage was beckoning, standing between them in a way, as he knew it always would, adding zest to both their lives. He kissed her long and tenderly.

"I'm sorry, Max. I'll make it up to you. If it takes me the rest of my life, I'll make it up to you."

"Miss Tindall. Your call please. Your call please, Miss Tindall."

Charles pushed the door open. "You're sure you're okay, Sara?" She nodded, her eyes bright. "I'll see you later, then. Come on, Max. I'll get you to the hospital. Then I think I'll dash out and see poor old Lil. I once saw a body hanging from a ceiling. It was not a pretty sight."

"You're a saint, Charles," Sara said.

Patrick Delvaney, small, quietly triumphant, was standing in the passageway. Sara turned to flash him one of her beautiful, flooding smiles. Max caught her hand, kissed her again. "I love you."

Raine was dancing from one foot to the other, swinging her Jassy skirt. Charles thought he had never seen her looking more lovely. He moved obsessively toward her. "Raine . . ."

She hesitated only slightly. Her mind was already fleeing toward the footlights. She blew him a kiss and ran. Charles shrugged his shoulders and sighed.

Max gave him a quizzical look. He was thinking that as a husband or potential husband Charles was a pretty good doctor, a pretty good detective, and perhaps, as Sara had suggested, something of a saint. "Come on," he said, "let's get a taxi. My arm is hurting like hell."